RAPTURED SOULS

RAPTURED SOULS

By Jeremy Reis

ISBN: 978-0-9760043-7-0

DISCLAIMER

This is a work of fiction. Names, characters, businesses, places, events, locales, and incidents are either the products of the author's imagination or used in a fictitious manner. Any resemblance to actual persons, living or dead, or actual events is purely coincidental.

The views and opinions expressed in this book are those of the author and do not necessarily reflect the official policy or position of any agency or organization. Readers should not take any content or characters as literal or as a representation of reality.

The publisher and the author make no representations or warranties with respect to the accuracy or completeness of the contents of this work and specifically disclaim all warranties, including without limitation warranties of fitness for a particular purpose. No warranty may be created or extended by sales or promotional materials.

To Jennica, the love of my life

Chapter 1: People Mover

David Mitchell maneuvered through the dimly lit, smoke-filled room, his heart thudding in his chest. The neon signs cast an eerie glow over the pool tables, and the bar's dull roar did little to calm his jangled nerves. The jacket he wore did a good job hiding the gun strapped to his side, but it did nothing to mask his tension.

David took a seat at the end of the bar, using the mirrored wall to keep a discreet watch on the entrance. He'd been chasing leads on this domestic terror group for months. Intel had it that tonight, in this bar, a major arms deal was going down, and David was there to stop it.

Fiddling with a forgotten coaster, memories of the last failed sting operation flooded back. The SAC had given him one more chance, reminding him that this was costing valuable FBI resources with little to show for it. But more importantly, the safety of countless innocent people was on the line.

A familiar face appeared in his peripheral vision. Mark Harris – one of the middlemen David had been tracking. Mark took a seat two stools away, ordered a whiskey, and tapped his fingers impatiently on the counter. David knew that when Mark started tapping, something was off.

His instincts screamed at him that tonight was not going as planned. He mentally recounted every step leading up to this moment. He had left no trace of his investigations, no loose ends, but the palpable tension in the room suggested otherwise.

His phone buzzed, a message from a colleague: *"Deal's moved. Docks. Warehouse 12. Be careful."* David's heart sank. They had been compromised. He needed to act fast.

But just as he prepared to leave, two men cornered him. One was big, with tattoos sprawling down his arms. The other, thin and wiry, with a scar running across his cheek. David didn't need to know their names to realize they were trouble.

"Leaving so soon?" the big one growled, grabbing David's arm.

He had trained for moments like this, yet, the gravity of the situation was not lost on him. With a swift motion, he used the man's weight against him, flipping him onto the ground. But the wiry one was quick, lunging at David with a switchblade.

A struggle ensued, glasses shattering, patrons shouting. David disarmed the man but not before the blade sliced across his arm. Ignoring the sting, he dashed out, knowing he needed to make it to the docks.

Outside, the cold air slapped him awake. The bleeding was manageable, but he couldn't afford to lose much time. The pain was a stark reminder of what was at stake - not just the mission, but his reputation, and more importantly, the countless lives in the balance.

With grim determination, David started his car and sped off towards the docks, ready to confront whatever lay ahead.

The docks were shrouded in an unsettling silence, broken only by the occasional distant horn of a ship and the lapping of water against the pier. The fog made everything look ghostly, casting Warehouse 12 in an eerie, faint light.

David approached cautiously, using the stacks of crates and shadows to mask his movement. His heart pounded in his chest as he neared the slightly open door of the warehouse. Inside, he heard the murmurs of hushed conversations and an occasional, stifled sob.

Drawing his gun, he peeked through the door's gap. He expected to see men huddled around weaponry, discussing the particulars of an arms deal. Instead, he saw a scene that shook him to his core.

Rows of people—men, women, and children—were standing in lines, eyes wide with terror. Guards patrolled the area, while at the far end, Mark Harris discussed something animatedly with another man. Instead of crates filled with guns or explosives, David was staring at groups of men, women, and children.

David felt a rush of anger and despair. This was far more than a domestic terror group; this was likely a human trafficking operation, possibly on a scale he'd never encountered before. He fumbled in his pocket for his phone, intent on alerting his team and calling for immediate backup.

But as he reached for his cell phone, he discovered it was damaged – most likely during the altercation at the bar. Cursing under his breath, he felt the weight of isolation heavily. Confronting the group directly was suicide. He was outnumbered, and any attempt to intervene would likely endanger the hostages even more.

David remembered the tracker device in his pocket—a small magnetic chip with GPS capabilities. If he could plant it on one of their vehicles, the FBI could track their movements, leading them to the traffickers' main base of operations.

Slipping around the side of the warehouse, David identified a couple of vans, likely used to transport the victims. Moving silently, he attached the tracker to the undercarriage of one of them.

But just as he was about to retreat, what sounded like a child's soft cry echoed from inside the warehouse. David hesitated, torn. Every fiber of his being screamed at him to burst in and free the victims. But the reality of his situation—outgunned and alone—made it clear that doing so would be a death wish.

Fighting back a torrent of emotions, he retreated to a safer distance. From there, he watched as the captives were loaded into the vans, their eyes conveying a feeling that would haunt him.

The other vans started to move out, leaving behind only the one David had tagged. His heart sank as he realized the tracked van was not part of the convoy – his gamble hadn't paid off.

David felt a crushing weight of guilt and frustration. His intel had been so off the mark. While he had been preparing for an arms deal, innocent people had been ensnared in this vile trade.

He watched from the shadows, a heavy feeling of despair settling in, as the other vans, presumably carrying the victims, disappeared into the night. Every instinct told him to follow, but without backup and a clear plan, it could jeopardize the lives of the innocent victims even more.

Defeated, David decided to head back to FBI HQ. He felt like he was leaving a piece of himself behind at that dock, the desperate eyes of the captives haunting his every step.

At the FBI headquarters, the operations room was a hubbub of activity, but it all fell silent as David walked in. His face, etched with the grim events of the night, told a story before he even spoke a word.

"They're moving people, Lisa. Not weapons," David's voice was raw, edged with guilt. "I placed a tracker on one of their vans, but it wasn't one they used when they left the warehouse."

Agent Lisa Reynolds looked at him sympathetically, placing a reassuring hand on his shoulder. "We'll find them, David. This is just a setback."

David shook his head. "There wasn't time. And I didn't know..."

His voice trailed off, the weight of what he'd witnessed pressing down on him. He hadn't been able to save them tonight, but he was determined to bring the culprits to justice.

Lisa looked at him, searching for words to comfort him, but even she, who had seen many harrowing scenes throughout her career, was shaken by the depth of the operation they had stumbled upon.

"David, this is bigger than just tonight. It's bigger than one failed tracker or a damaged phone. We are up against an organized, vile operation. We'll regroup, get more intel, and strike back. They won't get away with this."

David looked up, meeting her gaze. "I know, Lisa. But for tonight, they did. And I can't help but wonder what those people are going through right now because I couldn't do enough."

Every second counted in operations like these, and the mistakes of the night weighed heavily on him. He thought of the victims, now possibly transported to a new hell, all because he'd acted on wrong intel and faced unfortunate setbacks.

Retiring to his office, David sat in the dim light, the shadows seemingly echoing his own dark thoughts. He replayed the events over and over in his mind: the docks, the warehouse, the faces of those innocent victims. Every decision, every misstep, felt like a personal betrayal to those he had vowed to protect. The weight of failure bore down on him, suffocating any glimmer of hope he tried to hold onto. Alone in the stillness, he couldn't shake the sinking feeling that his mistakes had cost those innocent souls' freedom, if not their lives. The room grew colder, his thoughts darker, as David wrestled with the enormity of his failure.

Chapter 2: Artifacts

T he salty sea breeze tugged at David's worn jacket, a tangible reminder that he was deep in the belly of the dockside district. The acrid smell of oil and diesel mingled with the mustiness of the damp air. An unsettling quietness settled over the dock area, disturbed only by the distant cries of gulls and the low hum of machinery.

David Mitchell, young and brash, had risen quickly through the ranks of the FBI. His success was undeniable, but it came with a restless energy, a constant need to prove himself further. His boots, well-scuffed to fit his undercover profile as a dockworker, echoed dully on the wooden planks beneath him. Each step was measured, deliberate, as he wove between stacks of shipping containers and abandoned equipment, making his way towards Warehouse 43. It was an unassuming structure, much like any other on the pier, but intel had led him to believe it was the current base of operations for the group he was tracking.

David couldn't shake the weight of his failure from a week ago, how he'd let the human smugglers slip through his fingers. Every fiber of his being ached to correct that mistake. He believed, with a certain desperate fervor, that this group was more than just smugglers; they were planning something big, something deadly.

Approaching the warehouse's entrance, he quickly assessed the situation. A single dim light flickered through a cracked windowpane, casting eerie shadows that danced along the walls. The soft murmur of voices reached his ears – an indication he wasn't alone.

Slipping on a pair of gloves, David carefully pushed the side door, which, to his relief, was unlocked. The dim interior of the warehouse was maze-like, filled with stacked crates and tarp-covered machinery. Every shadow could be a hiding spot, every echo a potential threat. He felt the weight of the situation pressing on him from all sides.

Moving deeper into the warehouse, he kept his senses sharp, eyes scanning for any clues that might confirm his theory about the group's terrorist intentions. The faint voices grew louder, and David found himself drawn towards a makeshift office at the far end of the warehouse, its contents hidden by a grimy, drawn curtain.

His breaths were shallow, controlled, as memories of the previous mission flooded back. The faces of the trafficked victims, their despair, the feeling of being so close yet so far - he couldn't fail them again. This group had to be stopped, and David was determined to gather the evidence needed to bring them down.

Pressing his back against a stack of crates, David peered around the corner, trying to get a glimpse of what lay within the office. His heart raced in anticipation, knowing that every discovery, every piece of evidence, brought him one step closer to redemption.

But for now, he needed to be patient, observant, and ready for whatever lay ahead. The risks were high, but David Mitchell was a man on a mission, driven by guilt and a burning need for justice.

Continuing his exploration of the warehouse, David soon came across an area cordoned off by heavy, dust-laden drapes. The filtered light created an almost sanctified atmosphere, a sharp contrast to the grim, industrial feel of the rest of the building. As he stepped past the drapes, the sight before him momentarily stopped him in his tracks.

Laid out on long wooden tables were an array of artifacts that looked like they had been untouched by time. There were intricately carved tablets, their surfaces etched with symbols and writings that seemed ancient. Scrolls, sealed with wax and bound with faded ribbons, lay next to what appeared to be fragile parchments. Each artifact looked meticulously preserved, waiting for someone to unlock their secrets.

This was unexpected. David had prepared himself for many things—weapons, plans, blueprints—but not artifacts that looked like they belonged in a museum or a sacred temple.

Puzzled, he approached one of the tablets, leaning in to decipher the markings. They looked familiar but foreign— possibly of Middle Eastern origin? The scrolls bore writings in languages David couldn't immediately recognize. This wasn't the domain of your everyday terrorist. Why would a domestic group be dealing in ancient relics?

Realizing the potential importance of his discovery, David took out a small camera from his jacket pocket. He began photographing the artifacts, capturing every detail. The eerie silence of the warehouse was occasionally punctuated by the soft click of his camera shutter.

His mind raced. Were these stolen? Were they being used as a front for smuggling, or did they serve a more sinister purpose? It didn't align with what he knew of the group. It added a layer of complexity to an already perplexing investigation.

David's focus on cataloging the evidence was so intense that he momentarily forgot the inherent dangers of his environment.

As the last image was captured, he tucked his camera away, feeling an urgent need to share this discovery with his team. But for now, he had to continue his surveillance, find out more about the group's intent, and most crucially, remain undetected.

David's heart rate was just returning to normal when a soft, static-filled voice broke into his ear, "David, heads up. We've got a drone overhead, and it's picking up two vehicles approaching your location."

It was Lisa, her voice laced with a mixture of caution and concern.

"Copy that," David responded, swiftly retreating further into the shadows. The warehouse was massive, with numerous hiding spots, but he needed to be close enough to listen in, yet hidden enough to avoid detection. He found an alcove behind a stack of wooden crates, providing him with a vantage point of the warehouse's main floor and the entrance.

The distant hum of engines grew louder. The sound of car doors slamming echoed through the vast space, followed by muffled voices.

Six men entered, their demeanor immediately setting them apart from the typical dock workers. They were dressed in a mix of business attire and rugged outdoor wear, looking out of place in the dimly lit warehouse. Two of the men stood out. One, tall with a silvering beard, seemed to command respect from the others, while the other, younger and clean-shaven, walked with an air of arrogance.

The leader, as David mentally labeled him, spread out a series of documents on one of the tables next to the artifacts. The group huddled around, their conversation initially hushed.

David strained to listen, adjusting the small amplifier he had. It wasn't perfect, but it would give him the edge he needed to pick up their conversation.

"...ensured that the artifacts from the dig were safely transported," the younger man was saying, a hint of pride in his voice. "Every piece is accounted for, and the paperwork... well, let's just say they won't raise any eyebrows."

The leader nodded. "Good. The organization has spent years ensuring that these pieces make their way out of the Middle East undetected. We can't afford any mistakes now."

Another man, with glasses perched on his nose, chimed in, "The mislabeling was a better idea than trying to smuggle these in. By the time anyone realizes these aren't mere replicas, they'll be safely in the hands of our specialists."

The mention of the Middle East and the 'organization' piqued David's interest. What was their game? The illegal sale of antiquities was lucrative, sure, but it was hardly the MO of a domestic terror group.

"Our time is nearing," the leader continued, his voice taking on a grave tone. "We need the funds to ensure everything goes off without a hitch. These artifacts are key to understanding what is to come."

David's mind raced. What were they planning? These artifacts didn't fit the narrative he'd been building. He tried piecing the puzzle together, the talk suggested something significant was in the works.

As the group continued discussing logistics and potential buyers, Lisa's voice crackled in his earpiece, "David, we're picking up two more suspicious SUVs heading that way. They might be heading to the warehouse. I suggest you find an exit."

But David was reluctant to leave. He was on the cusp of understanding the group's broader intent. Every word, every hint could be crucial.

Suddenly, a distant metallic clang echoed in the warehouse, followed by the unmistakable bark of a dog. The group instantly went silent.

David's heart raced. He knew he had moments, if not seconds, before the dog and its handler would be upon him. The shadows that had been his concealment could now be his trap.

Slipping out from his alcove, David moved silently along the perimeter of the warehouse, ducking behind crates, and using the stacks of artifacts as cover. The barking grew closer, echoing eerily in the cavernous space.

David located a side exit. Glancing back one last time at the artifacts, he slipped through the exit, disappearing into the fog-covered docks.

Once a safe distance away, he pressed his earpiece, "I'm clear, Lisa. But we've got more on our hands than we initially thought."

And while he had evaded immediate danger, the gravity of the situation weighed heavily on David. The stakes had been raised, the mysteries deepened, and he knew he was only scratching the surface of something monumental.

Chapter 3: Referral

Rebecca "Becca" Lawrence sat in her dimly lit office at the CIA headquarters, three monitors casting a cool glow across her face. Becca was a tall, athletic woman in her mid-thirties with an air of focused intensity. Auburn hair, always tied back in a neat bun, framed a face that held piercing blue eyes. Those eyes had seen more than their fair share of covert operations, especially in the labyrinthine politics and espionage games of the Middle East.

Becca had made a name for herself within the agency with her expertise in Middle Eastern affairs. Fluent in both Arabic and Farsi, she'd been pivotal in tracking high-value targets, intercepting clandestine communications, and, on occasion, running deep undercover ops that took her into the very heart of tumultuous regions. The scars on her body and soul bore witness to the dangers she'd faced and the sacrifices she'd made in the line of duty.

Today, though, she was tracing arms sales from Eastern Europe to Yemen, trying to pinpoint which groups might be about to escalate their activities. As she sifted through data, something caught her eye—a curious link that hinted at the involvement of a U.S.-based group in the weapon supply chain. She zoomed in on the details and found connections to a potential domestic terror organization.

Becca hesitated. While the information was compelling, her focus was international, not domestic. She was torn between pursuing this lead, which wasn't directly in her purview, and passing it on to those who specialized in domestic threats.

Finally, after considering her options, she picked up the phone and dialed a direct line to her contact at the FBI.

"John," she began when her call was answered, "It's Becca. I think I've stumbled onto something that's more in your wheelhouse than mine. You might want to take a look at this."

The conversation was concise, efficient. Both professionals, they quickly shared the necessary information. After hanging up, Becca felt a pang of uncertainty, hoping that she hadn't inadvertently overlooked something critical. But she pushed the thought aside. She had to trust her colleagues just as they trusted her, and her expertise lay elsewhere.

With a sigh, she turned her attention back to the Middle East, knowing that for every lead she chased down, countless more awaited her.

Chapter 4: Dressing Down

T he hum of the engine was a comforting background to the cascade of thoughts running through David's mind. The safety of his car was a stark contrast to the dangers that lurked in the warehouse just moments ago. As he tried to process the night's discoveries, the artifacts kept pulling his attention.

The fog outside settled like a blanket, mirroring the haze of his thoughts. His fingers drummed on the steering wheel, the rhythmic motion providing a sense of calm. He tried to rationalize the presence of the ancient tablets and scrolls, but they didn't fit with what he knew of the group. Their operations had always been about power, control, and immediate financial gain. The world of antiquities, with its slower returns, seemed out of place for them.

Pulling out his phone, he flicked through the images he had taken. The intricacy of the carvings, the delicate calligraphy on the scrolls, it was clear these artifacts were valuable. But in the grand scheme of things, with a potential terror plot looming large, they seemed less relevant.

Perhaps they're a smokescreen, David mused, a distraction from their real intentions.

He pondered on this idea. Misdirection was a commonly used tactic, drawing the attention of law enforcement to one area while the real operation unfolded elsewhere. The artifacts could be a brilliant diversion, leading investigations down the wrong path while the group continued their nefarious activities unchecked. Maybe they were trafficking these historical relics to raise funds. After all, the black market for rare antiquities was lucrative.

Lost in thought, David asked his phone to call Lisa.

"Lisa, it's David."

"I figured as much," she replied, a touch of humor in her voice. "What do you have for me?"

"They're moving something big, but it's not what we expected," David began, cautiously choosing his words.

"What do you mean?"

He hesitated for a moment before answering, "I found artifacts, ancient ones. Tablets, scrolls. But I couldn't find any evidence of weapons or explosives."

Silence greeted him from the other end. David could picture Lisa, brow furrowed, processing the information.

"You think this is their new operation? Trading in antiquities?"

"It's a possibility," David admitted. "The artifacts could just be a means to fund their other activities. Maybe they're using it to mask their real intent."

Lisa sounded skeptical. "It's a leap, David. From terror plots to antique smuggling. It doesn't fit their profile."

"I know," he conceded, frustration evident in his tone. "But it's all I've got for now. The meeting I overheard was cryptic, but they were discussing some organization moving Biblical artifacts and mislabeling the paperwork for smuggling."

Lisa sighed, "Alright. Get back here. We need to unpack this. If they've changed their MO, we need to be ahead of them."

David agreed, switching off the call. But as he drove through the fog-laden streets, doubt clouded his thoughts. The artifacts felt like a piece in a larger puzzle he wasn't seeing. He had relayed the immediate threat to Lisa, but he couldn't shake the feeling that there was more to the relics than met the eye.

Parking in the underground lot of the FBI headquarters, he paused, taking a moment to gather himself. Deep down, something nagged at him, a gnawing sensation that he was missing something crucial.

Stepping out of the car, David hoped that the team could shed more light on the situation. As he headed towards the elevator, the weight of responsibility pressed on him. He had a duty to prevent any potential threat, but he also had an obligation to uncover the truth, no matter how convoluted it might be.

The large glass doors of the FBI headquarters slid open with a soft hiss, revealing the familiar sterile corridor beyond. Fluorescent lights bathed the hallway in a cold, clinical glow. For David Mitchell, he had always felt out of place, a realm where order and protocol reigned supreme. Today, as he stepped onto the sleek, polished floor, the atmosphere felt worse.

The hallway was bustling, agents engaged in hushed conversations, their eyes darting around, a tangible unease in the air. David's entrance didn't go unnoticed. Heads turned, conversations stilled, and there was an immediate, almost tangible shift in the room's energy. The usual courteous nods and friendly smiles from colleagues he'd worked alongside for years were conspicuously absent. Instead, averted eyes and hushed whispers filled the void.

David could feel the weight of scrutiny on him. Every step he took seemed to echo louder, every gaze he met seemed to question his recent actions. Word had undoubtedly spread about the botched operation at the docks and the dark implications it held. The murmurs, though inaudible, seemed to resonate with the same frequency – disappointment, concern, doubt.

A young analyst, whose name David couldn't immediately recall, quickly stepped out of his path, eyes cast down. It was a subtle move, but the message was clear. David's recent decisions, his perceived failures, had caused ripples throughout the bureau, ripples that now threatened to become tidal waves.

Drawing a deep breath, David continued down the hallway, steeling himself against the palpable tension. He could feel the weight of expectation, the collective hope that he'd provide explanations, shed light on the murky situation they all found themselves in.

The closed door of the Special Agent In Charge loomed ahead, a silent testament to the reckoning that awaited. And as David approached, hand poised to knock, he took a moment to gather his thoughts, preparing himself for the confrontation that lay beyond.

The office door was imposing, a solid block of polished oak with a frosted glass pane that bore the stenciled title: "Special Agent In Charge – Robert Carlsen." David took a deep breath, feeling the weight of the situation, and knocked twice.

A curt "Come in" sounded from within.

Pushing the door open, David was immediately met with the piercing gaze of SAC Robert Carlsen. Carlsen was a tall man, silver-haired with a stern demeanor that had been carved from years in the field and countless high-stakes operations. His office was meticulously organized, a testament to his by-the-book nature. Today, however, it wasn't the usual pristine haven. Papers were strewn across the desk, alongside open folders and a screen displaying various news websites.

Carlsen motioned for David to sit. "Agent Mitchell," he began, voice cold, "care to explain yourself?"

David took the seat opposite Carlsen, trying to formulate a response. "Sir, I understand your concerns. I believed I had enough information to proceed—"

"You believed?" Carlsen interjected, his tone incredulous. "Your belief has jeopardized this entire operation! You discovered a potential human trafficking ring, and there wasn't even a SWAT team on alert!"

David tried to defend his stance. "I was working with the intel I had. The arms deal—"

Carlsen cut him off, slamming a hand on his desk, making the scattered papers flutter. "Forget the arms deal! We've got human lives at stake, and the media is having a field day!" He motioned to the computer screen where various news headlines blared:

- "Human Trafficking Ring Unearthed in City Warehouse?"

- "FBI Blindsided: Innocent Lives in Jeopardy!"
- "National Security at Risk: Where is the Oversight?"

David swallowed hard, each headline hitting like a punch to the gut. He knew the media's power to shape narratives and the pressure those narratives could exert on the Bureau.

Carlsen leaned forward, eyes cold. "Your recent decisions on this case are bordering on negligence, Mitchell. It's like you're working without a strategy. You've been in this game long enough to know better."

David clenched his fists, feeling the sting of the reprimand. "I'm doing my best with the cards I've been dealt."

"Your best?" Carlsen scoffed. "I'm beginning to doubt that. Maybe this case would be better off with another lead."

David's heart raced. The thought of being pulled off this case, especially now, was unbearable. He leaned forward, voice laced with desperation. "Sir, please. I've dedicated months to this investigation. I know the players, the stakes. One misstep doesn't invalidate all the groundwork."

Carlsen regarded him for a moment, a tense silence filling the room. The weight of their shared history, of years working together, hung in the balance. "You know, David," Carlsen began, his voice softening, "I worked with your father on a few cases back in the day. He was a great agent, one of the best I've seen." Carlsen gazed out his office window.

David's exterior remained composed, but internally, a storm of emotions raged. He had always heard stories of his father's brilliance in the field, but growing up, he had felt a void, an absence of warmth and connection. He never truly felt like he knew his father, never felt the love that a son should.

After what felt like an eternity, Carlsen finally spoke, his voice softer, but still edged with concern. "David, I've always trusted your instincts. But you need to understand, the stakes have never been higher. Mistakes aren't an option. Not anymore."

"I understand, sir," David replied, his voice steady, though inside he grappled with the memories of a distant father and a challenging upbringing.

Carlsen sighed, leaning back in his chair. "See that it doesn't. Because next time, there might not be a case for you to come back to."

David acknowledged the gravity of Carlsen's words, realizing that he was being given a second chance, but also a warning. The path ahead was clear – he had to rectify his missteps and ensure that the culprits were brought to justice. No matter the cost.

The door closed behind David with a muffled thud, echoing the weight of the conversation that had just transpired. The dimly lit hallway of the FBI headquarters, a path he'd tread countless times, felt alien. The familiar hum of activity around him—the chatter of agents, the distant ringing phones, the rustling of papers—all seemed distant, drowned out by the rush of thoughts clouding his mind.

Each step away from the SAC's office felt heavy, every footfall echoing the doubts that were now gnawing at him. The once-clear lines of his mission blurred, muddied by unexpected turns and the sting of Carlsen's words.

The covert world, with its shadows and uncertainties, had always been a realm where David felt a sense of belonging. It was a place where his instincts thrived, where the rules were flexible, where every challenge was just another puzzle to solve. The adrenaline of the chase, the intricacies of unraveling plots— it had always been his strength.

Yet, in the 'ordinary' world of the FBI, where operations followed protocols and decisions were scrutinized, David felt an overwhelming pressure. A world where every mistake was magnified, every failure a mark against his record.

He paused for a moment, leaning against the cool wall, and closed his eyes. The darkness seemed comforting, a brief respite from the glaring lights of judgment. The memories of past successes, of the accolades and commendations, now seemed like distant echoes, overshadowed by recent events.

Was he losing his edge? Had he grown too comfortable in the shadows, too reliant on gut instincts? The whispers of doubt grew louder, questioning his every decision, making him second guess himself.

Shaking his head, David tried to push away the crippling self-doubt. He had faced adversity before, had come up against challenges that seemed insurmountable. This was just another test, another obstacle to overcome. But the longing for validation, the burning desire to prove his worth, was undeniable.

He needed to set things right, not just for the sake of the case or the victims, but for himself. He had to prove that he still had what it took, that his years in the field hadn't dulled his senses.

Drawing a deep breath, David straightened up, determination replacing hesitation. He'd delve back into the investigation, retrace his steps, find the missing pieces. He'd been knocked down, yes, but he wasn't out. Not yet.

With renewed vigor, David headed towards the operations room. The weight of Carlsen's warning still pressed heavily on him, but so did a newfound resolve. The journey ahead was uncertain, but David Mitchell was a fighter, and he wasn't about to give up.

The operations room was abuzz with activity—agents hunched over desks, analyzing data, phone conversations overlapping in a cacophony of urgency. Yet amidst the hustle,

Lisa Reynolds stood apart, her gaze fixated on the entrance. She was waiting for David to enter. The moment their eyes met, she motioned him over, her expression a mix of concern and resolve.

David approached her desk, the weight of the previous conversation with the SAC still palpable. But Lisa, with her uncommon ability to read him, seemed to sense the undercurrents of his thoughts.

Without preamble, she said in a mocking voice, "Mitchell, you've failed me for the last time!" She laughed and remarked, "I can guess how it went with Carlsen. But remember, our mission is larger than the politics of this office."

David sighed, rubbing the bridge of his nose. "You know, for once, I wish he'd see the bigger picture. It's not about ticking off checkboxes, Lisa. We're dealing with lives here."

Lisa leaned in closer, her voice dropping to a hushed whisper. "David, I've known you for years. God has gifted you with your dedication, your passion—it's what makes you a great agent. But sometimes, passion can blind us."

He bristled at her words, a defensive retort forming on his lips. But he stopped, his eyes searching hers. "You think I've lost objectivity on this?"

Lisa hesitated for a moment, choosing her words carefully. "I think you're so driven to make things right, to rectify past oversights, that you might be missing the forest for the trees."

David leaned back, absorbing her words. The recent failures, the constant second-guessing, had indeed left him on edge. Was he indeed developing a tunnel vision, honing in on specifics while missing the broader narrative?

"You know," Lisa continued, her tone softening, "sometimes, stepping back, gaining a fresh perspective, can give us clarity."

David considered this, his brow furrowed. "I just feel... responsible. For all of it. And every day we don't act, they gain ground."

"I understand that," Lisa replied gently, placing a comforting hand on his arm. "But we're a team, David. You don't have to bear the weight alone. Maybe it's time to lean on the rest of us a bit more."

A heavy silence settled between them. David's eyes, often so sharp and focused, now looked wearied, introspective. "Maybe you're right. Maybe I've been so caught up, so obsessed with piecing it all together, that I've missed some obvious signs."

Lisa gave a reassuring smile. "All I'm saying is, trust in your team. Trust in me. We've got your back. And together, we'll see this through."

With a nod of acknowledgment, David took a deep breath, feeling the weight of the past few weeks slowly lifting. Lisa's words, while hard to digest, had given him a moment of clarity.

David's gaze was anchored to the floor, a battleground of thoughts storming through his mind. Failures, missed steps, lost opportunities—they all danced in his consciousness like specters, mocking, deriding. But amongst the clashing tumult of self-doubt and regret, there sparked a defiant, indomitable spirit, unwilling to be quenched.

David looked up, his gaze meeting Lisa's. In her eyes, he saw a reflection of his own internal war. But there was something else—a silent assertion of faith in the man he was, in the agent he had proven himself to be time and time again.

"I'm not done, Lisa," David declared, his voice echoing the resolute fire rekindling within him. "I've fought too long, come too far to be undone by mistakes, however grave."

A smile, faint but unmistakable, traced Lisa's lips. It wasn't a smile of jubilation but of recognition—a silent acknowledgment of the fierce determination that had always defined David Mitchell.

David retreated to his desk. The files, teeming with evidence, insights, and yet, unsolved mysteries, lay sprawled before him. Each piece was a fragment of a jigsaw puzzle, chaotic and seemingly incoherent, yet David knew that somewhere within this disarray lay secrets that could unravel the enigmatic terror group they were relentlessly pursuing.

On his desk, David found a file with a note on top, *My CIA contact sent this file over, thought it might be related to the case you're working on – John.* He scanned the contents before moving back to the evidence he collected in the warehouse.

He picked up the photographs of the ancient artifacts. Could there be more to these artifacts than met the eye? Each inscription and etching a potential thread to discovering this group's plans.

As he sorted through the photographs, a particular image of an artifact caught his eye—a stone tablet inscribed with ancient script. As he peered closely, recognition sparked. He'd seen these symbols before during his studies on Middle Eastern history and lore.

"This..." David muttered, his voice trembling with realization, "This is a prophecy."

Lisa, hearing the tremor in his voice, approached. "What did you find?"

David pointed to the inscription, "This speaks of end times, monumental changes, and events that were said to unfold at the climax of humanity's journey."

Lisa looked skeptically at him. "Prophecies? David, you think this is their angle?"

"I don't know," David admitted. "But it's clear they believe in this enough to risk smuggling it. This might be a clue to discover their motives."

Chapter 5: Sauce

The dim lights of the bar bathed the room in a subdued glow, the ambiance complemented by the soft tunes playing in the background. The rustic wooden counter, worn and polished from years of use, hosted an array of patrons — some in animated conversation, others lost in thought.

David occupied a stool at one end of the bar, his posture slightly hunched, his gaze locked onto the glass of whiskey in front of him. It wasn't his first of the evening, and the bartender knew it wouldn't be his last.

Maddie, the lively bartender with striking brunette locks and a sparkling personality, had seen David many times before. Their exchanges typically ranged from light banter to slightly flirty chats. However, tonight she sensed a difference in his demeanor. The usually self-assured David seemed distant, his eyes reflecting a depth of turmoil.

Making her way over to him, she placed another glass of whiskey before David. "On the house," she said with a hint of playfulness, though her eyes radiated genuine concern.

David looked up, forcing a faint smile. "Thanks, Maddie."

Leaning on the counter, Maddie lowered her voice. "You've been here often enough for me to notice when something's bothering you. Want to talk about it?"

He took a sip, letting the liquid warmth spread before replying, "Just one of those days."

Before Maddie could press further, a confident-looking woman with high heels approached the bar, positioning herself next to David. With a coy smile, she addressed him, "Is this seat taken?"

David turned to face her, the weight of his day making him more direct than usual. "I'm really not in the mood for company right now."

A bit taken aback by his bluntness, she nodded curtly and chose another spot further down the bar.

Maddie, eyebrows raised, gave David a teasing look. "Passed on that? She seemed intrigued."

David ran a hand through his hair, exhaling slowly. "Not tonight, Maddie. Just... not tonight."

Understanding his need for space, Maddie simply patted his hand. "Alright, but if you need a chat or another drink, I'm right here."

David nodded in appreciation, continuing to find solace in his drink, hoping the warmth of the whiskey would blur the edges of his disconcerting thoughts.

As the minutes ticked by, the bar's ambient noise faded into the background for David. The weight of his memories pressed down on him, and he found himself transported back to a time when he was just a boy, eagerly waiting by the window for his father to come home.

The image of a young David, sitting on the living room floor with his toy police badge and handcuffs, was vivid. He'd often play pretend, imagining himself catching bad guys just like he believed his father did. Every evening, he'd wait, hoping that today would be the day his father would walk through the door, sweep him up in his arms, and tell him stories of his adventures.

But more often than not, the door remained closed. And when it did open, it wasn't to the loving embrace of a father, but to a distant, preoccupied man who barely acknowledged his presence. David remembered the countless nights he'd go to bed, clutching his toy badge, tears streaming down his face, wondering why his father didn't love him enough to be there.

The bar's atmosphere grew heavier for David as he recalled a particular evening. He had won a school award, and his heart had swelled with pride. Racing home, he'd placed the certificate on the dining table, hoping his father would see it and finally have a reason to be proud of him. But when his father came home late that night, he barely glanced at the certificate, muttering a distracted "That's good" before heading to his room.

David's heart had shattered that night. He had yearned for validation, for a sign that he mattered to his father. But it never came. And as the years went by, the distance between them only grew.

The pain of those memories, the yearning for a father's love, still haunted him. It was a void that no amount of success or accolades could fill.

Maddie, sensing his distress, walked over and placed a comforting hand on his shoulder. "Hey, you okay?"

David looked up, his eyes glistening. "Just memories, Maddie. Old wounds that never really heal."

She squeezed his shoulder gently. "Sometimes, talking about it helps."

David nodded, taking a deep breath. "Maybe someday. But not tonight."

Maddie gave him a sympathetic smile, understanding that everyone had their own battles and scars. She left him to his thoughts, but not before refilling his glass, hoping it would offer some temporary solace.

Chapter 6: The Alarm

T he dim glow of the overhead lights cast an eerie ambiance over the FBI meeting room. David, having spent countless hours in this space, felt an unfamiliar tension in the air today. Across the table sat the SAC, Robert Carlsen, a seasoned agent whose stern face bore the scars of many battles fought in the line of duty. Carlsen's piercing eyes seemed to challenge David, skepticism evident in every glance.

"David," Carlsen began, his voice deep and resonant, "I've reviewed your report. It's... complex."

David took a deep breath, feeling the weight of the situation. "Sir, the evidence is clear. The smuggling of these artifacts isn't just about their historical value. It's intertwined with the human trafficking operations."

The room's walls were plastered with evidence supporting David's claim. Photographs of ancient relics were juxtaposed with images of terrified faces, victims of trafficking. Maps pinpointed locations of artifact discoveries alongside known trafficking routes. Color-coded strings connected the dots, weaving a sinister tapestry of crime that spanned continents.

Carlsen studied the web of evidence, his brow furrowed. "You're suggesting that these artifacts are not just being smuggled for their monetary value, but they're somehow linked to the trafficking operations?"

David nodded, his conviction unwavering. "Exactly, sir. The patterns are too consistent to be coincidental. Wherever we find these artifacts, we find evidence of human trafficking. They're using the same routes, the same contacts. There's a deeper connection here, and I believe if we can unravel the mystery of these artifacts, we can strike a significant blow to the trafficking ring."

Carlsen leaned forward, his skepticism slowly giving way to intrigue. "It's an ambitious theory, David. But if you're right, this could be groundbreaking. However, we need to tread carefully. We're dealing with forces that appear that they won't hesitate to react."

David met Carlsen's gaze, determination burning in his eyes. "I understand the risks, sir. But we have a duty to these victims. We can't let this slide."

Just as David was wrapping up a response, determined to convince Carlsen of the case's strange connections between the Biblical artifacts and human trafficking, an earsplitting wail shattered the room's stillness. The lockdown sirens, unmistakable and urgent, blared throughout the building. Red warning lights began to flash, casting an eerie, pulsating glow over the two men.

David and the SAC exchanged a startled glance. The intensity of their previous conversation was instantly overshadowed by the pressing emergency. The building's lockdown protocol was reserved for only the most severe security breaches or immediate threats.

"What on earth...?" Carlsen murmured, rising from his seat, his seasoned instincts kicking in.

David, equally alert, responded, "This isn't a drill. We need to find out what's happening."

The room, which moments ago had been a battlefield of wits and wills, now became a starting point for an entirely unforeseen crisis. The two men were united in the face of a larger, incomprehensible threat.

Their steps synchronized, David and Carlsen moved toward the door pulling out their service weapon, prepared to confront the chaos that awaited them outside. The blaring sirens, a haunting soundtrack to their uncertainty, only deepened the mystery of what was unfolding in the corridors beyond.

The stark silence that followed the cessation of the blaring alarms was deafening. The halls of the FBI headquarters, typically a bastion of order and control, had morphed into corridors of confusion and terror. David and Carlsen emerged from the confines of the meeting room, their eyes widening at the spectacle unfolding before them.

A haunting stillness lay where the fervent activity of seasoned agents once thrived. The alarm's sinister wails were replaced by frantic shouts, a cacophony of fear and disbelief. Agents, their usual composure shattered, swarmed the hallways in a desperate search for explanation and safety.

David's heart raced in his chest, the pulsating beat a grim soundtrack to the surrounding chaos. His eyes, trained for crisis and threat, darted across the room. The sprawled bodies of his comrades, still and lifeless, punctured the organized chaos. Every agent down was a comrade lost, every still form a silent testament to an inexplicable horror.

And then, amidst the storm of chaos, David's eyes froze. There, amongst his fallen brethren, lay Lisa. Her once radiant eyes, windows to a soul teeming with vigor and determination, now stared vacantly. Her face, always the source of stern encouragement, was frozen in an expression of shock, a silent scream echoing the horror of the unspeakable event.

"No..." The word escaped David's lips, barely a whisper amidst the surrounding turmoil. He rushed forward, his heart, and his soul rejecting the brutal reality before him.

Special Agent in Charge Carlsen's firm hand on his shoulder was the only anchor in a world that seemed to have slipped into an abyss of unreason. Agents, those still on their feet, were a mix of hysteria and militant order. Their training willed them to action even as their humanity grappled with the unimaginable.

Cries for medics, orders to secure the premises, the directive shouts attempted to carve a path through the fog of panic. But amidst the commands and the frenzied rush, a chilling silence from the fallen agents bore the gravest testimony. Something inexplicable, something terrifying had invaded their sanctuary of law and order.

As David stared at Lisa's lifeless form, he became an island of silent devastation.

Carlsen's voice, urgent yet surprisingly steady, attempted to pierce David's stupor. "Mitchell! Snap out of it! I need you with me."

And as SAC Carlsen pulled David up, forcing him into action amidst the pandemonium, a grave realization seeped into every corner of the FBI headquarters. They were no longer just the hunters of hidden threats and unseen enemies. Today, they had become the hunted, thrust into a narrative of horror where the rules of engagement had been horrifyingly rewritten.

David's surroundings seemed surreal. The once familiar hallways of the FBI headquarters now felt like an alien landscape, marred by the haunting stillness of the departed and the raw grief of those left behind. Every step was a challenge, the weight of loss-making the soles of his shoes feel like they were made of lead.

Shaking off the overwhelming sorrow, David tried to focus on the task at hand. He approached the wall-mounted intercom, pressing the button to connect with other departments, hoping to find some semblance of reason amidst the madness.

"Operations? This is Agent Mitchell. Anyone on this line?" he called out, his voice echoing in the silent corridor. The only response was a disconcerting static, like a forlorn whisper in the vast void of communication. He tried another line, then another, but each attempt yielded the same lifeless hiss. It felt as if the building itself was in mourning, cutting off any link to the outside world.

From the corner of his eye, David noticed Carlsen, his usually unflappable demeanor now etched with worry. "Mitchell! We need eyes on this situation. Get to the security room. Maybe the surveillance feeds can give us some insight into what the hell just happened."

David nodded, acknowledging the order, even as a fresh wave of despair threatened to engulf him. Lisa's image flashed before his eyes, the lifelessness of her face a stark contrast to the vibrant agent he had known. The urge to mourn, to break down was powerful, but his training, his years of dedication to the badge, propelled him forward.

As he navigated the labyrinthine corridors, the aftermath of the mysterious event was everywhere. Some agents sat in stunned silence, their faces reflecting a mix of disbelief and sorrow. Others were locked in tender embraces, their tears flowing freely, unburdened by the confines of professionalism. Amidst this tableau of sorrow, David saw the profound strength of the FBI family, a unity that, even in the darkest of times, refused to break.

An agent, her face streaked with tears, approached David, her voice quivering. "Do we... do we know what happened?"

David looked at her, the pain evident in his eyes. "I'm trying to find out. Stay strong," he urged, his voice gentle yet firm.

Reaching the security room, David swiped his card, the door clicking open. Inside, a bank of monitors displayed a patchwork of scenes from around the building. Some screens showed agents tending to their fallen colleagues, others displayed empty hallways and offices.

David began rewinding the footage, hoping to find a clue, a hint, anything that could explain the inexplicable. The scenes played out in reverse, a morbid dance that ended with the haunting moment when agents, mid-stride or in conversation, simply collapsed.

But there was no external threat, no sign of any intrusion. The agents seemed to have been struck down by an invisible force, a silent killer that left no trace. David felt a chill run down his spine. Whatever had caused this was beyond the realm of conventional threats.

He saved the footage onto a secure drive, knowing that it would be vital for any subsequent investigation. Exiting the security room, David's resolve hardened. The tragedy that had befallen his colleagues was a mystery, but he was determined to unravel it. The path ahead was uncertain, fraught with unknown dangers, but David Mitchell was not one to back down, especially not now. The quest for answers, for justice, had taken on a deeply personal dimension, and he would stop at nothing to uncover the truth.

The operations room, usually a hub of controlled activity, was now an epicenter of confusion and dread. Fluorescent lights overhead bathed the room in a sterile glow, starkly contrasting the wave of emotions displayed on the agents' faces. Eyes which usually held determination and focus now reflected a profound shock.

Every available TV screen flickered with images that felt more at home in an apocalyptic movie than the evening news. As one, the room turned towards the largest screen on the wall, where a prominent news network broadcasted live footage.

The images were terrifying. An airplane, smoke billowing from its engines, descended rapidly, crashing into an open field. The news report then changed to major city intersections, where bodies lay strewn amidst halted traffic. Pedestrians, having witnessed the sudden collapse of friends or strangers, were screaming and running, their faces painted with fear.

A reporter, trying to maintain composure, spoke into her microphone, "Reports are coming in from across the nation, and indeed from around the world. The cause of these sudden deaths is still unknown. Authorities urge everyone to stay indoors and remain calm."

Carlsen, his eyes never leaving the screen, muttered, "What in God's name is happening?"

David, transfixed by the footage, felt an icy dread in his stomach. He'd faced countless threats in his career, from terrorists to criminals, but this was something entirely different. An unknown enemy, unseen, unfathomable.

The news feed shifted to an airport terminal, where travelers were in a state of pandemonium. Some were trying desperately to contact loved ones, while others prayed fervently, hoping for divine intervention.

David felt a tap on his shoulder and turned to find Carlsen, his face etched with concern. "Mitchell, we can't take any chances. We need to treat this as a potential biohazard situation. Assemble a team. We'll wear hazmat suits and begin moving the bodies to a secure location."

David nodded, his professionalism taking over. "Right away, sir."

But as he set out to gather his team and the necessary equipment, a thought persisted. Was this a mere terrorist attack or a pathogen? Or were they witnessing something far more profound, an event that defied any logical or scientific explanation?

SAC Carlsen's voice echoed in the operations room, barely cutting through the cacophony of shock and fear. "Stay alert, everyone! We don't know the cause, and we can't predict who might be next. Safety first."

And as agents began to prepare, the weight of the situation sank in. They were in uncharted territory, faced with an inexplicable phenomenon. The journey to uncover the truth would be arduous and fraught with challenges, but the commitment to their duty and to one another remained unwavering.

David's thoughts were interrupted by the SAC, whose face showed the strain of the situation. "Mitchell," he began, his voice carrying a hint of exhaustion, "we're in uncharted waters. I've dealt with crises, but nothing like this. We need to stabilize, take stock, and lead."

David looked at his superior, admiring the man's unwavering strength in such dire circumstances. Carlsen continued, "We've lost agents today, friends, colleagues. But we're still standing, and we have a duty. A duty to those who've passed, to our nation, and to each other."

David nodded in agreement, his thoughts starting to overwhelm him. "What's our plan, sir?"

"We establish a central command," Carlsen replied, determination evident in his eyes. "We collate every piece of information, no matter how insignificant. We maintain communication with other agencies and offer assistance where needed. We must adapt and respond."

"And the bodies?" David asked hesitantly.

Carlsen exhaled deeply, the weight of the decision evident on his face. "We start by moving our fallen colleagues to the morgue. We treat each one with the dignity and respect they deserve. Once the morgue is full, we'll need to use the walk-in freezers in the cafeteria."

David swallowed hard, the grim reality of their situation hitting him. "I never imagined we'd ever face a situation like this."

Carlsen put a hand on David's shoulder, squeezing gently. "Neither did I, Mitchell. But we'll get through this."

David nodded, feeling a mix of gratitude and resolve. "I'll get started on the arrangements."

The task ahead was as solemn as it was gut-wrenching. The quiet corridors of the FBI headquarters echoed with an eerie silence as a somber procession began. Agents, some visibly shaken, others wearing masks of grim determination, began the heartbreaking task of moving their fallen colleagues.

David stood with a group of agents outside the morgue. The room, which had seen its fair share of victims of crime, now faced an overwhelming influx of the very people who once sought to bring justice to those victims.

Each body was handled with the utmost respect. Two agents were assigned to each fallen colleague, gently lifting them onto a stretcher. They proceeded slowly, the only sound being the muted shuffle of their feet and the occasional stifled sob. As they entered the morgue, each agent took a moment to recognize their fallen comrade, some offering a silent salute, others whispering a prayer.

As the hours wore on and the morgue's capacity was stretched to its limit, the grim reality set in. They would have to use the walk-in freezers in the cafeteria. The very space where these agents had shared meals, celebrated birthdays, and discussed cases would now bear witness to the aftermath of this inexplicable tragedy.

The freezers, usually stocked with food supplies, were quickly cleared. The task was undertaken with swift efficiency, a testament to the agents' training and discipline, even in the face of personal loss.

After the heartrending task of moving the bodies was completed, a silence heavy with unspeakable grief and confusion lingered in the air. David found himself drawn back to the operations room. The array of monitors that adorned the walls cast an ominous glow in the dim lighting, a stark reminder of the unreality they were all now involuntarily a part of.

David's gaze was fixed on the live news feeds, each channel painting a picture of chaos and incomprehension. The broadcasters, usually so composed and articulate, struggled to relay the unfolding horrors with their usual poise. Their voices wavered, betraying the terror and disbelief that had gripped the nation – the world.

David's usually sharp and analytical mind struggled to process the influx of information. The spectrum of emotions running through him was as vast as the scenes of devastation he was witnessing. Each broadcasted segment, each news headline seemed like a punch to his gut, intensifying the surreal nightmare they were all living.

He watched as a reporter, standing outside a major hospital, tried to maintain her composure while describing the scene behind her. Medical personnel were frantically moving between ambulances, attempting to triage and attend to the flood of incoming patients. The reporter spoke of overwhelmed morgues, just like their own situation at the FBI headquarters.

Turning his attention to another screen, David saw aerial footage of a major city intersection, where it seemed time had come to a standstill. Cars had stopped mid-route, their drivers and passengers having succumbed to the mysterious event. Pedestrians lay where they had fallen, turning bustling crosswalks into graveyards.

Every channel, every image underscored the enormity of the crisis. This wasn't a localized event; it was global, indiscriminate, and ruthless. And the more David watched, the more he felt the weight of responsibility bearing down on him. As an FBI agent, he was trained to face threats, to unravel mysteries, and to bring those responsible to justice. But this? This was unlike any challenge he had ever encountered.

Pulling himself away from the screens, David ran a hand through his hair, the reality of their situation sinking in. They were in uncharted territory. The rulebook, so to speak, had been thrown out the window.

David made his way to his office, the weight of the day's events evident in each heavy step. As he entered the familiar space, memories and moments from countless cases flashed before his eyes. He moved to his desk, its polished surface reflecting the dim light, and slowly sank into his chair. The soft leather creaked slightly, a reminder of the countless hours he had spent there, poring over evidence and planning operations.

But this time, his thoughts were consumed not by a case, but by a personal loss. He remembered the last conversation he had shared with Lisa, his fellow FBI agent and the one person who had always understood him, even when words were unnecessary. Their laughter, their shared frustrations, and their unwavering support for each other resonated in his mind. Lisa had been more than just a colleague; she was his closest confidant, the voice of reason amidst the chaos, and the pillar he often leaned on during challenging times. Now, the silence left in her absence was deafening, and David was left grappling with a profound sense of loss.

Chapter 7: Rigor

T he soft hum of sophisticated machinery and the faint glow of computer monitors illuminated the forensic laboratory. The room, with its gleaming white surfaces and orderly arrangement of scientific equipment, was a sanctuary of logic and reason in a world that currently defied both.

David Mitchell stepped into this sterile environment, the weight of the world heavy on his shoulders. The lab's cool air felt almost too clean after the chaos he'd witnessed over the past two days. His gaze settled on Dr. Samuel Owens, bent over a microscope, the lines on his face betraying hours, maybe even days, of work without rest.

David watched as the doctor, with practiced precision, slid a glass slide out of the microscope and carefully placed it on a nearby tray. The action, so simple and methodical, was a stark contrast to the complex mystery they were trying to unravel.

Breaking the silence, Sam's voice, wearied by hours of investigation and its disturbing implications, resonated with deep concern. "David, it's like nothing I've ever seen. We've run every test, exhausted every possible theory, but there's no trace, no markers. Whatever took these lives left no footprint."

David, taking a moment to digest the information, glanced at the screens displaying the statistical data of the global impact. Pie charts and bar graphs showcased the uneven devastation across continents. "The disparities, Sam... It's alarming."

Dr. Owens, nodding solemnly, tapped on one of the graphs. "This, David, is what's most baffling. Parts of Africa, South America, and North America show fatality rates as high as 20%. Yet, regions like Asia, the Middle East, and Russia... their numbers are staggeringly low, in many cases less than 1%."

David's sharp eyes caught on to another display showing a DNA helix. "What's this?" he inquired, pointing at it.

Sam took a deep breath, "That's where things get even murkier. We're seeing indications that this... event, might be targeting specific genetic markers. It's like a precision strike on a molecular level."

David felt a chill run down his spine, the implications sinking in. "So, you're suggesting that this is an engineered virus? Specifically designed to affect certain genetic profiles?"

Dr. Owens sighed, running a hand through his greying hair, "It's one of the few theories we're left with. But the technology required to pull off something of this magnitude... it's beyond anything we know."

David leaned against a counter, the weight of their discoveries pressing down on him. The idea that someone, or something, had the capability to launch a targeted genetic attack on such a massive scale was almost too much to fathom.

The stark differences in mortality rates across continents meant that global reactions would vary wildly. Nations most devastated might look upon the less affected ones with suspicion, potentially accusing them of being the culprits behind this biological nightmare.

"Sam," David started, his voice somber, "if this is true, we're not just looking at a global health crisis. This could spiral into geopolitical tensions, accusations, maybe even conflicts."

Sam nodded gravely, "I know, David. It's a tinderbox, and it's our job to find out who's holding the match."

Both men were lost in thought, the gravity of the situation evident. The lab, with its promise of answers, had only deepened the enigma. The quest for the truth was more urgent than ever.

In the days and weeks that followed the unprecedented global catastrophe, the world found itself in the throes of a cleanup operation of a scale never before witnessed. Countries from every corner of the planet joined hands, not in celebration or diplomacy, but in the somber task of tending to their dead and making sense of the disaster.

Africa, with its vast landscapes, saw entire villages and towns decimated. Fields that once echoed with the lively sounds of children playing were now silent, save for the sorrowful cries of those left behind. The sprawling savannahs, once witnesses to the circle of life, became the resting places for countless souls taken too soon. The local communities, already strained by decades of challenges, now faced the seemingly insurmountable task of burying their loved ones, often resorting to mass graves as the sheer number of the deceased became overwhelming.

The United States, a superpower and beacon of hope for many, found its cities and towns paralyzed. From the skyscrapers of New York to the vast expanses of the Midwest, every state, every community felt the weight of the tragedy. The mighty machinery of the nation was repurposed, with factories that once produced cars and gadgets now manufacturing coffins and body bags. Sports stadiums, symbols of entertainment and unity, were transformed into relief centers, providing shelter and solace to those in need.

Europe, though less affected compared to other continents, was not untouched. The ancient streets of Rome, Paris, and London, steeped in history and culture, now carried the heavy burden of sorrow. The Seine and the Thames, rivers that had witnessed centuries of human civilization, now mirrored the grief of their cities, their waters carrying tributes to the departed.

In contrast, Asia and the Middle East, for reasons yet unknown, were largely spared the scale of devastation seen elsewhere. While they did not remain untouched, the number of deaths was significantly lower. However, this geographic distinction did not mean they were immune to the pain. Every life mattered, and every loss was mourned. The regions, with their ancient traditions and cultures, offered prayers, lighting lamps, and incense in remembrance.

The initial shock and grief were compounded by the palpable fear of a potential viral outbreak. Was this an act of bioterrorism? A new, unknown pathogen? Nations ramped up their efforts, not just in handling the dead, but in understanding the cause. Every body was treated as a potential carrier, leading to heartbreaking scenes of hazmat-clad individuals performing last rites, devoid of the usual personal touch and warmth. Research labs worldwide collaborated like never before, racing against time to ascertain the cause and ensure there were no secondary outbreaks.

The suddenness of the deaths, combined with the absence of any clear cause, led many to speculate about a potent and swift-acting pathogen. Hospitals and health centers were inundated with the living, individuals frantic and fearful of infection. Nations scrambled to set up quarantine zones, and international travel came to a near standstill, with countries sealing their borders in a desperate attempt to prevent the potential spread of a contagion.

But as days turned into weeks, with no signs of any viral or bacterial outbreak, this theory began to wane. Instead, the world was left with a growing list of questions and an ever-deepening mystery. Why were some regions affected more than others? What was the connecting thread between the deceased?

Global organizations like the World Health Organization and the United Nations coordinated relief efforts, offering aid, resources, and expertise. Borders, often sources of contention, were momentarily forgotten as nations leaned on each other, sharing their pain, their resources, and their hopes for understanding and recovery.

Cleanup operations became a top priority. Streets once filled with joy and commerce now bore the grim sight of bodies awaiting transport. Trucks, previously used for transporting goods and produce, were now repurposed to transport the deceased. World leaders, in a rare display of global unity, coordinated efforts to ensure that the cleanup operations were carried out with dignity and respect.

The massive global cleanup, though rooted in tragedy, also laid bare the indomitable human spirit. Communities came together, setting aside differences of race, religion, and nationality. They grieved together, worked together, and hoped together, embodying the resilience of humanity in the face of unimaginable adversity.

Chapter 8: Pwned

Becca Lawrence's Virginia home, with its suburban charm, seemed a world away from the dark and intricate web she delved into daily as a CIA agent. The room was a testament to a mother's love for her child; Leila's drawings tacked on the walls, colorful blocks and plush toys dotting the carpet. Sunlight streamed through the window, casting warm patches over the cool tiles.

On a wooden coffee table, a manila envelope lay slightly ajar, revealing a photograph and the bold type: "Nadia Idris." Next to it sat Becca, her eyes showing traces of sleeplessness. She held a delicate teacup, its content untouched, her gaze fixed on her daughter, Leila, as she slept curled up on a plush sofa. The serenity of the scene contrasted starkly with the turmoil churning within her.

The sharp buzz of her phone disrupted the quiet, pulling her back from the precipice of her thoughts. Taking a steadying breath, Becca answered, "Mike."

"Becca," a voice acknowledged, its tone professional. "I understand the situation is tough. But we've got a brief window with Nadia. We need to act."

She hesitated, her eyes never leaving Leila. "Every moment I'm away, I risk not being here if... if something happens. With what the world's going through, I can't leave her side."

There was a pause on the other end. "Becca, you know as well as I do that we're in uncharted territory. Nadia might have insights. It's vital."

Gazing at the photograph poking out from the envelope, she whispered, "I never imagined I'd be making choices like this. I wish things were simpler."

Mike responded, "Don't we all? But duty calls. It always does."

Her fingers subconsciously played with the locket around her neck, a gift from Leila last Christmas. "I need a few hours, Mike."

He nodded, the gesture almost audible. "Alright. But time is of the essence. Do what you must, and then we proceed. Remember, we're all feeling the strain."

Hanging up, Becca was caught in the confluence of her duty and the fierce need to protect her child. The world had changed, but the choices remained just as hard, if not harder. She leaned over, gently brushing a strand of hair from Leila's face, the touch a silent promise.

After hanging up, Becca picked up her phone once more, dialing a number she knew by heart. Mrs. Martinez, her elderly neighbor, answered after a couple of rings. The kind-hearted woman had always shown an affectionate fondness for Leila. "Mrs. Martinez," Becca began, her voice urgent but composed, "I need a favor. It's important. Can you look after Leila for a few hours?" There was a pause, followed by the gentle voice of Mrs. Martinez assuring her that she'd be there in a heartbeat. Relieved, Becca whispered her thanks, the weight on her shoulders slightly lifted by the knowledge that her daughter would be in caring hands.

The café, tucked away from the bustling streets, always had an aura of secrets. Dimmed lights reflected off polished wooden tables, and the faint aroma of espresso mixed with whispered conversations, creating an atmosphere of clandestine rendezvous. It was the kind of place where conversations evaporated into the ether, leaving no trace.

Becca sat, scanning the dim room until her eyes settled on a familiar face. Nadia Idris sat in a shadowed corner, her eyes darting around nervously. Her fingers, once nimble and sure when typing away at a keyboard, now trembled slightly as they wrapped around a mug.

Their greeting was a blend of professional acknowledgment and shared history. "It's been a while, Nadia," Becca started, taking the seat opposite her.

Nadia looked up, her eyes searching Becca's, "Not long enough considering the state of the world." She paused, taking a shaky breath. "You said this meeting was urgent?"

"I believe you might have information we need, given your... expertise." Becca's voice was calm, but the urgency was evident.

Nadia leaned in closer, her voice dropping to almost a whisper. "It's not what they're saying, Becca. It's what they aren't." Her eyes were intense, hinting at the depth of her findings. "I've seen encrypted messages bouncing between shadow networks, things that don't add up, especially now."

Becca leaned in, her interest piqued. "What have you found?"

A pause hung in the air, tension mounting. Nadia's eyes darted to the exit and then back to Becca. "Not here. And not without my payment first."

As Becca mulled over Nadia's demands, a distant memory of her daughter, Leila, crept into her mind, juxtaposing the stakes at play. The information Nadia possessed could be crucial. Still, Becca had to tread carefully, not only for her sake but for Leila's.

The cold wind continued to howl outside, but the cafe's interior was thick with tension. The two women, from their corner booth, eyed each newcomer suspiciously, the last interruption still fresh in their minds.

"You're taking a big risk meeting with me, Nadia," Becca began, trying to ease back into their conversation.

Nadia laughed bitterly. "Aren't we all? Every time we step outside now."

Becca leaned in, her voice stern. "You hinted at something bigger. Multiple groups? Talk to me."

Nadia sighed, glancing out the window before replying, "You've seen the chatter. Groups from every corner of the world are coming out of the woodwork, claiming responsibility."

"But?"

"But it's noise, Becca. Smoke and mirrors. Boasts from groups desperate to appear more influential than they are. Many are just capitalizing on the chaos."

Becca's frustration was evident. "So, you're telling me we're back at square one?"

Nadia hesitated, her voice dropping to a whisper. "Not exactly. There's a pattern, an anomaly in the digital chaos. Bursts of data, too precise, too coordinated."

"And? What does it mean?"

Nadia seemed to retreat further into her shell. "I don't know. But it's different from the regular claims. Whoever they are, they're more sophisticated, more... controlled."

Becca sighed, rubbing her temples. "Nadia, I need more than just hunches. We're grasping at straws."

A vulnerable look crossed Nadia's face. "I told you what I know. Maybe it's not much, but it's a lead."

The seasoned CIA agent studied Nadia for a moment, gauging the hacker's reliability. Nadia's brilliant mind was evident, but the events had clearly taken a toll on her. The weight of the world seemed to rest on both their shoulders.

"I need you to dig deeper," Becca pressed, "You're onto something. I can feel it."

Nadia looked away, her expression unreadable. "I'll see what I can find. But Becca, be careful. If I'm right, this isn't just a game of claims and boasts. This... this is a whole new level of danger."

The eerie silence that followed the power outage was almost palpable. Nadia's laptop, a small island of light in a sudden sea of darkness, hummed softly. Becca's senses, honed by years of fieldwork, instantly snapped to high alert.

Nadia chuckled nervously. "I'd been waiting for this. Digital footprints indicate Russian hackers are having a field day with the chaos."

"Stay safe, Nadia," Becca commanded, her voice carrying the authority of someone who knew the perils of their line of work all too well. She hesitated, her gaze lingering on Nadia a moment longer before she pivoted, her silhouette merging with the darkness.

The cold night air stung Becca's face as she stepped into the desolate streets. The world was a shadow of its former self. A silence, deeper than the usual quiet of the night, punctuated the unease that had spread since the incident.

As Becca made her way towards the subway, every step echoing in the empty street, she felt it - the unnerving sensation of being watched. She quickened her pace, her keen eyes scanning her surroundings.

There – a shadow detached itself from the darkness, a man with wrap-around glasses, his build betraying a military background. Every instinct screamed danger.

She weighed her options. Engage or evade?

Evasion won. A confrontation, especially given the unknowns, was ill-advised.

Thinking quickly, she dashed into a nearby Chinese restaurant, the bright neon sign offering a momentary distraction. The aromatic scents of stir fry and spices hit her instantly. Waitstaff shouted orders while customers chatted away, oblivious to her sudden entrance.

Becca weaved through tables, narrowly avoiding a waiter carrying a tray full of hot soup. She could hear the muffled curses of her pursuer as he tried to navigate the same path she had just taken.

Reaching the kitchen, she shoved open a back door, finding herself in a tight, dimly lit alley. She could hear the distant hum of city traffic and the clinking of dishes from inside the restaurant.

Making her way out of the alley, she spotted a taxi idling by the curb. Without hesitation, she threw open the door and jumped inside, urging the driver to go. As the taxi sped away, she took one last look back, seeing her pursuer emerge from the alley just in time to see the taillights fade into the distance.

Chapter 9: Contemplation

T he rhythmic hum of Washington D.C. below gently penetrates the thick windows of David's midscale apartment. High up in his living space, a large room with sparse modern furnishings, he stands with his arms crossed, his silhouette darkened by the piercing glare of the massive wall-mounted television.

On the screen, a news anchor with a polished demeanor presents the latest findings with an overly enthusiastic tone, "Leading scientists now believe there's a bizarre correlation between a disruption in the Earth's magnetic field and the sudden, worldwide deaths. Preliminary reports seem to suggest..." she hesitated ever so slightly, "...that the unvaccinated against COVID have been disproportionately affected."

David scoffed, moving closer to the TV as if challenging its absurd proclamation. "The Earth's magnetic field? Really? This is their best explanation?" He muttered, fingers drumming agitatedly on the cool glass of his coffee table. Clips played of officials in lab coats, discussing charts and pointing at sun diagrams. But to David, their words felt empty, rehearsed. He'd been in the business long enough to recognize when a narrative was being pushed, and this? This was textbook deflection.

His phone vibrated, casting a pale blue light on the dark wood of the table. Ignoring it, David leaned back, memories of countless briefings and redacted documents flooding his mind. He recalled hushed conversations in the shadowy corridors of the Bureau, of theories and speculations whispered but never documented. Could this be another one of those situations? A truth so colossal that its very acknowledgement could send the world spiraling further into chaos?

Taking a deep breath, he turned off the TV, casting the room into a somber dimness. The only light now was the city's glow, refracted through his blinds. The official narrative might be solar flares and strange correlations, but David's gut told him a different story.

David reached for the file he brought home with him. He carefully opened the envelope, pulling out a series of photographs, documents, and transcripts. The first photo showed a man in his mid-40s, with sharp features and a cold, calculating gaze. Mark Harris.

The next few photos were surveillance shots. Harris at a rally, Harris meeting with known extremist leaders, Harris entering a warehouse late at night. David's eyes narrowed as he studied each image, trying to piece together the narrative.

A transcript of a wiretapped conversation caught his attention. Harris was speaking with an unidentified male.

"The time is coming," Harris said. *"We've been preparing for this for years. The world is distracted, and that's when it's going to happen. Wars and rumors of wars."*

The unidentified male responded, *"What about our people? Are they ready?"*

"More than ready," Harris replied with confidence. *"It's something we've been preparing for."*

David felt a chill run down his spine. This wasn't just talk; Harris was planning something big. He skimmed through bank statements, showing large sums of money being transferred to various accounts, all linked back to Harris.

David leaned back in his chair, rubbing his temples. The weight of the evidence was overwhelming. Mark Harris wasn't just a threat; he was the suspected leader of a well-organized domestic terrorist group. And with the world distracted by the bizarre magnetic field phenomenon, they had the perfect cover to execute their plans.

David's cell phone buzzed, lighting up the dimly lit room of his apartment. He reached for it and saw the name "Jacob" flashed on the screen.

"Hey," David said, answering. "What have you got?"

There was a brief pause. "I've located Mark Harris."

David's brow furrowed. Mark had been a thorn in their side, a mysterious player in a series of dangerous operations they'd been monitoring. "Mark Harris? Seriously? Where is he?"

"Cell phone believed to be his just pinged. It's in an urban housing area in Baltimore."

David felt a rush of adrenaline. This could be a significant breakthrough. "Have you alerted the local field office?"

"Not yet. Thought you'd want to be the first to know. Considering... well, considering everything."

David's mind raced. They could bring in a full team, but Mark had a knack for evading capture. A quieter approach might be more effective.

David spoke into the phone again. "Thanks, Jacob. Keep tracking any movement from that phone."

"I got it," Jacob replied, his voice sympathetic. "I'll let you know immediately."

David hung up, feeling a mix of apprehension and hope. Questioning Mark Harris could bring answers, or more questions. But either way, he was determined to get to the bottom of it.

Chapter 10: Boko

B ecca Lawrence, a formidable presence even in the echoing vastness of the CIA briefing room, waited as the entrance sealed behind her. The large screen at the front displayed Boko Haram's emblem, a black flag inscribed with white Arabic script — a symbol of terror that had wreaked havoc across West Africa for years.

She took a moment to scan the room. Fluorescent lights bathed the stark white walls, interrupted only by black-and-white satellite images of Nigerian territories. She noticed Assistant Director Harris standing near the screen, a remote in hand. His steel-gray hair was a stark contrast to his deep blue suit.

"Becca," he greeted, nodding towards the chair opposite him. "I assume you're wondering why I called you here on such short notice?"

She raised an eyebrow, "It's not every day that Boko Haram's insignia is the centerpiece in our briefing room. So, yes, you've got my attention."

He motioned for her to sit.

Harris clicked the remote, and a series of transcripts filled the screen. "These are intercepted communications from various Boko Haram cells. We've translated them from Hausa and Kanuri."

She leaned forward slightly, scanning the documents. "What am I looking for?"

Harris pointed to a specific line. "Right here. 'The heavens blessed our cause. The West will fall, and our ascension is imminent.' And here," he clicked again, "This one says, 'The reckoning has begun. Allah's judgment on the non-believers is here.'"

Becca frowned. "Harris, they've always been spouting religious prophecies and threats. How does this relate to the mass deaths?"

Harris leaned back, his expression graver. "Normally, I'd agree. But the frequency of these types of messages has surged since the event. It's as if they were expecting it or knew of it beforehand."

She crossed her arms, her professional exterior unwavering, but inside, her gears were turning. "You think they're responsible?"

"Not directly," Harris admitted, "But there's a possibility they might have been tools or pawns. The real players could be lurking in the shadows. Boko Haram might just be the tip of the iceberg."

Becca's brows knitted in thought. "Then I'm heading to Nigeria?"

Harris nodded. "Yes. We need to know what they know. But, Becca," he paused, looking her squarely in the eyes, "This isn't just a fact-finding mission. We need actionable intel. The world is in chaos. Misinformation is spreading like wildfire, and the public is scared. We need a solid lead, something concrete to act upon."

She smirked slightly, "And you think sending me into the lion's den will get us those answers?"

Harris's gaze didn't waver. "I wouldn't send you if I didn't believe you were the best for this mission. You've dealt with similar factions in the Middle East. You've worked in Nigeria. You know how to navigate the terrain, both physical and political."

Becca took a deep breath, memories of her past missions flooding back. "Harris, Boko Haram is unlike most groups I've dealt with. They're unpredictable."

"That's why you're not going in alone," he responded, pressing another button on the remote. A photo of a tall, dark-skinned man with piercing eyes appeared. "This is Jason Jackson. He's been our inside man in northern Nigeria for the past three years. He'll be your contact."

Becca recognized the face. "Alright, good, I know Jackson, he's a good agent. When do we start?"

Harris stood, stretching out his hand. "Immediately. Time is of the essence, Lawrence. But remember —"

"—Find out what they know. I know the drill."

The two exchanged a knowing glance, acknowledging the magnitude of the mission. As Becca turned to leave, she felt the pressure on her shoulders. But she was ready.

The events that had thrown the globe into turmoil were still a blur to many. But for Becca Lawrence, they were quickly sharpening into focus. Whatever lay ahead in Nigeria, she was determined to get to the heart of the matter.

Chapter 11: Kano

The safe house in Kano was inconspicuous from the outside, an architectural camouflage blending seamlessly with the surrounding buildings. Inside, the structure split its identity between a nondescript front room, painted in fading beige, and a dim, dingy backroom where a few powerful laptops blinked with an eerie blue light. The rooms whispered of secrets, covert operations, and hasty evacuations – the place was as transient as the intelligence it harbored.

Jason Jackson sat amidst the room's sparseness, the weight of his mission evident in every line of his posture. A tattered t-shirt clung to his frame, absorbing sweat that was half due to Nigeria's heat and half the internal fires of caffeine. Multiple mugs, each in various stages of emptiness, littered the space. It was clear that Jackson had been running on coffee fumes for hours, if not days.

When Becca entered, the room's dense atmosphere seemed to thicken, charged with the mutual recognition of shared responsibility. She observed him for a moment: the way his hand trembled slightly around the mug handle, the dark shadows under his eyes, the jeans that had seen better days. Here was an agent pushed to his edge.

"Jackson," Becca's voice was steady, but her concern was evident. "What have you found?"

He exhaled, setting his coffee aside. For a moment, he simply stared at the dark liquid, as if trying to discern answers from its depths. "It's a mess out here, Becca. Ever since the event, everything's been chaos. Communications are haywire. We've lost contact with a few informants, and the ones we do get in touch with... they keep mentioning 'Sabuwar Rana'."

Becca leaned forward, intrigued. "Sabuwar Rana? That's Hausa for 'New Day,' isn't it?"

Jackson nodded, taking a moment to clear his throat. "Exactly. At first, I brushed it off. Figured it was just talk – coded messages or maybe just the ramblings of scared individuals. But the more I heard it, the more it started to feel significant. It's being whispered in corners, painted on walls, even found it on some digital chatter."

Becca tapped her chin, thinking. "You think Boko Haram might be using this phrase as a sort of rallying cry? Trying to capitalize on the chaos?"

"It's a possibility," Jackson replied, looking up at her. "With everything that's been going on, there's a power vacuum. Governments across the world are struggling, and Nigeria's no exception. It wouldn't be unlike Boko Haram to seize this moment."

She leaned back, mulling it over. "'New Day' could imply a fresh start, a reset. Maybe they're planning a significant move, perhaps even an attempt to overthrow the government?"

Jackson shook his head, "Could be."

Becca's eyebrows knitted in skepticism. "I'm not sold on the idea that Boko Haram has any global desires or had anything to do with the events of 3/16. Boko Haram is ruthless, yes. But orchestrating something on this scale, with such precision? I'm not sure they possess that level of sophistication or resources."

"You're probably right," Jackson conceded. "But it's hard to put anything past them. They're unpredictable, and that makes them dangerous."

She sighed, "It does. Either way, 'Sabuwar Rana' might be our best lead right now. If they're planning something big, we need to get ahead of it."

The room fell silent, punctuated only by the soft hum of the laptops and the distant murmur of Kano's nightly activities. The implications of their conversation hung heavily between them, a web of complexities and potential dangers.

Finally, Jackson broke the silence. "We'll comb through every bit of data we have, chase every lead. 'Sabuwar Rana' is the clue, and we need to decipher its true meaning."

Becca nodded, her expression hardened with resolve. "We will. This 'New Day' they're heralding? We need to ensure it doesn't spell doom for Nigeria and beyond."

Jackson cleared his throat, taking a sip from his cooling coffee as he tried to gather his thoughts. The room seemed to grow quieter, the tension thickening.

Becca looked at Jackson, her sharp gaze unwavering. "Talk to me about assets, Jackson. What are we working with?"

Jackson sighed, glancing at the computer monitors before meeting her eyes. "We've got a couple of Ground Branch operators here. Good men, been on the ground a while. There's also a driver – knows the terrain like the back of his hand, and a few local assets. Oh, and a translator. As you can imagine, he's been invaluable."

She nodded. "Firepower?"

He held up a hand, cautioning her. "Becca, we're keeping things low profile here in Kano. High-risk moves would draw unnecessary attention. Only low kinetic operations are authorized for now."

She raised an eyebrow, the hint of a smirk playing on her lips. "Low kinetic? You know that's not exactly my style."

Jackson gave a weary chuckle. "Trust me, I remember."

Becca leaned in, resting her elbows on the table between them. "What about sources? There has to be someone on the inside, someone close to Boko Haram's operations."

Jackson hesitated, clearly wrestling with whether to divulge more. "We have a few low-level foot soldiers on the payroll. Just enough to keep us informed of minor movements. But..." He sighed heavily, "There is someone else. Someone higher up."

Becca straightened up, her interest piqued. "Go on."

He met her gaze, his face serious. "Look, it's a high-level source. I can't just let you meet him. It's sensitive, and I've been cultivating this relationship for a while. He's not just another informant; he's deep inside. We can't jeopardize that."

Becca leaned in closer, her voice low and firm. "Jackson, I didn't fly halfway around the world to get a filtered version of events. If he's as valuable as you say, then I need to meet him. The sooner I do, the sooner I can piece this together and get out of your hair."

Jackson ran a hand through his own disheveled hair, exasperated. "Becca, you don't understand. If this source is compromised in any way, it's not just the mission that's at stake."

She leaned back, considering him for a long moment. "You know as well as I do that every lead counts. And right now, your high-level insider might be our best chance."

Jackson sighed, leaning back in his chair, defeated. "Alright, but on my terms. He's my asset, my responsibility."

Becca nodded, her expression softening slightly. "Agreed. Let's get to work."

Jackson pinched the bridge of his nose, a deep breath escaping him. The dim lighting of the safe house revealed the weary lines etched into his face. "Alright, Becca," he began, his voice low and controlled, "I'll reach out to my asset, see if we can arrange something. But these things take time, and the utmost discretion."

She nodded, appreciating his predicament, but anxious all the same. "Thanks, Jackson. I know the stakes."

"We need to be careful here. Let me handle it. Meanwhile, you should get some rest." He gestured towards a hallway. "There's a guest room, second door on the right. Not exactly a five-star hotel, but it'll do."

She gave a small, tired smile. "Thanks. I could use some downtime."

Chapter 12: The Source

R etiring to the room, the sparse furnishings and a single dim light gave it an almost haunting ambiance. Becca slowly settled onto the bed, her spine protesting. She pulled out her encrypted phone, dialing a familiar number.

A moment later, the screen lit up, revealing the innocent face of her 10-year-old daughter, Leila. Her curly hair was a mess, and her big blue eyes gazed up, searching for her mother's face.

"Mommy!" Leila's voice was tinged with joy and relief.

"Hey, sweetheart." Becca's face softened, her own relief evident. "How are you holding up?"

Leila bit her lip, looking down momentarily. "I'm scared, Mom. Why did so many people...just...go? And why isn't school starting again? I miss Jenny and Amy."

Becca swallowed hard, feeling the sting of guilt. How could she explain to her daughter that the world outside was unraveling? "I know, baby. Things are a bit topsy-turvy right now. But remember what I told you about staying brave?"

Leila nodded, a small tear escaping her eye. "I'm trying, Mom. But I miss you. When are you coming back?"

Before Becca could reply, another face appeared on the screen, the familiar, kind eyes of her mother, wrinkles giving testimony to years of wisdom.

"Becca," her mother's voice was warm but assertive. "You look tired."

"Hey, Mom." Becca managed a smile. "It's been a long day."

Her mother's gaze was unwavering. "I know you're not going to tell me where you are or what you're up to. But promise me, Becca, promise you'll stay safe."

Becca's eyes filled with tears, feeling the weight of her dual responsibilities. "I promise, Mom."

Her mother leaned closer, her voice softer now. "All we have left in this world is family. I don't want to wake up one morning and hear you've... just vanished. Or worse."

Becca nodded, finding it hard to speak. "I know. I won't let that happen. I have Leila to come back to."

Her mother smiled, tears glistening in her eyes. "That's my girl."

Ending the call, Becca sat in the quiet of the room. The chasm between the worlds she inhabited was gaping. On one side, the innocence and simplicity of her daughter's life, a life she'd do anything to protect. On the other, the harsh realities and dangers she faced daily in her line of work. She saw it as her duty to shield Leila from the horrors of the world, but the weight of that responsibility was sometimes overwhelming.

The interior of the safe house was insufferable. Becca leaned against a wall, the moist air sticking to her skin, as she glanced around the room. The rigid edges of the maps pinned on the wall clung desperately to their hold, succumbing slowly to the damp air.

"You alright, Lawrence?" Jackson asked, pulling a chair and sitting down.

She nodded, wiping the beads of sweat forming on her forehead. The vigorous climate of Nigeria had a way of siphoning the energy out of a person.

Before she could answer, the front door creaked open. Noah Thatcher moved with an ease that belied the ruggedness of his physique. His attire was carefully curated to blend into the local environment: faded jeans worn from both design and desert sand, a sand-colored shirt which hung loosely enough to conceal the gear underneath, and worn-in boots that had seen miles of both city streets and uncharted terrains. The clothes were tactical without being overtly so; every item chosen not just for its ability to blend, but also for functionality. Even the simple leather band on his wrist, upon closer inspection, revealed itself to be a compact tool kit.

His face bore the stories of countless covert operations, the faint scars mapping out regions of conflict and territories of secrets. Deep-set hazel eyes, always alert and constantly scanning, betrayed a history of trust hard-won and easily lost. His hair, a dark cascade of waves cropped short, was peppered with gray, likely more from stress than age. Yet, amidst this battle-hardened demeanor was an air of discerning intellect. It was clear that Noah's strength wasn't just in physical prowess but in an analytical mind that had, time and again, outmaneuvered foes in situations that were as much about wits as they were about weapons.

"Lawrence, meet Noah Thatcher, CIA Ground Branch," Jackson introduced the man. Noah extended a firm, yet restrained handshake to Becca.

"Agent Lawrence," Noah acknowledged, his words laced with a hint of a southern twang that caught Becca's attention momentarily. It was a subtle note in his voice, reminiscent of long summer nights and the deep South. "I arrived in Juba about two months after you rolled out. We were still cleaning up after your operation there – in a good way!" Noah laughed thinking about some of those missions.

Jackson proceeded to explain the dynamics of the impending mission. "Noah will be accompanying you to meet the asset. We have a local driver, and there's no need for a translator - the asset speaks passable English."

Becca, weary and irate from the draining heat, scrutinized Noah. "Listen, Thatcher, I don't need a babysitter. Stay out of my way when I'm talking to the asset," she said with a cold firmness.

Noah held her gaze, his expression unchanging. "Understood," he replied succinctly.

Jackson continued explaining the meet. "The asset is Isma'il Al-Sabah. He's the third in command in the Kano area for Boko Haram. Has connections that spread like the roots of a baobab," Jackson revealed.

Jackson motioned for Becca to sit as he delved further into details. "The meeting will take place in a café in the heart of the city. It's one of Isma'il's properties. His turf, his rules. That's the only way he would agree."

Becca's brow furrowed. "You think it's wise for us to be meeting on his home turf? It gives him too much leverage."

Jackson nodded, understanding her trepidation. "I've met with him there before. It's secluded, away from prying eyes, and believe it or not, it has been the safest option every time."

"As for Isma'il," Jackson leaned in, his voice lowering, "He's a survivor. Climbed the Boko Haram ladder not just because of his strategic mind, but because he wasn't afraid to get his hands dirty. He's eliminated any competition within the group. Literally. Assassinations, alliances, double-crossing - the man's done it all to secure his place."

Becca interjected, "So, how can we trust any information he provides? If he's as cunning and ruthless as you're making him out to be?"

"You don't," Jackson replied bluntly. "You assume every word out of his mouth might be a fabrication. But he's also aware that providing credible intel is beneficial for him. It's a game, Agent Lawrence, one of wits and trust."

She pressed further, trying to understand the nature of their asset, "What's his motivation then? Money? Power?"

Jackson shrugged, "Both. Plus a sprinkling of self-preservation. While he's deeply embedded within Boko Haram, he's also aware of the precarious nature of his position. Allies today can become enemies tomorrow. Our arrangement provides him a safety net, of sorts."

Becca took a moment to process the information. She was stepping into a complex web of politics, power, and treachery. But that's what she was trained for. She just hoped that the web wouldn't ensnare her in its intricate trap.

Becca's eyes narrowed; she was aware of the danger and the opportunities this liaison with Al-Sabah brought. With the chaotic spiral the world was in, a high-level asset like Al-Sabah could provide insights that were gold dust.

"Alright, let's talk tactics," Noah began, unfolding a satellite image on the table. The overhead shot showed the café, with its red-tiled roof and surrounding streets for two blocks in every direction. "Here's where the rubber meets the road."

Becca leaned in, absorbing the layout.

"Our driver will be stationed here," Noah pointed to a side alley about fifty meters from the café entrance. "He'll keep the Land Rover running, engine hot. I can't stress how important it will be for a quick exit if things go sideways."

The meeting spot within the café was shaded in blue. "You'll be in this room right next to the main entrance. Once we get there, I'll clear the room and ensure it's secure. Once that's done, you and Isma'il will have your chat. I'll be stationed here," he motioned to a spot near the door of the room, "keeping an eye on the entrance and listening in."

"Since we're operating in a non-permissive environment," Noah's tone grew grave, "we won't have any ISR—no drones, no overhead surveillance. We're going in blind from above."

Jackson chimed in, "I'll be here at the safe house, monitoring your comms. But remember, if you hit a snag, we don't have a QRF. No quick response. You're out there on your own."

Becca nodded, her face a mask of determination, "Got it."

Noah continued, "The meeting is capped at 45 minutes. At that mark, we exit, even if you feel there's more to discuss. The longer we're there, the higher the risk."

Highlighting two locations on the map, he explained, "If things go south and we can't get to the Land Rover, we have two fallback positions." He paused, ensuring Becca understood their importance, "Again, we're without a QRF. If we end up at either of these positions, we'll have to improvise our extraction."

Becca took a deep breath, letting the gravity of the situation sink in. She knew the risks but understanding the specifics made it all the more real.

"I want everything prepped and ready to move in an hour," Becca ordered, the exhaustion edging her voice, but the determination unyielding. As Noah nodded and left to check on arrangements, Becca's gaze lingered on the photos on the table.

Becca studied the map, her fingers tracing the routes and fallback positions. Every detail mattered. She took a deep breath, each inhale and exhale priming her for the task ahead.

The weight of their situation bore down on her. But it was more than just the mission; it was the nagging reminder of the face of a ten-year-old girl thousands of miles away. A daughter waiting, praying for her mother's safe return.

Jackson, catching her eye, saw the fire and determination, but also the touch of vulnerability. It was a balance, a tightrope she walked every day: the dedicated agent and the protective mother.

They held a momentary gaze, an unspoken bond between two professionals in the field. In Jackson's eyes, Becca saw recognition, not just of the risks but of the personal stakes she carried into every mission.

She gave a curt nod, then steeled herself, readying her mind and body for the challenges that lay ahead. The world was chaotic, but for now, her mission, her duty, was her beacon through the uncertainty.

Chapter 13: The Meet

The Land Rover rumbled to life, its engine groaning under the unforgiving sun. Kano sprawled around them, a medley of vibrant colors, bustling streets, and the echoing calls of vendors competing for attention. The city was a mesh of age-old tradition melded with the burgeoning hints of modernity.

In the driver's seat, a wiry man with dark sun-baked skin steered the vehicle deftly through the maze of narrow streets. Beads of sweat glistened on his forehead, mirroring the moisture accumulating on the car's dashboard. The midday sun was ruthless, casting stark shadows on the weathered cobblestones. Ancient trees, bearing witness to countless generations, offered occasional shade as children, unfazed by the heat, played in the streets, their laughter echoing amidst the honks and engine roars.

Noah, in the passenger seat, maintained a sharp vigilance, his eyes scanning the unfolding landscape. Every so often, his hand would subconsciously drift to the sidearm holstered by his hip. He felt the weight of responsibility - not just for the mission, but for Becca seated behind him.

Behind Noah, Becca absorbed the scenes passing by her window. Women in vibrant hijabs haggled over market prices. Elderly men, wrapped in flowing robes, sat in shaded areas, sipping tea and engaging in passionate conversation. The city was alive, buzzing, its heartbeat strong despite the shadows of uncertainty looming over the world.

However, the tension in the air was palpable. Military checkpoints dotted the roads, the soldiers' alert faces scrutinizing every passing vehicle. Graffiti messages, some political, others declarations of hope, adorned the walls. And every so often, the city's pulse would be interrupted by the sobering sight of burned-out buildings or remnants of conflict, silent testimonials to the battles Kano had faced.

The Land Rover navigated a particularly crowded street, the scent of sizzling kebabs and spicy stews wafting through the windows. A radio from a nearby stall played a melodic Hausa tune, its notes blending with the cacophony of city sounds.

"Five minutes out," the driver finally announced, his voice calm but firm.

Becca took a deep breath, the mosaic of Kano's sights and sounds imprinting in her mind. She was here, in the thick of it, ready to navigate the web of intrigue that awaited. She gripped the door handle, her anticipation tangible, as the Land Rover continued its determined journey through the heart of Kano.

The Land Rover pulled up outside a nondescript building. It was weathered, its walls bearing the stories of years gone by, its facade mingling seamlessly with its surroundings. A simple wooden sign hanging above the entrance read "Cafe Arewa," its paint faded but its name still proudly visible.

Becca stepped out, her shoes making soft crunching sounds on the sun-baked gravel. The ambient noise from the cafe reached her ears; muted conversations, the clatter of cutlery, the soft hum of a ceiling fan. She could smell the distinct aroma of freshly ground coffee beans mixed with the faint scent of roasted nuts from a vendor across the street.

Noah was already surveying the perimeter, his trained eyes scanning for any potential threats or irregularities. His senses were heightened, every movement, every sound registering with pinpoint precision.

They made their way into the cafe. Dimly lit, the interior was a stark contrast to the blinding sun outside. Vintage lanterns hung from the ceiling, casting a soft amber glow. Mismatched wooden chairs surrounded equally mismatched tables. It felt cozy, lived-in, a place where secrets could be shared without fear of them traveling beyond its walls.

Becca and Noah were led to a private room near the entrance. The door, intricately carved with geometric designs, creaked softly as they entered. Inside, the room was simple. Whitewashed walls, a wooden table in the center with two chairs opposite each other. On the table sat a gleaming coffee pot, steam gently rising from its spout, and two porcelain cups.

In the far corner of the room stood a tall, imposing figure. A bodyguard. His presence was unobtrusive, yet his demeanor left no doubt about his capabilities. His eyes, constantly moving, missed nothing.

Noah immediately went into action. Swiftly, he moved around the room, checking the windows, ensuring they were secure. His fingers brushed lightly against the table, feeling for any irregularities. He then lifted the coffee pot slightly, checking its weight, before setting it down gently.

After his quick risk assessment, Noah nodded subtly to Becca, signaling that it was safe. He motioned for her to sit, taking his position near the doorway, still inside the room. His stance was relaxed but ready, a silent sentinel ensuring Becca's safety.

Becca took a seat, her posture upright, her senses on high alert. She poured herself a cup of coffee, its rich aroma filling the room. As she waited for Isma'il, the room's stillness was palpable. The gentle tick of a clock somewhere, the distant murmur from the cafe outside, and the soft breathing of the bodyguard were the only sounds that pierced the silence.

The weight of the upcoming meeting pressed on Becca, the anticipation building with each passing second. She was in the lion's den, ready to face whatever lay ahead.

The private room's door clicked softly as it opened, revealing Isma'il's silhouette framed against the dim hallway light. As he stepped into the room, his features became more apparent. The man was tall, with dark penetrating eyes that radiated intelligence. A neatly trimmed beard contoured his sharp jawline, and his traditional attire hinted at a man deeply rooted in his culture.

"Agent Lawrence," Isma'il greeted with a smile, extending a hand as he approached the table. His grip was firm but brief, the handshake of a man accustomed to dealing with people on various sides of the spectrum.

A waiter slipped in behind him, pouring Isma'il a fresh cup of coffee. The rich, dark liquid steamed gently as he placed a cup on the table, the aroma intertwining with the already potent smell in the room.

The brief moment while the coffee was being served allowed both Becca and Isma'il to discreetly assess each other. Isma'il's confident demeanor suggested he was in control, while Becca's cool composure showed she wasn't one to be easily swayed.

"Your friend at the door," Isma'il motioned towards Noah, "does he not care for coffee?"

Noah, without shifting his gaze from the surroundings, replied politely, "I'm good, thank you."

Isma'il leaned back in his chair, intertwining his fingers. "So, Agent Lawrence, to what do I owe the pleasure? I hear many things, but what, in particular, brings the CIA to my doorstep?"

Becca took a measured sip of her coffee before answering, her gaze unwavering. "There are rumors swirling around, Isma'il. Disturbing rumors that connect Boko Haram with the recent global events. They're not whispers; they're loud, bold claims. The U.S. would prefer to stay out of Nigeria, but for that, I need answers. Concrete answers."

Isma'il chuckled, a sound that seemed more mocking than amused. "From where I sit, it looks like the U.S. has its hands full. Millions dead, cities in chaos. I doubt your country has any appetite for more problems, especially in Nigeria."

She leaned in slightly, her tone firm. "You'd be surprised. When pushed, we can be very motivated. And trust me, you don't want the weight of U.S. interest coming down on your operations."

His eyes flashed a hint of irritation, then settled back into amusement. "Fair enough. I'll tell you what I know. But every piece of information has its price."

She raised an eyebrow. "Name it. Though I assume money isn't what you're after."

A sly grin spread across his face. "Correct. Money I have. What I need, Agent Lawrence, is a favor. Just one."

The room seemed to constrict a little as Isma'il began to unravel the political threads of Nigeria post-disaster.

"There are those who see opportunity in calamity," he began, his voice carrying a grave undertone. "Some believe that the events unfolding are a divine call, a signal for the rise of a new power. They believe it's time for Boko Haram to step into a leadership role, not just in Nigeria, but across the African continent."

Becca's skepticism was evident. "You expect me to believe that Boko Haram, with its limited resources and disarrayed structure, pulled off this cataclysm?"

Isma'il's laughter echoed in the room, deep and genuine. "Oh, Agent Lawrence, even I wouldn't dare to make such a grandiose claim. We did not cause the recent events. But, there are factions within Boko Haram who believe this is a sign from above. A religious endorsement of sorts. They think it's a celestial nudge to challenge the existing order, take Nigeria, and subsequently aim for regional dominance."

She leaned forward, eyes narrowed. "And where do you stand in all this? Are you amongst those with such lofty ambitions?"

A smirk played on Isma'il's lips. "I'm a realist. While I do see the potential for Nigeria under Boko Haram's influence, I'm not delusional. We aren't built for regional conflicts. My only ambition is Nigeria. And under my guidance, you have my word that Boko Haram won't drag the continent into needless wars."

Her skepticism remained. "I'd need more than just your word, Isma'il. Concrete proof. Without it, this is just another layer in the games of deception."

Isma'il nodded, slowly, thoughtfully. "I expected as much. I do have information. Tangible, verifiable information that I am willing to share."

Her gaze hardened. "What's the catch?"

He leaned in, the gravity in his voice unmistakable. "Once you have the information, Agent Lawrence, you'll understand my demands. Until then, trust will be our only currency."

Becca felt the atmosphere in the room change, a subtle shift, as if they were transitioning from the dance of preliminary words into a more dangerous dance of high-stakes revelation.

"I'm listening, please continue," Becca said, her voice steady, her eyes unyielding.

Isma'il leaned back, his gaze never leaving Becca's. He gauged her, measuring every nuanced expression.

"Good," he began, his voice carrying a mixture of dread and revelation. "Ten days ago, our men kidnapped Professor Ephraim Goldman, a prominent Jewish scholar and expert in biblical artifacts. He was in Ethiopia, guest lecturing at Addis Ababa University, unraveling the mysteries of end times prophecies to a rapt audience."

Becca's eyes narrowed, the intrigue and suspicion threading through her veins.

"Professor Goldman is renowned for his works, Agent Lawrence. His understanding of the ancient texts and artifacts is... unparalleled," Isma'il continued. "Our leader, Amir Al-Masri, believes fervently that we are living in the last days. Apocalypse. Armageddon. Call it what you will. Al-Masri sees the mass deaths not as a tragedy, but as a divine revelation. A signal of the impending end."

"And why would Al-Masri be interested in end times prophecies?" Becca interjected. "I thought his interests lay more in the realm of power and terrorism than theology."

Isma'il chuckled, a sound devoid of humor. "Al-Masri is a man who believes he's destined for greatness, Agent Lawrence. He believes the end times prophecies hold a key to unprecedented power and dominion. Professor Goldman, with his extensive knowledge, is seen as the gatekeeper to that power."

The room seemed to drop a few degrees, the chilling implications of Isma'il's revelation seeping into the silence.

"You want us to rescue Goldman," Becca deduced, her voice icy. "Why should we trust you? And what's in it for you?"

Isma'il's gaze bore into hers, a deadly earnestness mirrored in his voice. "I'll provide you with the location. Your team goes in, extracts the Professor, and everyone walks away with something they want. Goldman is of no use to us dead, Agent Lawrence."

"And Al-Masri?" Becca pressed.

Isma'il's gaze hardened, "He is a madman, fueled by delusions of grandeur. He sees the world as his chessboard, every piece, every nation a pawn in his twisted game. You extract Goldman, and in the process, if Al-Masri were to meet his end..." he trailed off, letting the unsaid words hang in the charged air.

A silence ensued. Becca absorbed the revelation, the magnitude of the choices before her. The ethical conundrums, the geopolitical implications – they all swirled into a maelstrom of uncertainty. But, amidst it all, one mystery – could Professor Goldman be a key piece in this darkened puzzle?

As if reading her thoughts, Isma'il broke the silence, "We eliminate a global threat, and you gain a crucial piece of intelligence. In this apocalyptic dance, Agent Lawrence, even enemies can become unwitting partners."

Becca's gaze lingered on Isma'il - this dangerous, yet potentially indispensable ally in a world where lines between friend and foe were becoming increasingly blurred. The game was changing, and with it, the rules of engagement.

Becca leaned back, her gaze unwavering, yet cautious. "I'll need to consult my superiors. This isn't a decision I can make on the fly, especially with stakes this high."

Isma'il smirked, a half-smile playing on his lips. "We all have our chains, don't we? Whether it's a hierarchy or an ideology. We all answer to someone or something."

"True," Becca said slowly, considering her words. "But this is a game of high stakes, and the players are not just pawns. Lives are on the line, Isma'il. Yours, mine, Goldman's, and countless others."

Isma'il leaned forward, resting his elbows on the table. "When you get your answer," he began, his voice soft, but there was an edge to it, "Use the usual channels. I'll provide the location, and your team can do what they do best."

Becca considered him for a moment, then gave a curt nod. "Fine. But understand, Isma'il, that if this is a trap, if this is a game to you, there will be consequences. Ones even you cannot escape from."

Isma'il's eyes glinted with a mix of amusement and something darker. "Life itself is a game, Agent Lawrence. But rest assured, I have no intention of playing with fire. Not this time."

Becca stood up, shouldering her bag. "I'll be in touch."

Isma'il simply nodded, watching her go. As she exited the room, the weight of the conversation and the gravity of the decisions to come pressed down on her. The next steps were unclear, the path fraught with danger, but the mission was clear. The game was on, and the clock was ticking.

Chapter 14: The Plan

The drone of the secure satellite phone filled Becca's ears as she waited. The tension was palpable even through the static of the connection.

"Becca," her superior's voice finally came through. "Break it down for me. Who do you have with you?"

"We're light. It's me, Jackson, two operators from Ground Branch, and a local driver - he's got some military background but hasn't seen action in years," Becca explained hurriedly.

"Ground Branch? Just two?" her boss, Harris, shot back, a hint of surprise evident.

"Yes. This was supposed to be low-profile, remember?"

A heavy sigh came from the other end. "We can get three more operators in your AO within 48 hours. You think you can keep the lid on this until then?"

Becca inhaled deeply, the hot, dusty air stinging her lungs. "We'll have to. But it'll be dicey."

"Understood," Harris replied crisply. "You have the green light to proceed. But I can't stress this enough, Lawrence - keep it discreet."

She nodded, glancing over her shoulder at the dimly lit safe house room. "We'll be as silent as the desert night. But without a QRF—"

"I know," he interrupted, a hint of remorse in his tone. "Logistics and optics. It's not ideal, but it's the hand we're dealt. We can offer drone support, though. Eyes in the sky."

A brief silence ensued as Becca processed the situation. "Isma'il's the key?"

"For now. Play along. Get the details on the professor. But don't forget, he's not our friend. Just a temporary ally."

The edge in his voice was not lost on Becca. "I'll tread carefully. We'll get that professor out."

"See that you do," Harris responded. "And Becca? Watch your six."

"I always do, sir."

"And Al-Masri?" she asked.

"You're the operator on the ground. Handle it." With a final click, the connection ended, leaving Becca lost in the throes of the mission ahead.

In the dimly lit planning room of the safe house, tables were strewn with detailed maps, aerial photos, and clusters of intelligence data. The chalky residue of old wall paint peeled off, giving the room a battle-hardened look. Amidst the scent of old wood and musk, Becca hunched over a hand-drawn layout of the compound where Professor Goldman was believed to be held.

Breaking the stillness, Noah began outlining his strategy. "Code name 'Jordan' – it's symbolic. Crossing into the Promised Land, achieving what seemed impossible. Here's how we do it: Team Alpha, which I'll be leading, consists of me, Rodriguez, Carter, and Jenkins. We'll enter from the north entrance." He pointed at a subtle mark on the map. "Our main task is to create a diversion, sweep and clear any threats, ensuring the area is safe for Bravo to operate."

Becca interrupted, her tone meticulous, "And Bravo?"

Noah met her gaze, nodding at Mikey, who stood beside a stack of equipment. "Team Bravo, under your lead, Becca, will have you and Mikey. You'll enter from the west side, benefiting from the diversion Alpha provides. Your singular mission is to get to Professor Goldman."

Mikey unfolded a satellite photo, showing the building where the professor was supposedly held. "This is it. Intel suggests there's a single guard outside the door, probably more inside. While Alpha's noise keeps most of them occupied, we use the west wing's blind spot to slip in."

Becca's face tightened in concentration. "So, once we have the professor?"

Noah answered, "Rejoin Alpha for extraction. We rendezvous at point Echo," he tapped a marked point on the map, "then we get the hell out."

Her gaze sharpened, "What's our contingency? If we face resistance, or if it's an ambush?"

"Abort signal over comms from the driver," Mikey interjected, looking at both of them. "We disengage, retreat, and head straight for the extraction vehicle. Jackson will be monitoring everything from a drone 20,000 feet above our heads."

Noah added, his voice firm, "Every moment counts, Becca. This operation is high risk, high reward. But remember, this is what we're trained for."

She paused for a moment, then finally nodded, "Alright. Jordan it is. But I want everyone sharp. Professor Goldman is our top priority. We get him, and we get out. No unnecessary engagements."

"Understood," Noah responded with a resolute nod.

Becca took a deep breath, gathering her thoughts. "We need everyone on the same page," she said decisively. "Mikey, get the rest of the team in here. It's time to brief everyone on our plan and make sure we're synchronized in our approach." Mikey nodded, quickly moving to the door to beckon the waiting operators into the briefing room.

Carter, a tall figure with a chiseled jawline and an aura of confidence, sauntered into the room, giving a nod to each of the operators. With a half-cocked smile and an air of playful bravado, he exclaimed, "Alright, boys, let's get the intel we need and get this mission rolling. Woohoo!" His energy was infectious, lightening the room's tense atmosphere for a moment.

Rodriguez, always quick with a retort, shot a knowing glance at Carter, smirking as he said, "Seems like you've had a bit too much downtime lately, Carter." The rest of the team chuckled, familiar with the banter between the two seasoned operators. Carter just winked back, never one to let a jibe go unanswered.

Mikey, glancing up from the satellite images, asked, "Becca, what's our ROE? We need clarity before we step in there."

Becca, her voice steady but assertive, responded, "If they present a clear threat, especially if they're armed, neutralize them. We can't afford hesitation."

Mikey nodded, taking in the gravity of the directive. A brief silence filled the room before Becca continued, reaching into her bag and placing a photo on the table.

"This is Amir Al-Masri." The image displayed a stern-faced man with a graying beard and intense eyes. "He's a secondary, but crucial, objective. If he's on location, he can't be allowed to leave."

Mikey, taken aback, said, "Al-Masri? The one behind the Mali attacks?"

Becca simply nodded. "He's been tied to this. It's imperative we handle it if the opportunity arises."

Noah, sensing the mounting pressure, interjected, "Okay, so we've got a dual focus. Extract Professor Goldman and keep an eye out for Al-Masri."

Carter grinned, flexing his fingers as if anticipating action. "Keep an eye out? Nah. 'Eliminate the threat' is more my style. Don't worry, Becca," he said with a confident smirk, "If Al-Masri's there, he ain't walking out of that place. We got this."

Becca confirmed, "Every one of you should know Al-Masri's face. If you spot him, eliminate the threat."

Chapter 15: The Rescue

The old Land Rover rumbled on, tires crunching the uneven streets of Kano's northern neighborhoods. Its exterior, once a vibrant green, had faded with the dust and dirt of numerous missions, making the vehicle almost blend with the nocturnal shadows of the Nigerian city. The dashboard's faint luminescence threw sharp contrasts onto Noah's face, revealing his intense focus and highlighting the subtle scarring from missions past.

Every so often, a dilapidated building would come into view, the moonlight glinting off its corrugated iron roof. The hum of the Land Rover's engine was occasionally interrupted by distant, muffled sounds – a dog barking, the faint strains of a radio, the muted conversation of night owls. The air, though cooler than the day, was thick, laden with the scents of burning wood, spices, and the musky after-rain aroma.

Noah, sensing the need to rally his team, cleared his throat. "Listen up. We're in one of Kano's quieter sections, but that doesn't mean it's deserted. These streets are unpredictable. We need to move silently, and swiftly." Glancing again at the digital map glowing on the dashboard, he added, "We should be at the target in about ten minutes. Double-check your gear."

Rodriguez tapped his earpiece methodically, "Comms check. Alpha team?"

Carter's voice, steady and assured, responded, "Alpha team is green."

Becca chimed in, her tone business-like, "Bravo team, green." But beneath her professional exterior, a whirlwind of emotions churned. Butterflies danced in her stomach, a sensation reminiscent of her early days in the field. A rush of energy surged through her, threatening to cloud her judgment. She clenched her fists, drawing a deep breath to steady herself. She couldn't afford to let adrenaline dictate her actions tonight.

From the front, navigating the path with a well-practiced ease, Mikey raised a hand, signaling his readiness without breaking concentration on the road.

"How do we look Overwatch?" Noah inquired.

Suddenly, Jackson's voice cut through, a beacon from his remote vantage point. "Overwatch here. I've got eyes on Al-Masri's safe house. All quiet for now. We need this operation to be a ghost, move in and out without leaving a trace."

The Land Rover pressed on, its occupants poised on the knife-edge of action.

"All right," Noah's voice cut through the quiet, authoritative and low. "NVGs on."

A series of muted clicks followed as each member of the team brought down their night vision goggles, the world instantly transforming into a green-hued landscape of shadows and outlines.

Jackson's voice crackled in their earpieces, tension apparent even in his measured tones. "Alpha, Bravo, visual update. We've got two tangos stationed outside the main entrance. They seem alert but relaxed. Additionally, there's a single guard posted by what seems to be the holding room — likely where they have Professor Goldman."

The team exited the Land Rover and began moving towards the target house.

Becca, scanning the surroundings through her goggles, took a moment to adjust to the green overlay. Every detail was sharper, more pronounced. The house, an imposing structure, stood out like a fortress in the night, windows dark and walls foreboding. Her heart raced, and she could feel the weight of the mission pressing down on her. She reminded herself of the training, the drills, and the countless operations she had been a part of. This was just another mission, she told herself, trying to calm the storm inside.

Noah nodded, eyes still focused on the target. "Good copy, Overwatch. We are Charlie Mike here. Preparing to move in. Let us know if we wake the neighbors."

The teams, Alpha and Bravo, formed up swiftly, their movements fluid and synchronized from countless drills.

The ambient sounds of the night seemed louder in the close proximity of the safehouse. Even the slight rustle of leaves echoed in their ears as they huddled in a shallow ditch, using it as temporary concealment. The team's breathing was the only audible indicator of their nervousness; every other movement was silent, professional, and precise.

Peering through the optics of their silenced M4 carbines, Mikey and Rodriguez fixed their sights on the guards outside the entrance, their fingers poised over the triggers. Each man's breathing slowed, their concentration absolute, waiting for the word.

Noah, crouched next to them, turned his head slightly, his eyes scanning each member of the team. "Everyone good?" He received a series of minute nods and thumbs-up in response. Without a moment's hesitation, he whispered sharply, "Execute, execute, execute."

Almost instantaneously, two suppressed shots rang out, their sound muffled but final. The two guards outside the entrance collapsed, lifeless. The precision of Mikey and Rodriguez's shots left no room for error.

Rodriguez, leading the way with a determined pace, swiftly approached the entrance, Bravo team close on his heels. Their destination was the holding cell. As they moved, Alpha team, including Noah, branched off to clear the main house.

Bravo team, with surgical precision, neutralized the lone guard outside the cell with a silenced shot before swiftly working on the door. It took mere moments for them to break through the barricade. Becca, her heart pounding in her chest, felt a rush of adrenaline. Every mission was a dance with danger, and she had learned to harness her emotions, channeling them into focus and precision.

Inside the main house, Alpha team encountered more resistance than anticipated. However, their training and cohesion as a unit shone through. In a series of rapid encounters, they neutralized six armed combatants, their movements smooth and controlled.

As Noah entered one of the rooms, he was met with a defiant Amir Al-Masri. Eyes filled with rage, Amir reached for a gun concealed on his side. But Noah, with practiced reflexes, fired several shots in quick succession. Al-Masri crumpled to the floor, blood pooling around him. Noah, taking a moment to ensure the threat was neutralized, quickly radioed in, "Alpha leader to Bravo, Al-Masri is down. We're Oscar Mike to your location."

The night had a cold grip on the desolate landscape surrounding Al-Masri's safe house. In the lingering silence, the distant growl of an engine cut through the air, jolting every member of the strike team. Becca felt a knot tighten in her stomach. They were not out of the woods yet. The tension grew, becoming almost tangible, its icy fingers weaving through each member of the team. They had achieved their objectives, but they were not safe yet.

From his Overwatch position, Jackson's voice crackled over the comms, a quiet but urgent alert that filled the air around Noah and his team. "Overwatch to Alpha," Jackson relayed, a sense of urgency coating every syllable. "I think we woke someone up. A truck is on its way to your location with multiple tangos. 15 mikes out. I recommend RTB."

Noah's heart rate quickened, the dark veil of the night feeling suddenly suffocating. They were exposed, vulnerable. They needed to move. Fast. "Good copy, Overwatch," Noah responded, the weight of his responsibility as the team leader pressing down upon him. "We are returning to exfil. The doctor is secured, HVT is down."

The professor, shaken but responsive, was between the converging Alpha and Bravo teams. His eyes, wide with a mixture of terror and relief, darted between his liberators.

Noah and Becca's eyes met, a silent agreement passing between them. Becca's eyes conveyed a mixture of determination and concern. It was time to move, time to escape the danger that lurked in the encroaching darkness. With Noah leading Alpha and Becca leading Bravo, they moved, the Professor in the center, a diamond formation of protection and combat readiness around him.

They reached the Land Rover. The driver, alert and ready, had the engine running, its low rumble a soothing counterpoint to the frantic beats of their hearts. The doors opened swiftly, each member of the team and the professor bundled inside, weapons ready, eyes still scanning the dark perimeter.

As the Land Rover sprang to life and accelerated away from the safe house, the danger of the mission, the weight of their actions, the lives taken, and saved, hung heavily in the air. Becca leaned back, allowing herself a moment of relief. The weight of leadership, the responsibility for her team, and the lives they had just saved pressed down on her. Yet amidst the turmoil, a palpable sense of relief surged through each member - they had faced the darkness and emerged victorious.

Chapter 16: Professor

I nside the safe house, there was an odd sense of normalcy. The warm, ambient glow of the lamps created pockets of soft lighting. The aroma of a meal being prepared wafted through the air, a stark contrast to the adrenaline and chaos they had experienced earlier. They gathered around a wooden table, its grainy texture bearing witness to countless tales of espionage and covert operations.

Dr. Goldman, his hands shaking ever so slightly, picked up a glass of water. Becca watched him intently, her mind racing. She was trying to reconcile the man before her, seemingly so ordinary, with the whirlwind of danger and intrigue that surrounded him. His gaunt face, lined with fatigue and stress, seemed to carry the weight of a lifetime of knowledge. She wondered what it felt like to be so sought after, to have knowledge that could potentially change the course of history.

Taking a deep breath, Becca began. "Professor, can you help us understand why Boko Haram targeted you?" she inquired, her gaze unwavering.

Dr. Goldman sipped the water, contemplating his answer. "It's a tale of twisted ambitions and beliefs," he began. "Boko Haram, and especially Amir Al-Masri, has a deep-seated desire to bring about the end times. They believed I could offer them insights into the Biblical prophecies, particularly those about the Apocalypse."

Becca leaned forward, her heart rate increasing slightly. The gravity of the situation was becoming clearer. "End times? Prophecies?" she echoed, trying to wrap her head around the enormity of it all.

"Yes," Dr. Goldman's voice was tinged with a hint of sadness. "Al-Masri believes he can be the harbinger of the end times, and he sought to understand the prophecies to bend them to his will."

Becca felt a chill run down her spine. The idea of someone trying to manipulate religious prophecies for their own gain was both terrifying and unfathomable. "And what do you think, Professor?" she probed, her eyes searching his for any hint of doubt. "Do you believe these men can dictate the onset of the Apocalypse?"

Dr. Goldman looked around the table, his gaze finally resting on Becca. "I believe we might be living in the end times. Not because of Boko Haram's actions, but because of what's been written."

Becca's brow furrowed. "The rapture? Are you talking about the Biblical rapture?"

The professor nodded, "Exactly. The rapture is a biblical concept where believers are taken up to Heaven, while others remain on Earth, starting a period of Tribulation. The deaths on 3/16? I believe it might have been the rapture."

The weight of Dr. Goldman's words settled heavily on the room. Becca felt a mix of disbelief and fear. The implications of what he was suggesting were vast. Here they were, operatives trained to deal with tangible threats, being confronted with a concept so profound and deeply spiritual. The juxtaposition of their worlds was stark and unsettling.

The room was silent for a moment, each person lost in thought. Becca's mind raced, trying to piece together the events and the implications of the professor's words. Whether they believed Dr. Goldman's theory or not, they couldn't deny the magnitude of the events they were embroiled in. The world, it seemed, was on the brink of something far bigger than any of them had imagined.

Chapter 17: The Park

The tranquil Baltimore park was bathed in a soft twilight glow. City noises — the distant hum of traffic, faint conversations, and muffled footsteps — played out like a muted symphony. While most visitors meandered through their own thoughts, a man sat, lost in reflection, on a bench facing the setting sun. His profile, silhouetted by the dimming horizon, seemed contemplative and resolute.

That man was Mark Harris. Though the evening's serenity seemed to envelop him, an air of anticipation hung about him, as if he expected a disturbance.

Agent David Mitchell's footsteps were deliberate as he approached. The weight of his responsibility, the countless hours spent on this case, and the gravity of the situation pressed heavily on him. He felt a mix of anticipation and anxiety. Stopping in front of the bench, he took a deep breath, trying to steady his racing heart. "Mark Harris?"

Mark looked up, slightly startled. "Do I know you?"

"I'm Special Agent David Mitchell, with the FBI." David paused, gauging Mark's reaction. "I have a few questions for you. We've been monitoring your activities for some time now. Allegations of trafficking, artifact smuggling... That's why I've been tracking you."

Mark's eyes widened momentarily, but he quickly regained his composure. "You've got the wrong idea, Agent Mitchell. I think there's been some misunderstanding."

David, choosing to get straight to the point, leaned in slightly. The intensity of the situation was palpable, and he felt a mix of determination and trepidation. "Then perhaps you can clear things up for me. Explain your operations, the artifacts, the people you've been associated with."

Mark hesitated but then took a deep breath, his voice firm but weary. "It's not what you think, Agent Mitchell. We're not criminals. We're believers. Those artifacts? They're part of our studies, our preparation."

David frowned, clearly puzzled. The pieces weren't fitting together as he had anticipated. "Believers? Preparation for what?"

"Prophecies," Mark said simply, his gaze unwavering.

David's skepticism was palpable. The idea seemed far-fetched, but he had learned never to dismiss anything outright. "Prophecies?"

Mark nodded. "Yes, the events of 3/16? They weren't accidents or anomalies. They were signs, Agent Mitchell. Signs we've been preparing for."

David leaned back, attempting to piece together the puzzle before him. The weight of Mark's words, the implications of his beliefs, pressed heavily on David's analytical mind. "So, you're saying that these 'signs' have some kind of religious significance?"

Mark gave a small, almost rueful smile. "To some, they might seem like mere coincidences or unexplainable events. But to us, they are prophecies being fulfilled. The people who died on 3/16? We believe they were taken up."

David blinked, caught off guard. "Taken up? You're talking about... The rapture?"

Mark nodded solemnly. "Exactly. The rapture, as foretold in the Scriptures. Those who were taken were believers, true followers of Christ. Their souls were taken up to meet their Lord in the clouds. It's prophesized in Matthew 24."

David's mind raced. He had heard of the rapture, of course, but to think that it might have actually occurred was both unsettling and hard to believe. "So, you believe all those people...millions across the globe... were what, chosen? And the rest of us left behind?"

Mark's gaze turned distant, burdened with the weight of belief and sorrow. "It's not just about being chosen, Agent Mitchell. It's about faith, true faith. Those who genuinely believed were taken to be with Him. The rest of us, like me, have been left to navigate the tribulations that will come."

David felt a chill, despite the warm evening air. The implications of Mark's beliefs, whether true or not, were monumental. "And you truly believe this, that we are now living in the aftermath of the rapture?"

Mark met David's gaze directly. "With every fiber of my being. It's why we prepared, why we tried to understand the prophecies. And it's why I'm still here, trying to make sense of what's next."

David shifted uncomfortably on the bench, trying to process Mark's revelations. The weight of the situation, the implications of Mark's beliefs, pressed heavily on him. "I'm trying to understand all of this, Mark. If your group was full of genuine believers preparing for the end times, and if 3/16 was indeed the rapture... then why are you still here?"

Mark took a deep breath, pain evident in his eyes. "It's a question I've been grappling with, David. I did all the 'right' things. Went to church, studied the Scriptures, took part in acts of service. But after 3/16, when so many from our group vanished and I was still here, I had to face a devastating reality."

David looked at Mark intently, trying to understand the depth of his pain and confusion. "Which was?"

Mark swallowed hard, "That maybe I had everything in my head, but nothing in my heart. I knew about Jesus, I knew the Scriptures, but perhaps I never truly knew Him. I never genuinely repented for my sins or completely surrendered my life to Him."

David frowned, trying to understand. "So, you're saying that even though you believed in all this, you weren't... 'chosen'?"

Mark sighed, "The rapture wasn't about being chosen. It was about true salvation. It's not enough to just know about Jesus or to perform religious rituals. It's about having a genuine relationship with Him. And, despite all my preparations and studies, maybe I missed the most crucial part."

David leaned back, his mind racing. The implications were profound, and he felt a mixture of sympathy and confusion. "So, what now?"

Mark's expression was resolute, "Now, I seek the genuine relationship I should've had from the beginning. And I try to help others find it too. Because if 3/16 was indeed the rapture, then the world has entered a period unlike any other, and we need to be prepared, spiritually and mentally."

"I'll be in touch. You're still a person of interest in this investigation, don't leave town," David explained to Mark before getting up to walk away.

Chapter 18: Task Force

The cold morning air slapped General Henry Porter's face as he stepped out for his routine two-mile run. Even in the growing tumult of post-3/16, his habits remained unshaken. The rhythmic pounding of his shoes on the pavement was meditative, each step an affirmation of his discipline.

Once back home, steam curled up from the hot shower, enveloping him and providing a brief moment of solitude. Dressed in his crisply ironed uniform, he made his way to the kitchen. The aroma of freshly scrambled eggs mingled with the sizzling sound of bacon frying. It was this consistency, these patterns, that grounded him amidst the global chaos.

He took a moment to savor his black coffee, its bitterness sharpening his focus. Opening his laptop, he quickly scanned his emails, filtering out the crucial from the mundane. There was an anticipatory tension in the air today; his first meeting leading the team dedicated to unraveling the 3/16 events was mere hours away.

By 6:30 a.m., he was at the office. He walked the corridors that felt familiar yet foreign, given the weight of their new mission. The sterile lights of the conference room greeted him as he walked in, 90 minutes before the scheduled time. He wanted to be prepared, to have every detail in place, every document ready.

Spreading out the various files and reports on the vast table, he reviewed the timelines, the missing persons' data, and the scattered intelligence they had gathered thus far. As he did, he could feel the gravity of their task. 3/16 wasn't just a date; it was a marker, an event that had reshaped the world and their understanding of it.

Every so often, he would glance up at the clock, measuring the time, waiting. By 8:45 a.m., the room had started to fill up, the murmur of voices, the shuffling of papers. But in that hour and a half alone in the conference room, General Porter had fortified himself, ready to lead with clarity and determination. Today, they would start piecing the puzzle together.

General Porter's eyes scanned the vast conference room, taking in each face, each representative of the varied factions of the intelligence and defense communities. The stark overhead lights did little to ease the stress that showed on everyone's faces. He could see the weariness but also the unyielding determination in the eyes of those gathered.

The reality of their task pressed heavily on his chest. He had led countless operations, faced innumerable threats, but this? This was different. 3/16 was an event that defied understanding, a catastrophic moment that had shaken the world to its core. As he silently assessed the room, he couldn't help but reflect on the weight of the challenge they faced. Could this eclectic mix of intelligence officers, military brass, and private sector operatives come together to solve the unsolvable?

He recognized many of the faces — men and women he'd collaborated with in the past. But there were others, specialists in fields he was less familiar with — biowarfare, epidemiology, even theoretical physicists and theologians. The depth and breadth of the expertise in the room were staggering. The best and the brightest, pulled from every conceivable discipline to address the inconceivable.

Taking a deep breath, Porter stepped to the podium at the head of the room. He felt a pang of uncertainty, a feeling he wasn't used to. How do you even begin to address an event of this magnitude? The vast sea of expectant faces looked up at him, waiting for direction, for answers.

"Ladies and gentlemen," he began, his deep voice filling the room, "I won't sugarcoat it. We are here to investigate, to analyze, and to act upon one of the most perplexing events in human history. I don't need to remind you of the gravity of our task. Many of you have lost colleagues, family, friends on 3/16. The world is looking to us for answers."

He paused, letting the weight of his words settle. "I understand that this is an undertaking like no other. But I also know this: there's no other group, no other assembly of individuals, I'd rather have tackling this challenge. We have the skills, the resources, and the determination to get to the bottom of this."

A few nods across the room signaled agreement.

"We may not know where to start," he continued, "but we will find our way. I know it's been several months since 3/16, but we will sift through every lead, follow every trail, until we uncover the truth. It won't be easy. But I trust in the expertise and dedication of each person in this room."

The dim lighting of the conference room seemed even more subdued as General Porter clicked through slides detailing the Army's 7-step problem-solving process. On the massive screen behind him, bullet points and flowcharts laid out a systematic approach to understanding and tackling the mystery of 3/16.

"First, we identify the problem," General Porter began, tapping his laser pointer at the introductory slide. "Next, we'll gather information and knowledge, formulating possible hypotheses. From there, we develop criteria and generate potential solutions."

As the general continued, Becca's attention drifted. The meticulous, drawn-out methodology felt stifling. She was accustomed to moving on her instincts, making quick, yet informed decisions in the field. This methodical approach, while no doubt effective in some scenarios, felt painfully slow for the urgency of the 3/16 crisis.

Her eyes scanned the room, reading the body language of her fellow attendees. While some seemed to be soaking in the general's every word, nodding in agreement, others shared Becca's restless energy. She caught the eye of FBI Agent David Mitchell, seated a few rows across. He was leaning back in his chair, one arm resting on the backrest, his fingers drumming a silent rhythm on the table. His eyes, alert and questioning, met hers. A brief nod passed between them, an unspoken acknowledgment of shared impatience.

She'd heard about Mitchell, about his reputation for being a maverick within the bureau. In many ways, he was the FBI's counterpart to her own role in the CIA: willing to push boundaries, to take risks when the situation called for it.

"We then evaluate those solutions and make a decision," General Porter continued, oblivious to the silent exchanges happening around him. "The sixth step is to implement the solution, and finally, we'll assess its effectiveness."

Becca took a deep breath, trying to quell her rising impatience. She recognized the value in a structured approach, especially with so many agencies and moving parts involved. But she also knew that, in a situation as fluid and as critical as this, agility and adaptability would be key.

The general wrapped up his presentation, and the room was filled with the soft hum of whispered conversations. Becca seized the opportunity, rising from her seat and navigating through the maze of chairs and tables to where Mitchell was seated.

"Agent Mitchell," she said, extending a hand, "Rebecca Lawrence, CIA. Mind if I join you for a quick chat?"

Mitchell looked up, a hint of a smile playing on his lips. "Agent Lawrence. Heard a lot about you. Please, have a seat. Call me David."

"Please, call me Becca."

The conference room hummed with conversation, the collective voices blending into an ambient backdrop. As the various agents and representatives regrouped, Becca sought out David, finding him by the window, his gaze fixed on the cityscape below.

"David," Becca began, choosing her words carefully, "I've got a few leads, ideas that may be considered... unconventional. I'm not convinced they'd be welcomed by this group."

David turned to her, his expression contemplative. "Becca, after everything that's happened, I believe any lead, any idea, however uncharted, might be the key. Lay it on me."

She hesitated momentarily, weighing the risks. "Alright, some of the sources I've been tapping into... they're not standard intel. But they're giving me a perspective that's different, something that could potentially be the edge we need."

David looked intrigued. "That resonates with what I've been uncovering. Sure, there's a lot to sift through, but I've stumbled upon recurring themes that don't fit the usual narrative."

She glanced around, ensuring they weren't overheard. "How do we navigate this? I mean, present our findings without them getting disregarded or ridiculed?"

He thought for a moment. "It's about strategy. We need to find like-minded allies in this group. We won't win everyone over at once, but with enough insiders advocating for our leads, the others might just start to listen."

Becca felt a sense of camaraderie. "Sounds like a plan. Between the two of us, maybe we can steer this ship into less charted waters."

David offered a small smile. "I'm with you. Let's see where these leads take us."

"I have someone I need you to meet."

Chapter 19: Revealing

The Four Seasons in Washington D.C. is a beacon of opulence. Every corner of the grand hotel speaks of an elegance that intertwines the city's historical reverence with modern luxury. The private lounge, with its ornate chandeliers casting a golden hue, showcases panoramic views of the city's landmarks. Between the gauzy curtains, the Washington Monument stands tall, its silhouette kissed by the setting sun, casting elongated shadows on the streets below.

David took a moment to appreciate the ambiance as he entered. The distant hum of muted conversations blended with the soft notes of a piano playing somewhere in the background. Spotting Becca at a corner table, he approached, noticing the distinguished gentleman with her. The man was the epitome of scholarly gravitas, with deep-set eyes that looked like they held a universe of knowledge, framed by a beard that spoke of years of contemplation.

"David," Becca said, her voice slightly hushed in the quiet elegance of the lounge. She rose, indicating the man across from her. "This is Professor Ephraim Goldman, the expert I mentioned. Professor, this is Agent David Mitchell. Let's retreat to your room, Ephraim, to discuss further."

The two men exchanged firm handshakes, mutual respect evident in the gesture. "Agent Mitchell, it's an honor," the professor began, adjusting the old-fashioned spectacles on his nose.

"Please, call me David," he replied.

"Yes, yes, let's retreat to my room."

After entering the well-adorned suit, they sat on the couch and dove into the heart of the matter. Professor Goldman leaned forward, his voice earnest. "David, what occurred on 3/16 wasn't merely a global tragedy; it was, I genuinely believe, the rapture."

David raised an eyebrow, intrigue evident on his face. "The rapture?"

Goldman nodded, "Precisely. Scriptures in both the Torah and the Gentile Bible, especially in the New Testament books of Thessalonians and Corinthians, detail an event where true believers in Christ would be taken from Earth. On 3/16, it appears the souls of the faithful were snatched away by Christ, leaving behind what seemed like lifeless bodies."

As David absorbed this, Becca added, "I've seen and heard many theories since the event, David. But nothing has resonated like the professor's insights. The way the bodies simply... dropped, lifelessly, simultaneously, across the globe—it's too synchronized to be mere coincidence."

David looked pensive, taking a moment before replying. "It's a monumental claim, Professor. Can you elaborate on why you believe this is connected to the end times prophecy?"

Goldman sipped his water, placing it gently on the table, and began. "Certainly. Biblical prophecy outlines a series of events that will occur at the end of days. The rapture is believed to precede a period known as the Tribulation, a time of great turmoil and strife. The sudden and inexplicable nature of 3/16 matches scriptural descriptions of the rapture – where the righteous are taken up by Christ."

David's eyes darted between Goldman and Becca, the weight of the revelation sinking in. "So, if this is true, we're on the brink of...?"

Goldman nodded gravely, "Potentially the most tumultuous period in human history."

David leaned forward, the weight of Professor Goldman's words pressing on him. "Professor, if we're to accept that 3/16 was indeed the rapture, what's next according to the scriptures? What should we brace ourselves for?"

Goldman shifted in his seat, taking a deep breath before speaking. "David, the next set of events, according to Biblical prophecy, is quite complex. Firstly, there's a prophesied attack on Israel from various nations, which is detailed in Ezekiel 38 and 39. But God intervenes directly, and His people, Israel, are protected."

David interjected, a hint of skepticism in his voice. "An attack on Israel? That's not uncommon in history, Professor. How do we distinguish this attack from the many conflicts we've seen in the Middle East?"

Goldman raised a hand, his fingers lightly tapping on the table, emphasizing his words. "The scale and nature, David. Ezekiel's prophecy details a specific consortium of nations coming together for this attack, including Russia, Iran, and Turkey, among others. This isn't just another skirmish; it's a significant alliance against Israel."

Becca, her face contemplative, added, "And given the current geopolitical climate, such an alliance doesn't seem far-fetched."

Goldman nodded in agreement, continuing, "Following God's divine intervention, a figure will emerge – the antichrist. He will negotiate a peace treaty with Israel, lasting seven years. It's this treaty that marks the beginning of a period called the Tribulation."

David frowned, the term new to him. "The Tribulation?"

"Yes," Goldman answered. "It's a seven-year period where the world will experience calamities of unprecedented scales — wars, famines, natural disasters. Halfway through, the antichrist will break the peace treaty, setting off the worst part of this era, aptly named the Great Tribulation."

David's gaze was intense, his mind racing. "And throughout this, where does that leave us, the people who remain? What's our role?"

Goldman looked David straight in the eyes, "Our role, David, is to stay vigilant, understand the signs, and above all, hold onto hope. While these prophecies spell out doom, they also promise a new beginning."

The room was thick with tension, each of them absorbing the profound implications of the conversation. David's investigative mind, ever probing, had a whole new realm to explore, one that ventured beyond the tangible into the realms of faith and prophecy.

Chapter 20: New Leadership

The clinking of coffee cups and soft murmurs of conversation filled the air at the cozy D.C. café. David and Becca sat in a corner booth, away from the main crowd, a spread of notes before them.

The café's TV played softly in the background, its screen showcasing a press conference. Lucien Morreau, the charismatic 55-year-old Prime Minister of Belgium, stood confidently before a backdrop of fluttering flags. His resonant voice held an eloquence that made even the café's patrons pause and listen.

"In these uncertain times, following the cataclysmic events of 3/16, the world requires unity more than ever before," Morreau's deep voice declared, his gaze sincere. "We stand on the precipice of history, and now, more than ever, we need to come together. I call upon the global community, especially our leaders, to convene at the United Nations. We must set aside our differences and achieve the previously unattainable — genuine world peace."

David took a sip from his cup, his eyes narrowing slightly. "Morreau's been making waves recently. Seems like he's positioning himself as a major player on the world stage."

Becca nodded, her gaze fixed on the screen. "He's charismatic, no doubt. People are looking for a figure to rally behind, especially now. But is he the real deal or just another politician seizing an opportunity?"

David leaned back, considering, "Time will tell. But with the world in chaos, figures like Morreau become incredibly powerful. His talk of peace is refreshing. Perhaps for once, a politician who really means it. Or maybe he's just opportunistic."

Becca smirked, "Add him to the list, then."

The TV's volume lowered as their conversation shifted back to their primary topic, but Lucien Morreau's image, that confident stance and compelling rhetoric, lingered in their minds.

David took a sip of his drink, looking thoughtful. "Goldman's theories... they're hard to ignore. But it's a lot to take in. The rapture, Biblical prophecies coming true? I mean, what do you think, Becca?"

Becca ran her fingers through her hair, leaning back. "Honestly, David? I've always believed in the power of intel, facts, and evidence. But after what happened on 3/16 and everything Goldman shared? I'm questioning everything."

David nodded slowly, "I met this guy, Mark Harris, in Baltimore. At first, I thought he was involved in some sort of extremist activities, but it turns out he had a similar belief. That 3/16 was the Rapture. He's not the extremist I had pegged him for."

Becca looked at David, surprise evident on her face. "Mark Harris? I've heard of him. I saw his name in a potential domestic terrorist report that crossed my desk a few months ago. You think he's onto something?"

"Ah, you're the CIA agent who sent the file over to John." David shrugged. "Mark seemed genuine. After further investigation, we cleared him. We had all of the intelligence wrong. And there were things he said that align with Goldman's take."

"Like Israel being attacked?" Becca inquired.

David sighed, "Israel is a focal point in the Middle East. They're under constant threat. But if the prophecies are to be believed, this would be a conflict of a different scale."

Becca took a moment, then said, "Professor Goldman mentioned he's returning to Israel to counsel the new Prime Minister, Abraham Katz. If this theory holds any water, Israel would be the epicenter."

David contemplated her words. "We need to get to the bottom of this, Becca. Maybe we should meet Mark again, delve deeper into these theories. If 3/16 is just the tip of the iceberg, we need to be prepared for what's next."

Becca nodded, determination settling on her features. "Let's do it. It's high time we get some clarity on 3/16."

Chapter 21: Ally

T he room, stark and sterile, hummed with an almost palpable tension. General Porter's stern gaze was fixated out of the window, watching the city's lights twinkle, giving David and Becca an uncomfortable sense of scrutiny. They exchanged uneasy glances, sensing that the forthcoming conversation would be anything but pleasant.

Finally, Porter turned, facing them squarely. "David, Becca," he began, voice stern and formal, "I've been hearing some rather... disconcerting reports about your latest lines of inquiry. This Working Group was assembled to uncover facts and truth, not chase wild religious theories."

David tried to hold his ground, his voice even but cautious, "General, we are simply following the leads as they present themselves. Every theory, every possibility—"

"Every possibility?" Porter snapped. "I've been told you're suggesting that 3/16 was a... a rapture? A biblical event?"

Becca interjected, "Sir, with all due respect, we're in uncharted waters here. No scientific explanation has been definitive so far. Why wouldn't we look at every conceivable angle?"

Porter's eyes flared, his voice raising a notch, "Because we are a government agency, Agent Lawrence. We deal with tangible evidence, not scripture."

David could feel the weight of the conversation pressing down on him, but he pressed forward, "General, we respect the boundaries and the principles of this Working Group, but we also know that there are moments, rare moments, when the unimaginable happens. And for many, 3/16 was one such event."

The room went silent for a few long moments. Becca could hear her own heartbeat. The implications of their investigation being shut down now would be catastrophic.

General Porter took a deep breath, each inhale carrying the weight of memories, pain, and regret. The room's atmosphere seemed to thicken with the gravity of his next words. "When I walked into our home on 3/16, I found Evelyn... just... still. Her body was there, but her spirit, her light, was gone. I've been in war zones, seen loss in many ways, but nothing prepared me for that moment."

His eyes, which had always been sharp and alert, now held a depth of sadness David hadn't noticed before. "You ever believe in God, David?" he asked suddenly, searching the younger agent's face for an answer.

Taken aback by the abruptness of the question, David cleared his throat, "Yes, sir. I do."

General Porter's eyes softened further, a wistful smile tracing his lips. "Evelyn always had this... certainty about her. This radiant confidence in her faith. And as I stood there, over her, I knew. I knew she had been right all along. That moment broke something inside me, David. The scriptures she shared, the prayers she whispered at night when she thought I was asleep - it all became clear."

He paused, collecting himself, "I realize now that on 3/16, Christ took his believers home. Evelyn was one of them. And the anguish I feel isn't just for losing her, but for all those years I wasted not truly knowing Him. Not being open to the truth she tried to share."

His voice grew more fervent, "Despite the official government line, I now understand what 3/16 truly was. I missed the rapture, David. But I believe that one day, I'll be with Evelyn. For now, there's work to be done here. Truths to uncover, even if they challenge everything we've known."

David and Becca exchanged surprised looks. The revelation was unexpected.

General Porter continued, "I've had reports about a looming threat in Israel. There's chatter about several nations aligning against them. We have to share our intel. The official stance may not acknowledge the biblical theories, but if there's even a sliver of truth, we owe it to our allies to prepare."

Becca, still absorbing his words, responded cautiously, "So, you're saying...?"

"I'm saying continue your investigation," Porter stated firmly. "Go to Israel. Meet with Professor Goldman, liaise with Prime Minister Katz. Share our intel. We have a duty to our allies."

David, visibly relieved, nodded. "Thank you, General. We won't disappoint you."

General Porter returned his gaze to the window, "This isn't about me. It's about understanding the truth, no matter where it leads."

Chapter 22: Jerusalem

J erusalem at dawn is a spectacle of its own kind. As the first fingers of sunlight caressed the city, they ignited the stones of its venerable structures in a radiant golden embrace. Every inch of this place whispers tales that date back to antiquity, tales penned in scriptures, etched in walls, and carried forward through countless generations.

The Old City, encircled by thick, robust walls, stands as a testament to an ancient era. Towering gates, which have stood sentinel for centuries, open up to a maze of narrow, winding alleys. These paths, trodden by prophets, kings, and pilgrims of old, are lined with stones worn smooth by countless feet. The very air seems heavy with the weight of stories, of prayers whispered and shouted, of tears shed in joy and sorrow.

Every so often, one could glimpse an old man with a tale in his eyes, deep in thought, lost perhaps in reminiscences of yester-years. Children, their laughter pure and untainted, play along these paths, their feet tracing the steps of those who walked before them, reminding the observer of the city's continuity and undying spirit.

The sounds of Jerusalem are a symphony of faiths. As dawn approached, the deep, resonant toll of church bells merged with the soulful call of the muezzin. The whispering chants from synagogues, echoing age-old psalms, added another layer to this rich tapestry of devotion.

Yet, just beyond the historic heart, modern Jerusalem soars and buzzes. Sleek skyscrapers of steel and glass brush the sky. Busy streets, filled with the honks of cars and the chatter of diverse tongues, signify the city's pace with the present. Trendy cafes, their aroma of freshly ground coffee beans wafting through the air, sit beside stalls offering falafel and shawarma, their scents equally enticing.

In the markets, the air is heavy with the scent of spices—cumin, za'atar, and sumac—piled high in vibrant mounds. Shopkeepers, their voices a melodic blend of invitation and negotiation, showcase wares ranging from intricate silver jewelry to richly embroidered textiles.

Lush gardens and parks offer a respite from the city's hustle, where olive trees, some hundreds of years old, stand in silent contemplation, their gnarled trunks holding secrets of the ages.

The Israeli Parliament building, known as the Knesset, stands tall and proud, a symbol of the nation's tumultuous yet unyielding journey. Inside, its halls are adorned with art and symbols, recounting tales of old and visions of the future. Among these tales is that of Abraham Katz.

In one of the Knesset's spacious conference rooms, with tall windows allowing the golden Jerusalem light to filter through, Prime Minister Abraham Katz was ready for the meeting. The room was simple yet elegant, with an elongated mahogany table at its center, surrounded by plush leather chairs. On the walls hung portraits of previous leaders, each telling their own story of service and sacrifice.

Katz stood at the head of the table, his tall, commanding frame making him almost a part of the room's architecture. He looked out of the window momentarily, seemingly drawing strength from the city he loved so deeply.

His salt-and-pepper hair, neatly combed back, revealed a broad forehead, an emblem of his thoughtful nature. Those signature piercing blue eyes, which many journalists found intimidating during press briefings, today had a more contemplative, almost tender gleam. Those eyes had seen wars, had witnessed peace treaties, had watched friends fall and enemies rise.

Though his suit was sharp, hinting at a blend of traditionalism with modern leadership, it couldn't quite conceal the ridged scar that ran down his left arm—an old battle wound from his days in the Israel Defense Forces. It was a constant reminder, not just of his own sacrifices, but of the nation's ceaseless battle for existence.

Katz had always been a man of few words, believing in action more than rhetoric. Yet, those who truly knew him, who had seen him beyond the cameras and press, knew of the deep well of compassion that lay within him. He was a father, a grandfather, and carried the weight of his nation's hopes and fears as if they were his family's own.

Today, as he waited for the agents, he hoped, as he always did, for a future of peace, even in a land where peace seemed a distant dream. For Abraham Katz, every challenge, every negotiation, every decision was a step towards that dream.

As the heavy doors of the conference room opened, a hushed reverence settled over the space. The large windows that moments before were basking the room in a warm Jerusalem glow seemed to dim just slightly, emphasizing the gravity of the impending discussion.

Leading the way was Dr. Ephraim Goldman. His once-slender frame was more robust than when he'd been captive, his posture straighter. The horrors he endured under Boko Haram had left emotional scars, but his recent rescue and subsequent return to Israel had brought back some of the old fire to his eyes.

Following closely behind him were two figures. The man, David Mitchell, had an air of meticulous professionalism about him. He scanned the room quickly, his gaze sharp and assessing. Beside him, Becca Lawrence moved with a grace that belied her well-documented tactical expertise. The weight of her recent mission was evident in her eyes, but so was the pride of its success.

Prime Minister Katz, who had been gazing out of the window, turned and stepped forward as the trio approached. His eyes settled on Goldman first, a brief smile hinting at the depth of their shared history and the gratitude for the man's safe return.

"Ephraim," Katz greeted, his voice warm, extending a hand.

Goldman took it, replying, "Abraham. It's good to be back." He then motioned to the agents beside him. "May I introduce FBI Agent David Mitchell and CIA Agent Rebecca Lawrence."

David stepped forward, extending a firm handshake. "Prime Minister Katz," he nodded with respect.

Becca did the same, her demeanor confident. "Sir," she simply acknowledged.

Katz's gaze lingered on Becca a moment longer, the corners of his eyes crinkling slightly. "Agent Lawrence," he began, "I have been briefed on the mission in Nigeria. Words may not suffice, but thank you for bringing our dear Dr. Goldman back to us."

Becca offered a modest nod, "It was an honor, sir."

Katz gestured to the chairs around the table. "Please, let's sit. We have much to discuss." The weight of their task ahead was palpable, but for now, formalities and gratitude set the stage.

The weight of the impending situation was palpable as Prime Minister Katz shifted in his chair, locking his gaze on Becca, awaiting the details she'd brought. The usual distant clamor of the Knesset seemed to fade, replaced by a quiet tension in the room.

Becca began methodically, spreading out the assortment of documents, photos, and satellite images she'd procured. "Prime Minister Katz, our intelligence strongly suggests an imminent, coordinated assault on Israel, involving multiple state and non-state actors. Specifically, we've identified Libya, Iran, Syria, Turkey, and the factions within Hamas as major players."

David, skimming through a dossier, added, "There are significant troop movements in Syria near our borders. We've noticed amassed troops and artillery in Libya, potentially preparing for a northern assault. Turkey is holding naval exercises in the Mediterranean, a show of strength, but it's more than that. They are positioning. Hamas, as always, is a wild card but seems to be receiving additional backing from Iran."

Katz, running a hand through his hair, seemed to digest this information, murmuring, "The usual suspects."

But Becca wasn't done. Taking a deep breath, she dropped the next bombshell. "There's more. Our most recent intel, which we're still cross-referencing for validation, indicates potential involvement from Russia."

Katz looked up sharply, eyebrows furrowing in surprise and concern. "Russia? That's...unexpected."

David chimed in, "Their motivations remain unclear, but it appears they might be providing logistical and military support. Given Russia's nuclear capabilities and their history of asymmetrical warfare, this poses a different level of threat."

Katz sighed heavily, "If Russia is involved, even tangentially, the stakes are higher. A conflict of this nature, with a nuclear-armed power, isn't just a regional concern anymore. It becomes global."

Dr. Goldman, who had been quietly observing the exchange, commented, "This alliance, especially with Russia involved, echoes certain prophecies. They believe the current global chaos is an opportunity, but we should see it as a forewarning."

As the weight of the situation hung over the room, Dr. Goldman stood up, beckoning everyone to the wall where a large map of the Middle East was displayed.

"While our primary concern is the tactical and political maneuvering of these nations," he began, "it's essential to understand the deeper historical and prophetic implications."

He moved his finger along the territories of the nations involved, "The alliances forming now are eerily reminiscent of those prophesied in the Bible." He paused, his gaze taking in everyone in the room. "Ezekiel, in particular, spoke of a coalition, a northern alliance, that would come against Israel in the latter days."

Becca, ever the skeptic, raised an eyebrow, "Historical coincidence, perhaps?"

Goldman offered a patient smile, "Perhaps. But when we overlay current events with the prophecies, the patterns are uncanny."

He continued, "Ezekiel mentioned nations by their ancient names - Magog, which many scholars believe refers to parts of modern-day Russia. Persia, which is now Iran, Put, which correlates with Libya, and so on."

David interjected, "So you're saying that this predicted alliance from...how many years ago?"

"Over two and a half millennia," Goldman clarified.

David let out a low whistle, "That this ancient prophecy is manifesting now?"

Goldman nodded, "Precisely. These scriptures describe a time when Israel would be back in her land, thriving, a 'land of unwalled villages' and then, this coalition would form to plunder and loot."

Prime Minister Katz, deep in thought, said, "And what does this prophecy say of the outcome?"

Goldman hesitated briefly, choosing his words carefully, "It speaks of divine intervention. A defense of Israel that's so profound that it would be known globally that God had defended His people."

Becca shook her head slightly, processing the information. "So, if we follow this narrative, we're not just on the brink of a major regional conflict but a prophetic showdown?"

Goldman met her gaze, "That would seem to be the case."

Chapter 23: The Attack

The chilling siren sliced through their conversation, its haunting resonance a stark reminder of the ever-present threat that loomed over Israel. Prime Minister Katz's face immediately hardened, every ounce of his being focused on the imminent danger. "This way," he commanded, gesturing for them to follow.

Exiting the conference room, David's heart raced, his thoughts a whirlwind of concern and anticipation. The hurried footsteps of the group echoed through the corridor, intertwining with the muted sounds of chaos emanating from the world outside. With each step, the urgency heightened, and David felt a knot of anxiety tighten in his stomach.

Soon they reached a fortified door, which opened to reveal the bustling command center inside the bunker. The room was alive with the frenzied, yet organized, activities of military personnel. Multiple screens displayed aerial views of the region, while uniformed officers intently relayed and received information via headsets. Warning lights flashed, and digital maps plotted trajectories of inbound missiles.

Katz immediately stepped into the role of leader amidst the turmoil. He gestured for Becca and David to take seats at the back of the room, from where they could observe without hindrance. Professor Goldman was summoned to Katz's side, the two exchanging grave, knowing looks.

Becca and David exchanged glances as they settled into their designated spots. The intensity of the command center was palpable, each individual driven by the singular purpose of safeguarding their nation. Alerts and updates streamed across screens, with officers promptly disseminating the information to ground units and defense systems.

Prime Minister Katz turned towards Chief of the General Staff, Yosef Golan, a distinguished military figure with decades of service to his country. Golan's face was lined with concern, his eyes reflecting the weight of the moment.

"Yosef," Katz's voice was sharp, demanding. "What's our situation?"

General Golan shifted, straightening his uniform. "Prime Minister, it's a multi-pronged assault. Our early warning systems failed to detect a barrage of missiles launched from Iranian soil.

Simultaneously, Russian forces have initiated an aggressive push from Syria. We've spotted tank divisions and multiple squadrons of fighter jets advancing rapidly."

He paused, swallowing hard before continuing, "It doesn't end there. Our maritime systems have identified Libyan gunships advancing from the Mediterranean, aggressively posturing against our naval defenses."

Katz's face turned ashen, the gravity of the words sinking in. "It's a coordinated strike," he whispered, more to himself than anyone in the room.

General Golan nodded grimly, "Yes, sir. And there's more. Our Iron Dome, our primary defense against aerial threats... it's been compromised. We believe Russian hackers are behind its shutdown."

David's heart sank. He felt a cold dread wash over him, the realization that they were facing an unprecedented threat. The room fell into a stifling silence, punctuated only by the soft hum of the equipment. Becca and David exchanged wide-eyed glances, the enormity of the situation overwhelming.

The room fell into a stifling silence, punctuated only by the soft hum of the equipment. Becca and David exchanged wide-eyed glances, the enormity of the situation overwhelming.

"How long?" Katz finally asked, his voice shaking with a mix of fear and determination.

Golan hesitated before replying, "Our best estimates put the Iranian ballistic missiles making impact in approximately three minutes. Our Air Force is scrambling, but realistically, they won't be able to significantly deter the sheer numbers we're seeing."

Katz ran a hand through his hair, the weight of leadership pressing heavily upon him. "This could be the end for us," he murmured, eyes locked onto the map showing the advance of enemy forces.

Dr. Goldman, sensing the rising despair, quietly stepped forward, "Abraham, throughout history, Israel has faced insurmountable odds. Remember our roots, our faith, our purpose."

Katz nodded, taking a deep breath. "Prepare all defenses. Alert all shelters. We'll stand as one nation against this storm."

The command center's atmosphere was tense, with every heart beating in anticipation of the impending disaster. The massive display screens blinked with hostile red blips representing the incoming missiles, fighter jets, and tanks. A deep feeling of dread settled over the room.

General Golan, his face ashen, pointed at the screen. "The first waves of missiles are nearly upon us. The jets and tanks aren't far behind. We need to brace ourselves." There was an unsaid realization that without the Iron Dome, they were severely outmatched.

It was in this bleak moment that a young analyst, her face illuminated by the glow of her monitor, exclaimed, "General, something's happening! The missiles... they're... disappearing from our radar!"

Golan rushed to her side, watching in disbelief as the red blips representing the threats began to vanish, one after another. "What is going on?"

Another officer, stationed at the communication desk, began to relay real-time field reports. "Reports are flooding in from the border! There's a massive hailstorm. It's targeting the missiles. They're being struck down mid-flight!"

"And it's not just the missiles," another voice piped up, "The Russian tanks advancing from Syria are being pelted. Many missiles are being diverted into their path!"

An Air Force liaison added, "Our pilots are reporting the same. The Russian jets, they're being severely damaged by the hail. It's as if the very sky is fighting against them!"

A stunned silence enveloped the room. The various threats, so imminent just moments before, were now being neutralized in an inexplicable way.

Golan, his voice tinged with awe, murmured, "This is a miracle."

PM Katz nodded, eyes glistening, "This isn't the work of any man or technology. This is divine intervention."

Dr. Goldman, ever the scholar, softly spoke, "In our ancient texts, there are stories of God using nature to defend Israel. This... this is a modern-day manifestation of those miracles."

The command center's screens flickered as the ground trembled beneath them. The steady hum of the equipment was punctuated by the sound of rattling and distant alarms from the outer reaches of the facility.

"Stay calm, everyone!" General Golan shouted over the noise. "This facility is fortified. It's built to withstand such tremors."

But the tremor wasn't the only thing catching their attention. On one of the TVs, news anchors were urgently reporting a significant earthquake with its epicenter in the Mediterranean Sea. Footage showed streets cracking, ancient buildings trembling, and people pouring out of structures, praying and looking up at the sky.

"Sir, our early warning systems are detecting a large tsunami," an analyst said, his voice echoing the urgency of the situation. "But it's heading away from our shores."

Attention shifted to the Mediterranean, where the colossal wave could be seen from satellite feeds gaining momentum. The Libyan gunships, previously a major threat, now looked like mere toys against the might of nature. The roaring waves flipped them over, submerging them, and then, within moments, they vanished into the depths.

Over in the Golan Heights, cameras captured chaotic scenes. Russian tanks, previously advancing in intimidating formations, now lay overturned and mangled. Huge crevices had opened in the earth, swallowing military vehicles and troops. And in the midst of this pandemonium, the Russians, unable to discern friend from foe, began clashing among themselves.

Prime Minister Katz watched the screens intently, his expression unreadable. The general turmoil and the natural disaster's crippling effect on the adversaries was a tactical boon. Yet, the room's palpable relief was punctured when another analyst, face ashen, turned towards him.

"Prime Minister," the analyst started, taking a deep breath. "We're getting reports that the earthquake is damaging sites all over the region. But Prime Minister... the Temple Mount. Sir, it's leveled. The mosque at the Temple Mount has been completely destroyed."

A hush settled over the room. All eyes shifted to Prime Minister Katz, awaiting his reaction. This wasn't just a strategic or tactical concern anymore – the Temple Mount held deep religious and cultural significance for Jews, Christians, and Muslims alike.

Dr. Goldman, standing to the side, caught the Prime Minister's eye. They exchanged a meaningful look, both realizing the profound implications of this event. The tectonic upheaval wasn't just physical; it threatened to shake the very socio-political fabric of the region. Would this lead to an unprecedented unity, or would it be the spark that would ignite longstanding religious tensions?

The news footage showed a Russian commander, trying to rally his troops with a megaphone, but his calls were drowned out by the cries of confusion and fear from his own soldiers. The disciplined force had turned on itself, their ranks shattered, making them easy prey for the advancing Israeli counter-offensive.

The command center was in disbelief. First, the skies defended Israel, and now the earth and sea had risen to its aid.

Dr. Goldman, still trying to comprehend the turn of events, quoted an old scripture, "When the enemy comes in like a flood, the Spirit of the Lord will lift up a standard against him."

General Golan, gazing at the screens, muttered in agreement, "We are not alone in this battle."

Chapter 24: Dynamic

The opulent waiting room adjacent to the UN General Assembly chamber was hardly a place for reflection. Its golden curtains, expensive wall hangings, and the rich scent of mahogany created a distinct atmosphere of power and prestige. But for Lucien Morreau, it was just another room, another stage before he took on the world.

Seated on a plush sofa, he adjusted the cuffs of his crisp white shirt, making sure the emblematic ring he always wore was visible. Its design—a peculiar amalgamation of ancient symbols—glistened under the soft lights. Next to him, a table showcased an array of refreshments and drinks, but he ignored them. Instead, his piercing blue eyes were fixed on a screen silently broadcasting the current speaker at the General Assembly. Lucien didn't need to hear the words; he already knew the essence of the discussions and the weight of the day's agenda.

Aria DeLacroix, his chief advisor, approached, her heels clicking on the marble floor. "They're almost ready for you, Prime Minister."

He nodded, acknowledging her without breaking his gaze from the screen. "The world seeks direction, Aria," he murmured. "They're like children lost in a forest, crying out for a guide. Today, they will find one."

Aria, accustomed to his dramatic flair, responded, "The world will listen. Make them believe."

Lucien's lips curled into a subtle smirk. "Belief has always been the most potent weapon."

At that moment, a UN aide approached, signaling it was time. "Prime Minister Morreau, they're ready for you."

Standing up, Lucien smoothed his suit, took a deep breath, and followed the aide. As he walked towards the main chamber, the hushed conversations of the waiting room faded, replaced by the weighty silence of the hallway. This was his moment, a pivotal step in his carefully choreographed dance to power.

The large double doors of the General Assembly chamber loomed ahead, and as they opened, the murmur of hundreds of diplomats filled the air. The room was a sea of faces from every corner of the globe, all looking towards the central podium where he would stand.

As Lucien Morreau stepped onto the stage, the room settled into an expectant hush. With the world watching, he began to speak, his voice authoritative, his words promising hope, unity, and a new era of global peace.

The General Assembly chamber settled into a thick silence, all eyes on the silver-haired orator taking center stage. Lucien Morreau adjusted the microphone to his height, pausing for dramatic effect before beginning his speech.

"Ladies and gentlemen, esteemed delegates, and leaders from across our global community," his voice resonated with calm authority, "the events of 3/16 have shaken the very foundations of our existence. In a blink, millions of souls were taken from us. Families torn apart, countries left reeling in the aftermath of such an inexplicable tragedy. Our world, already fractured in many ways, suffered a cataclysmic blow."

He paused, letting the weight of his words sink in. "Yet, amid this immense grief and chaos, we are presented with an unprecedented opportunity. An opportunity to reimagine, reshape, and rebuild a world not bound by the chains of division and hatred, but one illuminated by the light of unity and peace."

The assembly was rapt. Every word Lucien spoke seemed to pierce through the heart of the pain everyone felt.

"As we collectively navigate through this labyrinth of sorrow, another pressing issue has emerged." His tone shifted slightly, a hint of urgency creeping in. "The 'security situation' in Israel some six months ago. What is portrayed by many as an act of aggression is, in essence, nations coming together to ensure peace and security. With the recent escalations by Hamas and the ensuing concerns, it becomes paramount to extend a hand of support, stability, and safety to the Israeli people."

There were murmurs in the assembly. Some nods of agreement, some skeptical glances. Lucien pressed on.

"The intertwining of these two monumental events—the heartbreak of 3/16 and the volatility in Israel—sends a clear message to us all. The time for global unity is now. We cannot, and must not, allow the traumas of our past to dictate our future."

His blue eyes scanned the room, capturing the gaze of many. "Today, I propose we embark on a journey towards achieving world peace. A comprehensive plan that addresses not only the geopolitical challenges we face but also bridges the divides that have kept us apart for far too long."

He paused again, leaning slightly forward. "We have before us a blank canvas. Together, we have the colors of hope, resilience, and unity. Let's paint a future where no child grows up in the shadows of war, where every individual can live without fear, where our world stands united against any adversity."

Lucien's gaze settled on the assembly, taking in the sea of faces from every corner of the globe. With each passing word, he could feel the attention ratcheting up, the atmosphere thickening with anticipation.

"For decades," he began, his voice deepening for emphasis, "the Middle East has stood as a cauldron of conflict, a constant challenge to the world's conscience. The heart of this unrest, more often than not, has revolved around the State of Israel."

There was an undeniable truth to his words. The Middle Eastern conflict had for years acted as both a symbolic and very real wedge driving the international community apart.

Lucien continued, "Throughout history, whenever we've seen peace with Israel, it has served as a beacon, an exemplar of what can be achieved in even the most challenging geopolitical landscapes. I believe, and I'm sure many of you will agree, that solidifying peace with Israel is the linchpin to broader global stability."

He leaned forward slightly, his piercing blue eyes scanning the audience. "And so, if peace with Israel is the key, why not turn it? Why not employ it as the binding force that pulls us together, not just in the Middle East, but worldwide?"

He let the weight of his proposition hang in the air, giving the delegates a moment to digest it.

"My esteemed colleagues, today, I bring before you not just a theory or a philosophy, but tangible action." Lucien's voice carried a sense of gravity and impending revelation. "I present a blueprint, a pathway towards global peace, beginning with one of the most historically volatile regions."

He paused, letting the anticipation build further, feeling the collective pulse of the room rising.

"After months of discreet, intense negotiations and diplomatic efforts, I am overjoyed—no, *honored*—to announce that all nations of the Middle East, including the State of Israel, have come together in an unprecedented show of unity."

Lucien unveiled a large, ornate document bearing the insignias of each country. "This," he said, holding it up for all to see, "is a 7-year peace agreement. An agreement that promises a cessation of all hostilities, mutual cooperation, and, above all, a shared commitment to a prosperous, peaceful future."

The room was silent for a beat, then broke into a cacophony of applause, cheers, and gasps of disbelief. The magnitude of Lucien's announcement, and the implications of such a pact, were not lost on anyone.

Prime Minister Abraham Katz, a tall, distinguished figure with a salt-and-pepper beard, stood up. He seemed composed, yet the subtle set of his jaw hinted at the weight he felt. The sheer gravity of this situation was not lost on him, nor on the countless generations before him who had longed for peace.

Katz waved to the assembly, a gesture of both gratitude and acknowledgment. His eyes, however, told a deeper story. They were the eyes of a leader who had seen his nation through its highest highs and lowest lows. And today, they held a blend of hope, caution, and determination.

As the applause began to subside, Lucien continued, "It's only by coming together, by laying aside our differences, that we can truly achieve what has eluded humanity for so long. Peace. Real, lasting peace. Today, we're not just witnesses to history; we're its architects."

The room, already thick with emotion, hung onto Lucien's every word. However, beneath the surface of this monumental event, undercurrents of doubt, suspicion, and unease lingered. In the world of geopolitics, things were rarely as simple as they seemed.

The green room, draped in opulence, felt miles away from the bustling UN assembly hall. Intricate wooden panels decorated the walls, and a grand chandelier cast a soft, golden glow. A long mahogany table occupied the center, holding a variety of refreshments.

Lucien, with a champagne flute in hand, emanated a powerful aura of calm assurance. He sipped leisurely from the glass, his eyes twinkling with the bubbles.

Israeli Prime Minister Katz, usually stoic and reserved, looked sincerely grateful as he approached Lucien. "Your vision and determination have given us hope, Lucien, hope that seemed impossible."

Dr. Goldman, a man of wisdom and contemplation, watched the two, intrigued. The tales of Lucien's charisma had not been exaggerated. There was something captivating about him.

Lucien, his voice smooth, responded, "Peace has been a dream, Abraham, an elusive one. But the landscape has shifted."

Katz gestured for him to elaborate. "You're referring to the recent catastrophes?"

Lucien nodded, taking another sip. "First, the tragedy of 3/16. Then, the nations that sought to devastate Israel were themselves befell to unfortunate circumstances. Natural disasters on an unprecedented scale. Earthquakes, storms, calamities that claimed tens of thousands of lives, ravaging their landscapes and infrastructures."

Goldman chimed in, "The world is reeling, trying to make sense of it all."

Lucien leaned in, "And in this chaos lies opportunity. Think of it, Abraham, Ephraim. A new world where governance is unified, where economies are interconnected, where humanity stands together. That is the path forward."

Katz frowned thoughtfully. "Getting nations to relinquish their sovereignty won't be easy. Especially in this climate of heightened nationalism."

Lucien's smile held a hint of mischief. "With the right financial incentives, nations will find the prospect... tantalizing. In our rapidly evolving digital age, the concept of paper currency is becoming more and more obsolete. A global economy demands a unified financial system. Imagine a single digital currency, universally accepted, which could spur exponential growth."

Goldman, ever curious, leaned in, "A digital currency? Like the cryptocurrencies we've seen rise and fall?"

Lucien nodded, "Similar in concept, but vastly different in execution. This currency would be state-backed, regulated, and would serve as the central economic pillar for every nation."

Katz looked intrigued but skeptical, "And this would benefit Israel how?"

Lucien's eyes sparkled with anticipation, "By ensuring global participation, we level the playing field. Debts are forgiven, majority world nations rise from poverty, and wealth disparities shrink. Israel, with its technological prowess, could lead the charge in implementing and maintaining this system. The economic prosperity will foster stability, and with stability, peace naturally follows."

Dr. Goldman, always searching for the underlying implications, questioned, "But would this not also consolidate immense power into the hands of the few overseeing this system?"

Lucien chuckled softly, "Power is always a double-edged sword, Ephraim. But with the right leaders and checks in place, we could usher in a new era of transparency and cooperation."

Katz looked contemplative, "Forgiving debts, creating a unified digital currency, these are monumental tasks."

Lucien, standing up, spread his arms wide, "Monumental challenges, Abraham, but think of the monumental rewards! A thriving, peaceful global community, interconnected and interdependent. This is the way forward, and together, we can make it a reality."

Chapter 25: The Target

D avid leaned back in his ergonomic chair, the cold light from his office computer illuminating his thoughtful expression. The walls of his office bore plaques of commendation and a framed photo of a younger David at the FBI Academy. It was an anchor to his roots, reminding him of why he joined the Bureau in the first place.

On his sleek, mounted TV screen, Lucien Morreau stood against the backdrop of a large, ornate hall, blue UN flags flanking him. Lucien's commanding voice resonated clearly, "In the wake of 3/16, we have the unprecedented opportunity to redefine our world. It's not merely about survival, but thriving, progressing. By expanding economic horizons for all nations, we step towards lasting peace. To oppose this initiative is to oppose human advancement and peace itself."

David's fingers drummed on the armrest of his chair, taking in Lucien's words. It was clear Lucien's charisma was a force to be reckoned with.

The TV feed quickly switched to the U.S. President at a White House press conference, "While we're still reviewing the specifics of this peace plan, let me be clear: We believe in peace. A peace agreement with Israel, under the right terms, could be monumental for global stability."

David cocked an eyebrow. The President's words were carefully chosen, non-committal, but the subtext was evident.

Without missing a beat, the broadcast switched to the Capitol's grand steps. A tall, burly senator from Kentucky, with thick white hair and piercing eyes, stood with a determination that contrasted sharply with the previous speakers. "America was founded on principles of freedom and self-reliance. We will not, and I emphasize, we will not surrender our values to this so-called 'new world order.' No matter the promises, no matter the allure, we will remain resolute."

David's computer emitted a soft chime, indicating a new message. The sender was labeled "SecureComm." It was the internal encrypted messaging system the FBI used for sensitive information.

Opening it, David recognized Becca's signature code at the bottom. Her message was concise: We have intel on a threat, high visibility, high impact. Meet me at the joint operations conference room for debrief.

The weight of the message hung heavily on him. "High visibility, high impact" typically meant a significant threat with broad implications, not just for the nation but potentially on a global scale.

Quickly locking his computer, David stood up and grabbed his jacket from the back of his chair. The hallways of the FBI headquarters were bustling with agents and personnel, all engrossed in their tasks. Yet, there was a silent undercurrent of urgency that David felt as he briskly made his way through the corridors.

Upon reaching the joint operations conference room, he saw Becca standing by the door, scanning her security clearance. The door hissed open, revealing a dimly lit room with a vast oval-shaped table at its center. The walls were adorned with screens, currently black, waiting to be activated.

Becca looked up, her face grim. "Took you long enough," she remarked, though there was no real heat in her voice.

"What do we have?" David asked, urgency coloring his tone.

Becca gestured to one of the seats. "I'm waiting on a few more. Then we'll get into it. This is... big, David."

David's pulse quickened. He took a seat, nodding for Becca to continue, bracing himself for the intelligence that could shift the paradigm once again.

Inside the joint operations conference room, David could hear the hum of computers and the faint clicks of keyboards. The muted light from overhead projectors highlighted the intense expressions on everyone's face.

Becca stood at the front of the room, remote in hand, next to a projector screen that currently displayed a satellite image of the Belgium Federal Parliament.

"Alright, listen up," she began, her voice firm, demanding undivided attention. "We've received intelligence about a significant threat to the Belgium Federal Parliament."

The room was deathly silent, all eyes fixed on her.

"Initial intelligence suggests that there will be a two-fold attack. First, a wave of gunmen will storm the building, followed closely by the detonation of multiple explosive devices."

A map of the Parliament popped up, highlighted areas showcasing potential entry points and blast zones. David's eyes quickly scanned the marked spots, analyzing their implications.

"The target day," Becca continued, "is tied to the return of Prime Minister Lucien Morreau from his UN trip in New York City."

David took a sharp breath. The implications of attacking such a high-profile target were massive, especially with Morreau's rising global influence post-3/16.

Becca switched the slide, revealing a network of suspects, their profiles, and connections. "Our intelligence has identified some key players, though we are still piecing together their hierarchy and full plan. What's clear is their intention to inflict maximum damage and chaos."

David leaned forward, absorbing the intricate web of connections. The professionalism and meticulousness of the plot made it evident that this was not the work of a run-of-the-mill extremist group.

Becca paused, her gaze sweeping the room. "Our primary objective is to prevent this at all costs. We need to coordinate with Homeland, ensuring that our response is swift and decisive."

"Becca, how credible is this intel?" An agent from the back of the room asked.

She nodded, "Credible enough that we're taking it very seriously. And so should every agency here. We've already briefed Belgium intelligence services."

David stood up. "We need to brief Morreau. If he's the high-profile target amidst this chaos, he needs to know."

Becca nodded in agreement, "I've arranged a meeting with him at his hotel in New York. David, I want you to accompany me."

"We're dealing with a very tight window here," she continued, "Time is of the essence. Let's get to work."

The room sprang into action, with agents and officers moving quickly, coordinating their next steps. The weight of the situation pressed on everyone's mind, but David couldn't help but feel a spark of determination.

The luxurious suite of the Parkview Hotel was bathed in a soft golden hue, emanating from the setting sun. As David and Becca sat opposite Lucien Morreau, the glistening skyline of Manhattan could be seen through the vast windows, but the beauty outside was starkly contrasted by the tension inside.

David, leaning forward, laid out the intelligence report in front of Lucien. His voice was measured but conveyed urgency, "Prime Minister, we believe this threat is real and imminent."

Lucien, ever the composed statesman, steepled his fingers, "I understand the gravity, Agent, but I trust the capabilities of my protective services in Belgium. They're quite competent."

Becca interjected, "Sir, this isn't just about competence. The intricacy and scale of this planned assault is unlike anything we've seen in recent times."

Before Lucien could reply, a sudden commotion from outside the suite broke the conversation. Raised voices, muffled shouts, and then – unmistakably – the chilling sound of gunfire.

David's and Becca's training kicked in instantly. They both drew their sidearms, with David pushing Lucien behind them.

The Diplomatic Security Service officers in the room had already assumed protective positions, weapons drawn, aiming at the suite's entrance. One of them urgently beckoned Lucien toward the bedroom.

But before anyone could make a move, the suite door exploded inwards. David's eyes caught the metallic flash of a thrown object – a stun grenade. Without hesitation, he lunged at Lucien, shielding him with his body as he tackled him to the plush carpet. Simultaneously, he closed his eyes tight and clamped his hands over his ears, bracing for the deafening blast.

A bright flash and a disorienting boom rocked the room. The air filled with a high-pitched ringing. David shook his head, trying to clear the effects. As his vision and hearing started to return, he saw shadowy figures charging into the suite.

Becca was already up, her gun spitting fire as she engaged the intruders. Her shots precise, she managed to down two of them before taking cover behind a luxurious couch.

David's senses heightened as he scanned the room, assessing the threat. Every second was crucial. In one swift motion, he gripped Lucien by the arm, pulling him up from the carpeted floor where they had taken cover. Adrenaline surged through

David, amplifying his strength as he steered Lucien with forceful determination.

"Move!" he urged, his voice barely audible over the chaos. Using his own body as a shield, David ensured that every step Lucien took was behind the safety he provided. Bullets whizzed by, embedding themselves into the lavish decor, shredding the opulent drapery, and shattering an ornate mirror.

As they approached the bedroom, David took a split second to glance over his shoulder, locking eyes with Becca who was engaging the intruders with fierce precision. Her face was set in a steely determination, but her eyes briefly flashed gratitude for David's cover.

David pushed Lucien into the bedroom and quickly turned back to the main room, taking aim and firing several shots, giving Becca the window she needed. She darted toward the bedroom, diving through the door just as David slammed it shut behind her.

With their backs pressed against the sturdy wood of the door, David and Becca worked in unison to barricade it, using every piece of furniture they could grab - a heavy dresser, a nightstand, even a plush chair. They moved with a practiced efficiency, each understanding their roles in this perilous dance.

Panting heavily, sweat dripping from his brow, David turned to Becca. Both of their chests heaved as they took a much-needed breath, the weight of the moment settling in. Their eyes met, a silent acknowledgment passing between them. They had managed a momentary reprieve, but both knew that this battle was far from over.

The dim lighting in the bedroom gave a hushed, surreal feeling to the space. David, with practiced efficiency, ejected the empty magazine from his gun and slammed in a new one, the familiar metallic click echoing in the heavy silence. His eyes remained firmly fixed on the bedroom door, anticipating the inevitable breach.

Becca, every bit the professional, guided Lucien toward the bathroom. "Stay down," she whispered, pushing him into the tub. She drew the shower curtain for minimal concealment, knowing its meager protection was only for show.

Making her way back, she took a quick survey of the room, searching for any advantage. David had already positioned the mattress upright, an improvised shield. His rapid breathing and intense focus betrayed the adrenaline coursing through his veins. The palpable tension between the two agents was electric, both knowing the importance of their next moves.

Without verbal communication, but a mere glance and a nod, David signaled Becca to take her position. As she ducked behind a heavy wooden dresser, its ornate carvings standing in stark contrast to the violence outside, she gripped her firearm with determination.

The muffled thuds of approaching footsteps became louder, overshadowing every other sound. Then, with a violent burst, the door was blown inwards. Almost simultaneously, two dark objects were hurled inside. David's instincts kicked in, and with a swift kick, he sent the mattress toppling over the stun grenades. The explosion was deafening, the force sending a shockwave through the room, rattling windows and shaking the very foundation. Smoke and debris filled the air, but David's focus remained laser-sharp.

Taking advantage of the temporary disorientation, both agents sprang into action. David rolled out, positioning himself at a right angle to the entrance, creating a deadly crossfire with Becca. Their synchronized barrage of bullets cut down the first wave of assailants.

As the smoke cleared, both agents moved cautiously but swiftly towards the living area. David spotted the final gunman attempting to take cover. Without hesitation, he aimed and fired, ending the threat.

Panting, ears still ringing from the blasts, David and Becca shared a brief moment of mutual relief, but both knew that their job was far from done.

The bustling press area was awash with the chaotic symphony of chattering reporters, flashing cameras, and frantic correspondents trying to secure the best vantage point. Behind the sleek black podium adorned with the official seal, Lucien Morreau, Prime Minister of Belgium, cut a poised figure amidst the cacophony.

As he began speaking, an almost immediate hush fell upon the crowd, as reporters hung on his every word. "I would like to start by expressing my deepest gratitude for the brave Diplomatic Security Service personnel who put their lives on the line today. Their courage and sacrifice ensured that many lives, including my own, were spared."

David and Becca, standing to the side, exchanged a glance. They felt the weight of the day's events, but their disciplined expressions gave nothing away.

Lucien continued, "This assault was not just an attack on me but on our collective vision for global peace. It is a stark reminder that there are forces out there who wish to drag us into chaos and conflict."

The media hung onto his every word, sensing the gravity of the situation. He looked straight into the cameras, eyes filled with resolve, "To those who believe they can terrorize us and halt our march towards a brighter, shared future, hear me now. We will not be deterred. You will be found. You will be stopped. And you will face the consequences of your barbaric actions."

Following his bold declaration, Lucien gracefully exited the platform, his security detail escorting him back into the opulence of the hotel. They briskly maneuvered through the marble-clad hallways, the echoes of their footsteps the only sound breaking the tense silence.

Reaching the dimly lit parking garage, a state-of-the-art armored SUV awaited him. Slipping inside, he was joined by David and Becca.

The intimacy of the vehicle allowed for a brief drop in formalities. "I wish I could have thanked you both publicly," Lucien confessed, his usually commanding voice filled with sincere appreciation.

David nodded, "We understand, sir. The anonymity protects us and the broader mission. The fact that you're here, safe, is all the thanks we need."

Becca added, "Operational integrity sometimes demands that our contributions remain in the shadows."

Meeting their gaze, Lucien responded, "Both of you have shown exceptional bravery today. If there is ever anything you need, any way I can be of assistance, please do not hesitate. You have my deepest gratitude and respect."

Chapter 26: No Case

T he old church stood solemnly at the end of the narrow alley, its bell tower silent and its grand wooden doors weathered by time. Its windows, once vibrant with stained-glass renditions of biblical scenes, now looked muted, casting soft kaleidoscope patterns on the worn-out pews.

As David walked in, he saw Mark Harris standing near the altar, staring up at the faded mural of Christ with arms extended, a symbol of divine embrace. The hushed ambiance and the lingering scent of incense provided a sense of tranquility, a stark contrast to the chaos outside.

"Used to come here as a kid," Mark began, without turning. "Every Sunday, rain or shine. Back when these pews were filled with folks, and the air echoed with hymns and hope."

David took a few steps forward, the creaking wooden floor breaking the profound silence. "Why keep coming back to an empty vessel, Mark?"

Mark turned to face him, his eyes reflecting a mix of sadness and solace. "Maybe because in times like these, there's comfort in holding onto relics of the past. Reminders that once there was faith, hope, community."

David nodded, taking in the solemn beauty of the old sanctuary. He decided to shift gears. "I've got some news. You've been cleared. The victims we interviewed confirmed your story. You were aiding refugees, not trafficking them. What appeared to us on the outside as a potential terrorist group was just the actions of a group trying to save people."

A palpable sense of relief washed over Mark's face. "Thank you," he whispered, visibly moved. "You don't know what that means to me."

They stood in companionable silence for a moment before Mark turned his gaze back to David, his eyes earnest. "David, start reading your Bible. Time's running out."

David raised an eyebrow, surprised by the abrupt shift in topic. "What do you mean?"

"The peace treaty with Israel," Mark explained, his voice filled with urgency. "It's a sign. The end times are near."

David smirked, his voice tinged with irony. "Mark, the Middle East has been at war for the past 6,000 years. What makes our generation so special?"

Mark looked at him intently. "Just remember what I said. It's all in there," he said, pointing towards an old Bible resting on a nearby pew. "And sometimes, it's the relics of the past that hold the answers to our future."

Mark took a deep breath, looking around the church, the place of many childhood memories. "David, ever think about why the media's not reporting all of the truth from the Israel war? Why they're omitting the divine intervention part?"

David's face darkened, memories flooding back. "I was there, Mark. Whatever happened... it was beyond human comprehension."

Mark paused, choosing his words with care. "It aligns perfectly with Ezekiel 38 and 39. An alliance, numerous and powerful, setting its eyes on Israel. But instead of Israel being decimated, there's divine intervention."

David raised an eyebrow, memories of his childhood Bible stories coming back. "Refresh my memory?"

Mark continued, "The prophecy speaks of a vast coalition, led by Gog, from the land of Magog. This force assembles against Israel, but it's not man who defeats them. God intervenes. There's mention of earthquakes, storms, fire from the skies... It's an unmistakable act of God. And now, Lucien Morreau ..."

David sighed, rubbing his temples. "Okay, I'm following. But where does Morreau fit in all this?"

Mark hesitated, "What's your take on Lucien?"

David shrugged slightly, "Seems like a visionary. Perhaps too idealistic, but overall, wants what's good for the world."

Mark's voice became urgent, "But what if he's playing a bigger role? The Bible speaks of a charismatic figure, one that the world will be enamored by. That's the antichrist."

David chuckled, "And you think that's Lucien? The antichrist?"

Mark nodded, conviction in his gaze. "I believe there's a chance. You see, David, the antichrist isn't a monster or a cartoon devil. He's likable, persuasive, and globally adored. And that's what makes him perilous."

Chapter 27: Backdoor

The soft hum of the apartment's air conditioner was the only sound as David sat on his worn-out couch, deep in thought. His apartment, usually a place of refuge, felt unusually still tonight. The dim light from a single lamp cast elongated shadows on the walls, giving the room a somber atmosphere.

He looked down at the Bible Mark had given him, the leather worn and pages marked with annotations. A pang of sadness hit him as he thought of Lisa. The way her laughter filled a room, the sarcastic quips she'd send him during particularly tedious briefings, the comforting presence she had when everything felt like it was spiraling out of control. She was his confidante, his partner in crime, and his closest friend. The void she left was impossible to fill.

David had always been wary of commitments, especially after witnessing the toll the FBI life took on relationships. The countless late nights, the secrets, the danger—it was a recipe for heartbreak. He'd seen too many colleagues go through painful divorces, and he had vowed never to let himself fall into that trap. But with Lisa, it was different. She wasn't just a colleague; she was his confidante, his rock. The thought of a life without her was unbearable, and the gaping void she left behind seemed insurmountable.

Running a hand over his face, he sighed and opened the Bible, flipping to the pages of Ezekiel. As he read through the chapters, the parallels between the ancient scriptures and the modern-day events became eerily clear. The descriptions, the alliances, the divine interventions—it all felt uncannily familiar.

David leaned back, his heart racing. The words on the pages seemed to jump out at him, each verse echoing the events of the past few weeks. The weight of realization settled in, and a shiver ran down his spine. He considered the possibility: Could the world truly be heading towards some sort of prophesied end? Could Mark be right?

Closing the Bible, he took a deep breath. Everything was changing so rapidly, the world spinning out of control, and here he was, çontemplating ancient scriptures in his dimly lit apartment. It felt surreal.

He picked up a framed photo of him and Lisa from his side table, her radiant smile contrasting with his own goofy grin. He missed her more than he'd ever admit. Tears welled up in his eyes as he whispered, "What do you think, Lisa? Are we on the edge of prophecy?"

His thoughts were swirling from the weight of the prophecies he had just read when his phone vibrated, pulling him back to the present.

Grabbing the device from the coffee table, he saw Becca's name pop up on the screen. "I need you to meet someone," the message read.

Raising an eyebrow, David quickly typed back, "Who? Where and when?"

There was a brief pause before Becca's response came through. "Old Crow Tavern, 8 pm. You'll know who when you get there. Trust me, it's important."

David frowned slightly. The Old Crow Tavern was an unassuming little dive bar downtown. It wasn't their usual meeting spot, which made the message all the more intriguing.

"Alright, I'll be there," David texted back, feeling a mix of curiosity and apprehension.

He quickly changed out of his casual wear, opting for a dark jacket and jeans. Grabbing his keys, he headed out. If Becca said it was important, it was. But who could this mysterious contact be? And why at such a secretive location?

The streets of the city were alive with the early evening bustle as David made his way downtown. The weight of the day, the prophecies, and the unexpected turn of events pressed on him. But whatever Becca had in store, David was ready. As he always told himself, expect the unexpected in this line of work.

David entered the Old Crow Tavern, the hum of conversation wrapping around him as he closed the door behind. He scanned the semi-lit room, spotting Becca sharing a booth with a woman whose raven-black hair and piercing blue eyes made her immediately noticeable.

"David," Becca greeted, rising to greet him with a nod towards the woman, "Meet Nadia Idris."

David reached out a hand, "A pleasure."

Nadia gave a slight smile, taking his hand firmly, "The pleasure's mine."

David settled into the seat, his curiosity evident. "Becca mentioned you had something to share?"

Nadia shifted uncomfortably in her chair, eyes darting between Becca and David, "Can I trust him?" she whispered to Becca, her voice laced with uncertainty.

Becca leaned forward, placing a reassuring hand on Nadia's, "I've been through hell and back with David. He's solid. You can trust him."

Nadia exhaled slowly, tension easing from her shoulders, "Alright. I was hired for what I thought was a routine job by The Wave Corporation. They pitched it as simple penetration testing."

David leaned in, "And?"

Her eyes darted back to his, "I wasn't hacking into The Wave. It was Access Unlimited. The largest ISP out there."

David's eyes widened in realization, "That's...massive."

Nadia took a deep breath, "It gets worse. They wanted a sniffer on the main backbone. The data they could intercept..."

"Why would they want that?" David interjected.

Nadia leaned in, her voice urgent, "I've reason to believe they're linked to the UN. Maybe even a front for some of their operations."

David's eyebrows knitted in confusion, "The UN? Why would they want control over the world's communications?"

Nadia hesitated, searching for words, "To consolidate power? Control narratives? If they're looking at a one-world government model, which isn't out of the realm of possibility, they'd need to silence or sway any opposition. The data they could pull? It's a goldmine for blackmail. Politicians, business magnates, anyone who could stand in their way."

David ran a hand through his hair, the weight of the revelation sinking in, "This goes deep."

Nadia nodded, a hint of fear in her eyes, "I'm scared. They know I know."

David gave her a reassuring nod, "We'll protect you. First, we need to unravel this further."

David raised an eyebrow, intrigued. "You put a backdoor into their system?"

Becca smirked, "She always does. So, Nadia, did you happen to do your usual sneaky trick?"

Nadia, looking slightly abashed but with a hint of mischief in her eyes, responded, "Well, I couldn't resist. And, yes, I did put a backdoor in. It's what I do; it's a kind of insurance."

David leaned forward, his professional interest piqued. "What did you find?"

Nadia hesitated for a moment, gauging the reactions of her companions. "A lot. More than I ever expected. I have their internal emails. It's... it's big, Becca. Really big."

Becca took a deep breath, sensing the gravity of the situation. "What are we talking about?"

Nadia ran a hand through her hair, her demeanor serious, "They're in deep. It's not just some corporate espionage or financial fraud. It's international. It's political. They have dirt on some very powerful people. I mean, we're talking about heads of state, major business leaders. If the hints in these emails are accurate, they have the kind of information that can topple governments."

David rubbed his temples, feeling the weight of the situation. "This... this isn't just espionage or corporate games. This is a global power play. Nadia, this is beyond anything we've seen before. It's too massive for just the FBI or CIA. And for your safety, you can't just go into regular witness protection."

Nadia, a stubborn set to her jaw, retorted, "You think I don't know that? I'm good at hiding, David."

Becca shook her head, her tone firm. "Not good enough, Nadia. They'll tear the world apart looking for you if they realize what you've done."

Nadia gulped, fear evident in her eyes. "So what are you suggesting?"

Becca leaned in, her tone conspiratorial. "I have contacts, networks outside of the CIA. I can get you somewhere safe, but it'll be off the grid. You need to be somewhere even the most seasoned agents wouldn't think to look."

Nadia nodded, determination returning to her eyes. "I want to be far away from any Western influence, someplace they wouldn't expect. Maybe somewhere in the East?"

Becca smirked, "I might have just the place in mind. Remote, with locals that aren't too fond of outsiders. You'd be a ghost."

David looked between the two women, realizing the magnitude of the step they were about to take. "We're about to embark on something bigger than any of us. We need to trust each other, more than ever before."

The bar's ambient noise provided the background soundtrack as the tension in the air slowly began to dissipate. Becca shifted in her chair, eyes locked onto Nadia's. "Tomorrow. Our usual coffee spot, 10 a.m. I'll give you the travel details then." She paused, choosing her words carefully, "But understand this, it's not going to be a walk in the park. You won't just hop on a direct flight and vanish. It's going to be a process, a discreet one."

Nadia, determination clear in her eyes, nodded. "I understand, and I'll bring the hard drive. You'll have everything."

With a final nod, Nadia stood up, throwing on her jacket and blending seamlessly into the crowd, leaving David and Becca alone.

Once she was out of earshot, Becca turned to David. "What's our play, David? We've got the intel, but this is bigger than both of us."

David took a deep breath, letting it out slowly. "We need help. We need someone with resources and influence. Someone outside the usual government channels."

Becca raised an eyebrow, "You're not suggesting..."

David nodded, "Lucien Morreau. He owes us, especially after the attack. And I think he's got the connections to not only protect Nadia but to also ensure this evidence sees the light of day."

Becca seemed to mull it over, then with a sigh she replied, "Alright, but we tread carefully. Morreau may be grateful, but we don't fully know his game yet."

David reached for his jacket, "Agreed. Let's set up a meeting. We're in too deep to turn back now."

The next day, the sun tried to pierce through the dense cloud cover of D.C. as David made his way through the morning bustle. Mid-step, he felt the familiar vibration of his phone. Becca's name flashed on the screen.

"Got the gift for Uncle. Liked it so much, I got two. One for him, one for us. Make sure we wrap it nicely?"

Despite the seriousness of the situation, a grin tugged at the corners of David's mouth. He admired Becca's talent for coded communication. Tapping quickly, he replied.

"Uncle's in town. Perfect timing. We can drop it before his birthday party. Meet?"

Her response was prompt. "Agreed. Usual spot? Noon?"

David's fingers danced over the screen. "Noon works. Stay safe."

As he continued on his way, David's thoughts were consumed by the magnitude of their discovery. They had vital information, and it was imperative they navigated their next moves carefully.

Chapter 28: The Offer

T he grandeur of the Belgian Embassy was evident from the moment David stepped inside. Marble floors gleamed under chandeliers, reflecting the soft gold light. The air smelled of old wood and polish, lending a sense of gravitas to the proceedings.

He was promptly met by stern-faced security personnel. Going through the meticulous pat-down and metal detector screening, David could sense the heightened tension. He was reminded of his reason for being there; things were escalating and the global landscape was changing rapidly.

Once cleared, he was guided to a plush waiting area outside Lucien's office. The room was decorated with artwork showcasing Belgium's rich history, from medieval tapestries to modern interpretations of its towns and cities.

Lucien's assistant, a sharp-featured woman in her early thirties with a kind smile, approached him. "Mr. Miller, can I offer you something to drink? A coffee, water, or perhaps a traditional Belgian lager?"

Chuckling, David replied, "As tempting as the lager sounds, a black coffee will do, thank you."

While David waited, he took the time to glance through a few documents he had brought with him, trying to calm the fluttering in his stomach.

The assistant returned shortly, leading David into Lucien's spacious office. Floor-to-ceiling windows dominated one wall, providing a panoramic view of D.C., while the other walls were adorned with accolades and photographs from Lucien's various diplomatic missions.

Lucien stood up from his desk, extending a warm handshake that turned into a hug. "Ah, David! So good to see you again. Please, have a seat."

David nodded in appreciation, settling into one of the leather chairs opposite Lucien's desk.

Lucien leaned back, his fingers steepled. "I heard you declined the lager. Pity, it's one of our finest. But I digress." His tone turned serious. "I must once again express my gratitude for what you did in the hotel. It was a close call, and I've not forgotten it."

David inclined his head slightly, "It's my duty, sir."

Lucien continued, "I've since bolstered my security detail. And, courtesy of the circumstances, the Secret Service has graciously extended their protective services for my visits to the U.S."

David nodded, understanding the implications. "That's wise. These are unpredictable times."

Lucien's deep blue eyes studied David for a long moment before he leaned back in his chair, interlacing his fingers. "David, it's always a pleasure to see you. While I value our conversations, I suspect today's meeting isn't just a casual visit. What brings you here?"

David hesitated, trying to find the right words. He cleared his throat, "You're right, Lucien. There's something I need to discuss. Something... explosive. I've been wrestling with this information, and after much thought, I've decided that you might be the only person with the global stature to handle it."

Lucien raised an eyebrow in intrigue. "That sounds dire. But before you proceed, understand this: Whatever you're about to share, if it threatens global stability, it's imperative we handle it with the utmost discretion."

David nodded gravely, "I'm aware. And, I wanted to give you the option to decline hearing it. Once I share this, there's no turning back."

Lucien smiled faintly, "David, I didn't rise to this position by playing it safe. I take calculated risks, always for the greater good. Besides," he paused, leaning forward, "I trust you. Your judgment, your integrity. If you believe this is something I need to know, then I'm willing to listen."

David swallowed hard, appreciating Lucien's faith in him. "Thank you, Lucien. I hope, after hearing this, you won't regret that trust."

Lucien's eyebrows furrowed as David relayed his findings. The weight of the revelation hung heavily between them. "The United Nations, compromised to such a degree? It's... it's reprehensible," Lucien muttered, genuinely disturbed.

David's gaze never left Lucien's. "This is bigger than any one nation or agency, Lucien. The ramifications of this information going public could destabilize the very fabric of international cooperation. But those at the helm of this operation must be stopped."

Lucien took a deep breath, his expression pensive. "David, I've always had a suspicion that the depths of corruption within the UN were beyond our comprehension, but this... this is something else entirely." He sighed heavily, raking a hand through his hair. "I've been wrestling with a decision for a while, and given what you've told me, I believe it's time to act."

David waited with bated breath, sensing Lucien was about to disclose something equally monumental.

Lucien leaned in, his voice barely above a whisper, "David, the challenges in working through the United Nations to bring about genuine global peace have been immense. The bureaucracy, the politicking, the hidden agendas – it's been a nightmare." He paused, choosing his words carefully, "Which is why I've been planning an alternative. In the next week, I'll be announcing the inception of a new organization: 'The Circle.' Our sole mission? To pave the path to genuine worldwide peace."

David blinked in surprise. "A whole new organization? How have you managed to keep this under wraps?"

Lucien smiled, a hint of mischief in his eyes. "It's been challenging, but we've been meticulous. The Circle will operate beyond the tentacles of corruption, free from the constraints that have bound the UN."

David pondered this for a moment. "So, the peace treaty with Israel...?"

Lucien nodded, "Will be facilitated through The Circle. The traditional frameworks have failed us, David. It's time for a new approach, one that puts the future of humanity first, without any ulterior motives. All facilitated by a single digital currency."

David leaned back, processing the enormity of Lucien's revelation. "This changes everything," he murmured.

Lucien's expression grew serious, "It has to, David. The future of our world depends on it."

David's eyebrows knitted together as he tried to process everything Lucien was saying. "That's ambitious, to say the least," he finally replied, trying to mask the incredulity in his voice. "Essentially, you're talking about a world order reshaped around a single currency. And you genuinely believe the superpowers will just... fall in line?"

Lucien's face broke into a sly smile. "They already have. Think about it, David. Every superpower, every nation, is tied together by a web of economic dependencies. The U.S., China, Russia – they all understand the value of a unified, stable global economy. In our interconnected world, the fallout from one country's economic collapse can send shockwaves across the globe. A single currency, one that's digital and not tied to any one nation's politics or policies, provides a safeguard against that."

David leaned forward, intrigued despite his reservations. "But how did you sell them on this idea?"

Lucien chuckled softly. "It's all about economic leverage, David. The promise of a prosperous, interconnected world is too alluring to resist. And with the backing of the major players, the rest will have little choice but to follow suit."

David frowned, "It sounds almost... coercive."

Lucien's expression sobered. "It's pragmatic. The world is on a knife's edge, David. We can't afford the luxury of waiting for every nation to come around organically. With the superpowers and Europe as the lynchpin, other nations will understand the benefits of joining The Circle. It's not about coercion; it's about presenting an opportunity they'd be foolish to miss."

David paused, mulling over Lucien's words. "And if a nation decides to hold out, to reject this new order?"

Lucien's gaze was steady. "Then they'll find themselves isolated, cut off from international trade and the global community. But I believe most nations will see the wisdom in joining us. After all, The Circle represents the future, a chance for a prosperous, unified world."

David leaned back in his chair, a whirlwind of thoughts swirling in his mind. "This is... monumental, Lucien. The implications of what you're proposing are staggering."

Lucien nodded, "The world is changing, David. And we're at the forefront of that change. Together, we can guide it towards a brighter, more harmonious future."

Lucien leaned forward, sincerity evident in his eyes. "David, I cannot express how much I value your integrity and the lengths you've gone to protect me. Bringing me this information about the UN, it just solidifies my trust in you."

David nodded, appreciative of Lucien's words but still processing everything he'd learned. "It seemed only right, especially given the magnitude of what you're trying to achieve with The Circle."

Lucien sighed, looking out the window briefly. "Ever since that assassination attempt, I've been made painfully aware of how precarious my position is. And as much as it pains me to say it, I feel let down by my own security team. The world is no longer just about national boundaries and their respective threats. It's global, interconnected. And with my transition from Prime Minister of Belgium to heading The Circle, the threats will only magnify."

David's eyebrows raised in surprise, "You're becoming the President of The Circle? I assumed it would be a democratically elected position."

Lucien nodded, "In time, yes. But right now, swift, decisive action is of the essence. A fledgling organization like ours can't afford to be bogged down by bureaucracy. We need to build our foundation, establish our vision, and then transition to a more democratic structure."

David mulled this over, understanding the logic but wary of potential pitfalls.

Lucien, sensing his hesitation, continued, "Which brings me to my proposition. David, I need someone I can trust implicitly to oversee security, not just for me personally but on a global scale for The Circle. I need an International Security Director. Someone with your background, your instincts, and your moral compass. Son, I need you."

David swallowed hard, the weight of Lucien's offer heavy on his shoulders. "Leave the FBI? That's a massive leap, Lucien."

Lucien met his gaze evenly, "Yes, it is. But think about it, David. With The Circle, you won't just be safeguarding one nation but striving for global stability. Your influence, your impact would be on an unparalleled scale."

David looked deep into Lucien's eyes, grappling with the gravity of the decision before him.

David took a deep breath, his mind racing with the implications of the decision he was about to make. "Lucien, the vision you're putting forth for The Circle, it's undeniably ambitious. But if done right, it could change the world. If I can be a part of that, ensuring the safety and security of such a monumental endeavor... I'm in."

Lucien's face lit up with genuine relief and happiness. "David, you have no idea how much this means to me, to The Circle. Your expertise and dedication will be invaluable."

David raised a hand, signaling a moment of caution. "But I'll need some time to wrap things up at the FBI. I can't just walk away overnight."

Lucien nodded, his smile unwavering. "Of course, take the time you need. Given the U.S.'s significant involvement in establishing The Circle, I'm confident they'll understand and support your transition."

David chuckled, "I hope you're right. It'll be quite the conversation explaining to my superiors that I'm leaving to join an organization seeking global peace."

Lucien grinned, "Well, when you put it like that, how could they refuse?"

Lucien leaned back in his chair, staring thoughtfully at the hard drive David had placed on the desk earlier. "David, that device right there might very well be one of the most important keys to our mission with The Circle."

David, following Lucien's gaze, shifted uncomfortably, "It's explosive material, for sure. What you're suggesting is that we use it as leverage?"

Lucien shook his head slowly, choosing his words carefully. "Not leverage in the traditional sense. More like a tool to clear the path. Corruption and deceit are like weeds in a garden. If you don't uproot them entirely, they'll strangle everything you try to grow."

David nodded in agreement, understanding Lucien's analogy. "So, we expose the corruption, bring down those responsible, and lay the foundation for The Circle's vision of global peace."

"Exactly," Lucien replied. "But it has to be done strategically. We don't want unnecessary chaos or conflict. We want accountability. We need to show the world that The Circle isn't just another empty promise. We're here to bring genuine change, and we won't let anything stand in our way."

David took a moment, absorbing Lucien's words. "You're asking me to dismantle an international spying ring spearheaded by the U.N., and expose high-ranking officials. It's a tall order."

Lucien locked eyes with David, his determination evident. "I wouldn't have chosen you if I didn't believe you were up to the task. The Circle's vision demands we face these challenges head-on. This is the moment, David. We have to seize it."

David straightened up, a newfound resolve forming within him. "Alright, Lucien. Let's bring in the dawn of a new era. Starting with this hard drive."

Inside the FBI headquarters, David stood in his office, surrounded by boxes filled with mementos from cases past and awards recognizing his service. The walls, which once held framed commendations and pictures, now stood bare.

Agent Paul Stevens, David's long-time colleague and friend, entered the room with a smirk. "Never thought I'd see the day where the great David Mitchell would be packing up his desk."

David laughed, carefully wrapping a framed photograph of his team from a successful operation years ago. "Neither did I, Paul. But sometimes, life throws a curveball you didn't see coming."

Paul picked up a plaque from one of the boxes, an award David had received for his exceptional service. "You sure about this, David? The Circle might be an incredible opportunity, but the Bureau... this has been your life."

David sighed, placing another item into a box. "I know. I've spent more hours here than I can count, but it's time for a new challenge. And Lucien's offer... it's a chance to create a more significant impact on a global scale."

Paul nodded, understanding the weight of the decision. "Just promise me one thing, David."

David raised an eyebrow, "What's that?"

Paul smiled, "Don't forget us little people when you're off changing the world."

David chuckled, "Never. You all are the reason I've had such a successful run here."

As they continued packing, other agents popped in, offering their well-wishes and sharing fond memories. The atmosphere was bittersweet, a mix of excitement for David's new journey and sadness for the end of an era at the FBI.

By evening, David's office was empty. He took one last look around, taking in the memories of the room where he had made so many pivotal decisions. With a final nod, he turned off the lights, ready for the next chapter in his life with The Circle.

Chapter 29: Prophecies

I nside a cozy café, the aroma of fresh coffee wafted through the air, accompanied by the gentle hum of conversations. David walked in with Becca, scanning the room before spotting Mark at a corner table, who waved them over.

"Mark," David began, "this is Becca. We've been through a hell of a lot together."

"Ah, the famed Becca! Pleasure to finally meet you," Mark said, shaking her hand. "David's mentioned you in passing."

"I hope it was all good," Becca replied with a smile. "And I hear you and David go way back."

Mark laughed, "I was under investigation by the FBI once, all thanks to him. Hope I'm not gonna be on the CIA's list now."

Becca smirked, "Oh, with the CIA, you wouldn't know about it. We'd just make you vanish."

David interjected with mock exasperation, "Alright, enough with the disappearing act jokes, it's still a sensitive topic."

Mark, noticing David's change in demeanor, quickly steered the conversation. "So, what's new in your world, David?"

David took a deep breath. "I've actually left the FBI. I'm now working with Lucien Morreau, heading up security for The Circle."

Mark's eyebrows shot up in surprise. "You need to tread carefully, David. The times we're entering, especially with this peace deal in Israel, are eerily lining up with biblical prophecies."

David leaned back, "Been keeping up with your Bible, I see."

Mark nodded, "More than ever. Anything strike you as you read?"

Before David could reply, Becca's inquisitive gaze met Mark's. "End times prophecies, you've mentioned them before. Can you delve deeper?"

Mark took a deep breath, gathering his thoughts. "Alright. The Bible, particularly the books of Daniel and Revelation, detail events leading to the end times. Central to this is a peace treaty signed with Israel that will last for seven years. But, it's not just any peace agreement. It's brokered by a significant global figure, often interpreted as the antichrist. The first half of these seven years seems peaceful, but it's a deceptive calm."

Becca leaned in, intrigued. "Go on."

Mark continued, "Midway through the seven years, this leader, the antichrist, breaks the treaty, leading to worldwide chaos. It signals the beginning of the Tribulation period, a time of unprecedented disasters and judgments. Wars, natural calamities, and more intensify, causing unparalleled suffering. And the antichrist, with a newfound zeal, persecutes those who resist his dominion and challenges the sovereignty of God."

He paused to sip his drink, his gaze distant, "The latter half of the Tribulation, known as the Great Tribulation, sees the antichrist consolidate global power. He institutes a singular world economy, religion, and government. And here's the catch: to partake in this new world order, one must pledge allegiance to him, often depicted as receiving a mark."

Becca, trying to bridge the gap between Mark's beliefs and the startling reality they were living, inquired, "Mark, who do you believe the antichrist might be?"

Taking a deep breath, Mark responded, "I've studied scripture and prophecy extensively, and everything seems to indicate that someone like Lucien Morreau fits the profile."

David's eyes widened, shock evident in every feature. "That's a strong accusation, Mark."

Mark nodded somberly. "I know how it sounds, especially considering your new role. It's just an educated guess based on what I know."

David's face tightened. "We're on the cusp of achieving real, lasting peace, Mark. The kind that hasn't been witnessed for generations. Perhaps ever. I don't need negativity clouding that vision."

David stood abruptly, the metallic scrape of his chair punctuating his displeasure. Mark reached out, trying to soothe the fraying nerves. "David, wait..."

But Becca's calm voice interjected, "David, he's just sharing what scripture suggests. Try to understand."

However, David was beyond reasoning. His footsteps echoed his tumultuous thoughts as he strode out of the café.

As the door swung shut behind him, Becca turned to Mark, her face a mix of concern and curiosity. "I'm sorry for David's reaction. These are high-stress times, but I'm genuinely interested. Please, continue. The connections between ancient scriptures and today's events... it's just so intriguing."

Chapter 30: Brazil

The opulent conference room, located on the top floor of The Circle's headquarters, held an air of tension. Floor-to-ceiling windows provided an expansive view of the city's skyline, yet all eyes were focused on the gleaming mahogany table where David, Lucien, and a host of others sat.

Carlos Santos, the stern-faced President of Brazil, sat with a demeanor that emanated authority. "Mr. Morreau, you might have the whole world wrapped around your finger, but Brazil has always stood on its own. We won't trade our sovereignty for some empty promises."

Lucien, ever the picture of calm, leaned back in his chair. "I understand your reservations, Carlos. And believe me, the last thing I want is to take away any nation's identity. But the world is changing. And The Circle isn't here to dominate but to unite."

Carlos raised an eyebrow skeptically. "With all due respect, it sounds like domination when you talk about bypassing elected leaders and taking away our self-rule."

Just then, an aide to Lucien, a tall woman in a sharp suit, handed Carlos a sleek tablet. "Please, Mr. Santos, take a look at this," Lucien's voice held a hint of an enigmatic tone.

As Carlos studied the screen, his confident demeanor shifted. David, sitting two chairs away, strained to get a glimpse but was too far to see the content. Carlos's face paled, his eyes widened slightly, and his grip tightened on the tablet.

"Even if I were inclined to agree," Carlos began, his voice faltering, "my party, the people of Brazil—they would never stand for it."

Lucien leaned forward, the soft light casting shadows on his determined face. "Carlos, leadership is about making difficult choices for the betterment of your country. Already, several minority parties — the Workers' Party, Brazilian Social Democracy Party, and Progressives — they all see the potential and are leaning toward joining The Circle. They recognize the advantages and the prosperity it can bring. If you lead, the rest of your party, and by extension the nation, will follow. They trust you, and rightly so. This isn't just about politics, it's about shaping the future of Brazil."

Carlos took a shaky breath. "And what of the Brazilian people? What of their voice?"

Lucien replied, "Guaranteeing you a leadership role for the next five years ensures that voice remains strong. Join us, and together we'll elevate Brazil to heights never before imagined."

David shifted in his seat, stealing glances at Carlos and the tablet in his hands. Every fiber of David's being itched with curiosity. What was on that screen that could elicit such a visceral reaction from Carlos? The president's once assertive posture had shrunk, his complexion pallid. David had witnessed countless negotiations and interrogations in his time with the FBI, but he had seldom seen someone so rattled. Lucien's composed demeanor was a stark contrast, almost as if he knew what the reaction would be before handing over the tablet. David's mind raced. The weight of the secret behind that screen gnawed at him, making him question if there were deeper, hidden facets to The Circle's operations that he hadn't yet grasped.

The atmosphere in the room grew even more tense as Carlos, still reeling from the impact of the tablet's contents, tried to regain some semblance of control.

"I... I need to consult with the National Congress. This isn't a decision I can just make on a whim," he stammered, his bravado from earlier entirely gone.

Lucien looked him squarely in the eye. "Carlos, sometimes a leader must make bold choices, ones that may not be immediately popular. The Brazilian people trust your judgment. They elected you to make tough decisions, and sometimes that means taking a leap of faith."

Carlos opened his mouth to protest, but Lucien waved over an assistant—a tall man with sharp features and an air of cold determination.

"This is Alejandro," Lucien introduced smoothly, "He will accompany you back to Brazil. If there are any... roadblocks, political or otherwise, Alejandro will provide the necessary... motivation, just as we did for you today."

Carlos swallowed hard, realizing the subtle threat veiled behind Lucien's words. With resignation weighing heavily in his eyes, he nodded, the fight all but drained out of him.

Lucien's demeanor immediately shifted from stern to jovial. "Fantastic!" he exclaimed, rising from his chair and pulling Carlos into an enthusiastic embrace. "Brazil has a dazzling future ahead, Carlos. Together, we'll ensure it shines brighter than ever!"

David sank heavily into his plush office chair, feeling its comfort but hardly acknowledging it. The room seemed smaller somehow, the air thicker. He reached up to rub the tension from his temples but found no relief.

The encounter with Lucien and President Carlos had shaken him. The transformation he'd seen in Carlos, a formidable leader, within a mere matter of minutes was jarring. The confident leader had devolved into a compliant puppet, and David was left with a barrage of questions.

He replayed the scene in his mind, focusing on the moment Carlos had been handed the tablet. What could possibly have been on that screen that had such a profound effect? Was it personal information, compromising photos, details of hidden financial misdeeds, or something even more sinister?

And then there was Lucien—charming, persuasive Lucien—who had presented himself as a beacon of hope and progress. But today, there had been a shift. What was he offering these countries in return for their allegiance? And perhaps more importantly, what was he threatening them with? There seemed to be an underlying menace that David hadn't noticed before, hidden beneath layers of charm and eloquence.

The more David pondered, the more he realized how little he knew about Lucien and The Circle's true objectives. He had joined, believing in the mission of worldwide unity and peace, but now he wondered if he was just a pawn in a more intricate game.

Is Lucien truly the harbinger of peace he claims to be? Or is he something darker, more manipulative? And where does David fit into all of this?

The weight of these questions bore down on him, making the room feel suffocating. He needed answers, but more than that, he needed to decide where his loyalties truly lay. The path ahead was uncertain, and every step had to be tread with caution.

Chapter 31: Backyard Party

The old streets of Beirut bustled with life. Locals meandered through the market, the aroma of spices and freshly baked bread mingling in the air. Amidst this, Ryan "Ry" Mitchell walked side by side with Becca Lawrence, trying to look as inconspicuous as possible. His unremarkable attire made him blend into the crowd, but Becca felt a pang of nostalgia. Her choice of traditional Lebanese clothing reminded her of the times she had spent undercover in the region, immersing herself in the culture and building connections.

As they neared a café, the soft strains of traditional Lebanese music wafted through the air, stirring memories of past assignments. Ry held the door open for Becca, and they stepped inside. The café was dimly lit with a rustic charm. At a corner table, Rashid Farouk stood up with a bright smile, greeting them.

"Becca!" Rashid exclaimed, embracing her warmly. "It's been far too long."

Becca smiled, her eyes reflecting genuine affection and a hint of sadness. "Indeed, Rashid. Too long." She remembered the times they had worked together, the close calls, and the trust they had built.

Rashid gestured towards the chair opposite him, and the duo sat. Ry remained silent, scanning the room and observing their surroundings, but Becca felt a rush of emotions. She was torn between the familiarity of the past and the urgency of the present.

"So," Rashid began in hushed tones, almost a whisper, leaning in, "When are you going to come work with me in the private sector?"

Becca smirked, "Oh, you know. CIA still has its charms. Every day, I get to do the usual—saving the world, one war at a time."

The atmosphere was light, but there was an underlying tension. Becca took a deep breath. "Rashid, I've lost touch with an old friend, Sami. I was hoping you might help reconnect us."

Rashid's eyes darkened. "That might be a tall order, Becca. You know how it is. Everyone's preoccupied with the... 'backyard party' they're planning."

Becca leaned in. "I've heard whispers. And that's why I'm here. I want to help with the 'party planning.' Perhaps Sami can fill me in?"

Rashid hesitated, his gaze fixed on Becca. "I'll see what I can do. But I need to be careful."

Becca nodded. "I understand, Rashid. But it's urgent."

Rashid sighed, "I promise, Becca. I'll be in touch."

The sun had begun its descent over Beirut, casting a warm golden hue over the ancient streets. Buildings, worn by time, stood as silent witnesses to the many stories that had unfolded on these pavements. Ry and Becca made their way through the narrow alleys, the sounds of daily life surrounding them—children playing, merchants selling their wares, and the distant calls of prayer.

Finally, Becca broke the silence. "Beirut... every time I come back here, it reminds me of when I first started. The vibrancy, the culture, the people—it's unlike any other place." Her eyes took on a distant, nostalgic look.

Ry, ever vigilant, continued to scan the streets and rooftops, but responded, "It's tragic, isn't it? How decisions made in offices far away can affect the lives of so many here. And all too often, those decisions lead to destruction."

Becca sighed deeply, "I remember my first posting here. I fell in love with the city. And now, thinking that all of this," she gestured around, "could be reduced to rubble because of another conflict? It's heartbreaking."

Ry nodded, "It's a pattern, Becca. We've seen it repeat itself time and time again in the Middle East. But we have a chance to make a difference this time. We just need that intel."

They continued their walk, the weight of their mission pressing heavily on their shoulders. The sun dipped below the horizon, casting long shadows on the streets of Beirut. As they approached a nondescript building, Becca entered a code, and the door clicked open. They stepped into the safe house, knowing the importance of the days ahead.

Elaine Ramirez, an expert in cyber intelligence, hunched over her desk littered with multiple monitors and keyboards, was the digital eyes and ears of the CIA's Beirut operation. Her fingers danced across the keys, bouncing between coding programs, encrypted communication platforms, and various regional websites. Her focus was on one particular Lebanese dating site, where a profile under the name "DesertRose89" had recently become active.

"Becca, I got it!" Elaine called out excitedly.

Becca, who had been in the middle of a strategy discussion with Ry, quickly approached Elaine's workstation. The dating profile displayed on one of the monitors showed a woman with dark flowing hair, amber eyes, and a cryptic bio that read,

"Seeking someone who knows the rhythm of the old streets and the magic of lunchtime stories."

"That's definitely Rashid," Becca confirmed, her eyes skimming the coded message. "Classic him, using a public platform in the least suspicious way."

Elaine nodded. "So, what's the next move?"

"Swipe right," Becca instructed, "And send him a little note."

Elaine swiped on the profile and quickly typed out, "Your stories always intrigue me. Perhaps we could share one soon?"

They waited with bated breath. After a few tense minutes, a reply pinged on Elaine's system. She read out, "I'm down to party. Let's meet two doors south from my old office. Lunchtime in two days?"

"That's near the old Beirut Times building," Becca filled in, looking at Ry. "Rashid's former place of employment. It's an inconspicuous spot, should work."

"Alright," Becca said, turning back to Elaine, "Confirm it. And keep monitoring for any unusual activity."

Elaine quickly typed her affirmative response, and the trio set to work, preparing for what was to come.

In the dim lighting of the safe house, Ryan stood by the table, dwarfed by a large tablet propped up on a stand. The illuminated screen showed an incredibly detailed satellite image of an old brick building nestled amidst a tangle of Beirut's narrow alleys.

"Here," Ryan pointed to the left side of the building, where the alleyway bent sharply, "is a blind spot, a perfect place for an ambush. And these," he motioned to various balconies and rooftops on surrounding buildings, "are all potential sniper nests. We'll be going in almost blind."

Becca, her face a canvas of concentration, studied the image. "What's our ISR status?"

"We won't have any real-time ISR support," Ryan responded, "But," he said, pulling out a small compact UAV from his bag, "I've got this. It can give us aerial visuals and should be small enough not to draw attention."

Becca nodded, contemplating their options. "I trust Rashid. We've been through a lot. But, like you, I know these meetings are never without risk." She took a deep breath, her mind racing. "We need intel from General Haddad. Understanding Lebanon's intentions, knowing if they're really gearing up for war or just posturing, is paramount."

Ryan paused, meeting her gaze. "Then we do this, together. We take all precautions and trust in our skills, our training."

Becca gave him a slight smile. "And hope our intel is right."

Chapter 32: Wired

The sun was at its zenith, casting sharp shadows on the streets of Beirut. The white Land Rover pulled up discreetly along a quiet stretch, a quarter mile from the meeting point. The area appeared calm, almost eerily so. Becca shut off the engine, the subtle purr dying into silence. The two agents exchanged a quick glance; their years of working together had developed a shorthand that required few words.

Ryan reached for a compact case in the backseat, flipping it open to reveal a state-of-the-art nano drone. He held it carefully, almost reverently. "Eyes in the sky," he murmured, stepping out of the vehicle. With a gentle toss, the drone ascended with a slight buzz, its small size allowing it to fade easily against the backdrop of the cityscape.

Back inside the Rover, Ryan plugged a feed into the onboard screen, granting them a bird's eye view. The drone provided a real-time visual as it hovered around the location. "Looks quiet so far," he said, his eyes scanning every inch of the feed, looking for anything out of place.

Becca leaned in, her sharp eyes taking in every detail, "Any signs of snipers or potential threats?"

Ryan toggled through different visual filters. "Infrared is clear. No signs of anyone on the rooftops or in any of the overlooking windows. The surrounding buildings also seem quiet."

The drone made a broader pass, capturing varying angles, especially the concealed nooks and possible hideouts. Minutes felt like hours, but there was still no sign of anything amiss.

Becca exhaled, her posture relaxing a fraction. "Time to move. We can't keep Rashid waiting too long."

She reached for her earpiece, pressing it as she spoke, "Stargate, this is Pegasus 1, we're Charlie Mike to the meet."

Almost instantly, Elaine's voice crackled through, "Good copy, Pegasus. Everything's quiet on the comms in the area. You're good to proceed."

Becca and Ryan shared another glance. It was time. Ryan pocketed the drone's remote after setting it on an automated surveillance loop, and they both stepped out of the Land Rover. The streets welcomed them with the faint aroma of spices, a hint of normalcy in their perilous world.

With every step, the two agents were alert, their senses tuned to the slightest anomaly. They had done this dance numerous times before, but the stakes now, with the world on the brink, felt even higher. As they neared their destination, both hoped that this meeting would provide the clarity they so desperately needed.

The alleyway leading to the door was dim, the sunlight barely filtering through the closely packed buildings. Each step was deliberate, the gravelly path beneath their feet crunching softly. The constant hum of the city seemed far away, replaced by the heightened awareness of their immediate surroundings.

Reaching the door, Ryan checked the UAV footage again. The overhead drone's perspective revealed no immediate threats. With a nod, he signaled Becca, indicating that the area still looked clear. He took a position a couple of steps behind her, eyes darting from window to window in the neighboring buildings, ensuring they weren't being observed.

As Becca gently started to pull the door, she noticed an out-of-place glint. A cable. Cautiously, she whispered into her mic, "Hold one, I see a cable attached to the door." With practiced ease, she retrieved a small mirror mounted on a telescopic rod from her tactical vest. Extending it to its full length, she held it up to the door's corner, angling it to get a view of the inside.

Her trained eyes quickly identified the cable's termination: an anti-personnel mine. "Stargate, Pegasus 1 here. We've got a problem. There's an explosive device at the entrance," Becca's voice was steady, despite the alarming discovery.

The reply came swiftly, concern evident in Elaine's voice, "Understood, Pegasus 1. We recommend immediate exfil."

Before Becca could acknowledge, Ryan's sharp whistle cut through the air. His eyes were glued to the UAV feed that showed a truck advancing towards them, five figures discernible in its bed. "They're closing in, less than a klick out."

Ryan's voice had that urgent edge, "Stargate, Pegasus 2. We've got company, and we're moving out." He grabbed Becca's arm. "Becca, Rashid played us."

Her eyes hardened, anger replacing shock. "Elaine, I want a location on Rashid Farouk. I have some questions for him."

Elaine's voice was firm, urgency pushing her words, "I'll find him, Becca. But you need to get out of there. Head back to the Land Rover, now!"

With a nod to Ryan, Becca turned on her heel.

Ryan and Becca drove in silence for a moment, with only the hum of the Land Rover's engine breaking the tension. The bustling streets of Beirut were a maze of sounds and sights. Market stalls selling colorful textiles, the aroma of kebabs grilling on an open flame, and the general hum of conversations all around them.

Becca's voice broke the silence, her tone all business. "Stargate, Pegasus 1 here. What do you have for me?"

The response was swift. "Pegasus, Stargate. I've pinged his cell. Looks like he's at the market near his flat."

"Feed his coordinates to my phone," Becca instructed.

Ryan glanced at Becca, his brow furrowed. "Becca, rushing into a crowded market, just the two of us, is asking for trouble. We should circle back, gather intel, maybe get some backup."

Becca's gaze remained focused on the road. "Ryan, the clock is ticking. If this situation escalates, it could trigger a regional war. I won't let that happen."

Ryan sighed, "Alright, but no snatch and grab. We approach this strategically. He knows we're onto him, and that market is the perfect place for an ambush."

Becca nodded, her determination evident. "Agreed. We'll go to his flat. Let's give him an option – give us the General, or face the consequences."

Ryan pulled the Land Rover into an alley two blocks from Rashid's apartment, ensuring they weren't followed. They quickly shed their tactical gear and made their way to the apartment. Ryan picked the front door lock and they stepped inside.

Inside the modern apartment, the sound of the city seemed distant. Natural light streamed through large windows, highlighting the neutral tones of Rashid's living space. The walls, lined with framed paintings and prints, showcased a mix of contemporary and traditional Lebanese art. One wall was dominated by a sleek bookcase crammed with titles ranging from political treatises to classic Arabic poetry.

A beautiful Persian rug lay in the middle of the living room, a hint of Rashid's perhaps more traditional side. The juxtaposition of the rich tapestry and the modern chrome-and-glass coffee table on top showed that Rashid had an eclectic taste. The ambient lighting, candles, and a faint scent of sandalwood incense made the place feel cozy, quite at odds with the man's recent actions.

Rashid's surprised gasp was muffled by Ryan's hand as he made his way inside, carrying groceries from the market. Ryan swiftly immobilized him, expertly handling the panicking man with ease. The zipping sound of the ties echoed sharply in the apartment's silence.

Becca, stepping into Rashid's line of sight, looked disappointed. "I thought we had an understanding, Rashid. We were supposed to be on the same team. We used a dating app to setup the meet Rashid, but it feels like you're not going to get a second date."

Rashid, looking terrified, tried to speak but Ryan's grip was firm.

Becca gently nudged Ryan, signaling for him to let Rashid talk. "Go on, Rashid. Explain."

Catching his breath, Rashid quickly spoke, "Becca, I wanted to help, I truly did. But they reached out to me first. They knew of our planned meeting with Haddad. They warned me... said that if I helped you, they'd... they'd hurt my family."

Ryan's stern face showed a flicker of sympathy. "So you set us up to save your own skin?"

Rashid's eyes welled up with tears. "I'm sorry, Becca. It was them or you. And I couldn't put my family in danger."

Becca's expression softened. The world of espionage was never black and white, and sometimes the gray areas were where agents like her were forced to operate. "Okay, Rashid. We need to know what they're planning. And you're going to help us." Rashid swallowed hard but nodded in agreement.

The tension was palpable in the dimly lit room, a sharp contrast to the airy ambiance of the rest of Rashid's apartment. Rashid's eyes darted around the room, settling momentarily on Becca's steely gaze.

"It's okay, Rashid," Becca started, her tone softening slightly, "I understand your situation. But you've put us all in a precarious position."

Rashid's face contorted with anguish, his voice shaky, "I did what I had to do for my family."

Becca sighed deeply, moving closer, "Your family isn't safe, Rashid. Not from us, and certainly not from the Lebanese government."

Rashid's eyes widened, and his breathing quickened, "What do you mean?!"

Becca continued, "You think they'll let you go after using you? No. You know too much now."

Rashid swallowed hard, the reality of his situation sinking in. "So, what now?"

Becca sat opposite him, locking eyes, "You're going to help us. And in return, we can extract your family. Take them somewhere safe. Western Europe? America? You choose. But first, I need information."

Rashid's eyes darted around, calculating the weight of his next decision. "What do you want to know?"

Becca leaned in, her voice firm and commanding, "I need names, Rashid. Who in the military or government is pushing for war with Israel? When is this attack planned? How will they attack? Air? Ground? Sea? Are there other countries in the fold?"

Rashid hesitated for a moment, drawing a deep breath, "I can find out, but it will take time."

Becca stood up abruptly, "You have 24 hours, Rashid. Get me the information I need, and I promise, we'll ensure the safety of your family. But if you fail, or double-cross us again..." she let the threat hang in the air, letting the gravity of her words sink in.

Rashid nodded vigorously, "I'll get you what you need."

Becca rummaged in her pocket for a moment before producing a small, nondescript card. Handing it to Rashid, she pointed to the jotted-down username. "Use the SharingFile service. Drop everything there."

Rashid's eyes scanned the card briefly before looking up at Becca.

"Do you remember the library where we first met?" Becca asked, a hint of nostalgia lacing her voice.

Rashid nodded, "Of course."

"The password is the library's name. All lowercase," Becca instructed.

Rashid swallowed hard, committing the details to memory. As he was about to speak, Ryan stepped closer, his tall frame casting a shadow over Rashid.

"Listen, Rashid," Ryan's voice was low, cold and calculated, "If you fail to deliver on your promise, believe me when I say, I'll personally make sure to fulfill every single one of Becca's promises. And trust me, it won't be pleasant."

Rashid's gaze darted between Ryan and Becca, the weight of their words pressing down on him. He nodded rapidly, "I'll get you what you need."

"See that you do," Becca said, her voice betraying no emotion. With that, both agents turned on their heels and exited the apartment, leaving a shaken Rashid to contemplate his next move.

Chapter 33: The Briefing

Lucien Morreau's office was a lavish one, dominated by a massive mahogany desk and panoramic windows that offered a sweeping view of the Washington, D.C. skyline. As General Porter stepped through the door, he scanned the room and saw David standing off to the side, engaged in conversation with one of Lucien's aides.

"David!" The General's voice boomed, filled with genuine warmth. Crossing the room, he reached out, shaking David's hand firmly. "It's good to see you. Seems you've settled in nicely. Congratulations on the new role. Word around the Beltway is you're doing wonders here."

David smiled, "Thank you, General. We're trying our best. It's a new chapter, but one filled with potential."

General Porter nodded before turning his attention to Lucien, who stood waiting with an expectant smile. The two men exchanged a crisp, professional handshake.

"Mr. Morreau," General Porter began, "I'm grateful for the opportunity to discuss these pressing matters with you. Your organization is making waves, and it's important we stay coordinated."

Lucien gestured towards the plush chairs arranged around a gleaming conference table. "Of course, General. We appreciate the trust you're placing in The Circle. Please, have a seat."

As they settled in, General Porter leaned forward, "Before we begin, I must emphasize that the information we'll be sharing is of the highest classification. Any leaks could jeopardize American lives and our sources in critical regions."

Lucien nodded solemnly. "We understand the gravity, General. You have my word—what's said in this room stays in this room."

David, looking every bit the seasoned security professional, added, "I've been on the other side of these briefings, General. I understand the risks. We'll ensure the information remains secure."

General Porter nodded, satisfied. The air in the room grew heavier as they prepared to delve into matters of national security.

General Porter straightened up in his chair, clearing his throat before speaking, "Mr. Morreau, on behalf of the President of the United States, I'd like to express our nation's deep appreciation for the steps The Circle is taking towards global peace. The President has personally conveyed his good wishes for the successful culmination of the peace treaty with Israel."

Lucien smiled, "That's kind of the President. We, too, are optimistic about this historic agreement and are doing everything in our power to ensure its success."

Porter's expression became more serious, "Mr. Morreau, part of the reason for my visit today is to share some intelligence that we believe is critical to your efforts."

Lucien raised an eyebrow, intrigued. "Please, go on."

"We've received credible intelligence," Porter began, "that Lebanon's threats aren't mere bluster. They're making concrete plans to launch an all-out offensive against Israel. And the timing couldn't be worse—it's set for the eve of the treaty signing."

David leaned forward, the gravity of the situation apparent on his face. "That would throw the entire region into chaos."

Lucien's fingers tapped on the table, his face reflecting concern. "Are you suggesting they have the capability and intent to halt the treaty?"

General Porter nodded, "It appears so. We have reliable sources indicating that Lebanon has been heavily arming Hezbollah. Their plan is a coordinated strike, attacking Israel from multiple fronts. It's an aggressive move, and given the fragile state of affairs, it could plunge the Middle East back into tumultuous conflict."

Lucien paused, absorbing the gravity of the revelation. "And what does the United States plan to do with this intelligence?"

General Porter met Lucien's gaze steadily. "Our priority is peace, Mr. Morreau. While we have our measures in place, we believe that The Circle, with its international influence, is in a unique position to mitigate this situation. We're handing this information over to you, trusting that you'll handle it in the best interests of global peace."

David nodded, "We'll do everything in our power."

Lucien's voice was resolute, "Rest assured, General, The Circle will take appropriate actions to ensure that peace is not derailed."

The large, dimly lit conference room was filled with tension. On one end of the wooden table sat Lucien Morreau, flanked by his closest advisors. To his right, David was clutching a pen, jotting down arguments, while on his left, Viktor leaned back in his chair, fingers steepled and eyes unyielding.

Antoine Dubois, seated opposite Lucien, looked between the two men, waiting for the tide of the conversation to turn. He tapped a finger rhythmically on his closed laptop, a beacon of neutrality in the rising storm.

"We cannot preach peace and then drop bombs on a sovereign nation, Viktor!" David's voice rose with conviction. "This entire mission, The Circle, is founded on the promise of diplomacy. A pre-emptive strike would be the ultimate hypocrisy."

Viktor scoffed, his cold eyes locking onto David's, "It's about being practical, David. Lebanon's ideology is unwavering, their path destructive. A surgical strike now could save countless lives later. Peace is our goal, yes, but we must be prepared to take the steps necessary to preserve it."

David shook his head, "But who are we to decide the fate of an entire nation? To play God? Our focus should be on dialogue, on understanding. War should always be the last resort."

"It's naive to think we can just sit down and have a chat with them, David. They've shown their hand, they're ready for war," Viktor snapped. "To them, peace is a sign of weakness. Sometimes, strength is the only language understood."

Antoine, rubbing his temples, interjected, "Gentlemen, this isn't getting us anywhere. Lucien, your guidance here is essential."

All eyes turned to Lucien. He had been silent throughout, absorbing each argument, weighing the pros and cons. He looked at David, then at Viktor, before finally speaking, "I understand both of your concerns. David, your commitment to peace and diplomacy aligns with our core values. Viktor, your pragmatism and foresight are also valid. However," he paused, taking a moment to gather his thoughts, "we must remember our ultimate goal. If we strike first, we set a precedent that might unravel everything we've worked for. Yet, we cannot simply sit idle and hope for the best."

David nodded, sensing a victory, but Lucien raised a hand to silence him. "Viktor, I won't sanction a strike, but I want to be ready. I want options, fallback plans, and I want them quickly."

Viktor nodded, "Very well, Lucien. We'll be prepared."

David let out a slow breath, "And I'll reach out to my contacts, see if there's any room for a peaceful resolution."

Lucien nodded, "We walk a fine line, gentlemen. Let's tread carefully." The tension in the room began to dissipate as Lucien's words brought a semblance of unity to their divided stance. "David, please stay a minute."

The last murmur of the meeting faded as the heavy oak door clicked shut behind Viktor and Antoine, leaving David and Lucien alone in the grandeur of Lucien's spacious office. Antique maps and paintings adorned the walls, creating an atmosphere that felt both historic and authoritative. An immense, polished mahogany desk sat between them, but

Lucien didn't retreat to his chair. Instead, he strolled to the large window that provided a bird's eye view of the city's shimmering skyline.

"I understand your reservations about Viktor," Lucien began, his voice measured. "Viktor grew up in a Russia where the lines between enemies and allies were constantly shifting. His tenacity has often been his armor, but I value his perspective just as I value yours."

David leaned against a nearby bookshelf, surrounded by meticulously arranged titles, many of which were on diplomacy and history. "Lucien, I respect Viktor's experiences, but we're on the brink of something unprecedented. The idea of preemptively striking Lebanon... it just doesn't sit right."

Lucien turned, locking eyes with David. "Your concerns are valid. The Circle isn't a monolithic entity. We're a tapestry of perspectives, each thread contributing to the larger picture. Viktor's aggressive stance is one such thread, but it's balanced by others, like your commitment to diplomacy."

David looked down, clearly grappling with his emotions. "I just don't understand how The Circle, a body committed to global unity, can even entertain the idea of a military strike."

Lucien sighed, choosing his words carefully. "Italy's commitment to our cause is profound. After the Pope endorsed The Circle, Italy joined our efforts and donated it's two aircraft carriers to the cause. With their military force, and the addition of Diamond Worldwide, the private military contractor, we have the means to defend our vision, or take proactive action if necessary. But David, understand this: it's my hope that we never need to resort to force."

"David, I want you to negotiate peace with Lebanon."

David's eyes reflected his inner turmoil. "You want me to negotiate with Lebanon. Lucien, I've been in tense situations, but this? It's geopolitics on a scale I've never encountered."

Lucien walked closer, placing a firm hand on David's shoulder. "You're underestimating yourself. I don't need a diplomat who's bound by protocols and niceties. I need someone who can navigate the unpredictability of a high-stakes situation, who can connect on a human level. Your background, your instincts – that's what we need. Lebanon is wounded, volatile, and you understand the psychology of such situations."

David met Lucien's gaze, uncertainty still present but mixed with determination. "Alright, but Lucien, we're walking a tightrope. One misstep, and it's not just The Circle's reputation at stake, but countless lives."

Lucien nodded, the weight of the situation evident in his eyes. "I'm aware, David. And I trust you to find the balance we need."

Soft light filtered into the opulent conference room through tall windows draped in heavy velvet curtains. David, Lucien, Viktor, and Antoine sat around a polished table made of dark mahogany. Neatly arranged stacks of papers and digital tablets lay in front of each person, showing the depth of the discussions and the preparations that had been in progress.

David cleared his throat, his posture confident. "After weeks of negotiations, Lebanon has finally agreed to step down. They won't openly endorse the peace treaty with Israel, but their official stance is one of non-interference. In return, France is stepping in with a generous $6 billion aid package to support Lebanon's post-war reconstruction."

Lucien nodded, smiling slightly, "Well done, David. Your diplomatic acumen is proving invaluable."

Viktor leaned back, his demeanor always reflecting a military readiness. "Impressive, considering we're on the cusp of making history in just a week. However, relying on their word until the last moment could be a risk."

Before anyone could comment further, the conference room door swung open. A young aide, her face pale and her steps rushed, entered. She quickly approached Lucien, leaning in to whisper something urgent into his ear. Simultaneously, a soft buzz emanated from David's pocket. Extracting his phone, he rapidly scanned the message displayed. His face turned ashen.

Heart pounding, David exclaimed, "Lebanon has initiated a rocket attack on Israel, and Hezbollah has joined in from Syria."

Viktor's eyes darkened. "I knew they were snakes. Deception is part of their game."

Lucien, always the picture of serenity even in a storm, took a deep breath. "We've given diplomacy its fair shot, and it seems they've reneged on their agreement. Viktor, take care of it."

Viktor stood up sharply, determination written all over him. "Consider it handled." He said and quickly exited the room.

As the door clicked shut, Lucien turned his gaze to David, his eyes compassionate yet firm. "David, don't blame yourself. They merely played their cards, feeding you what you hoped to hear, all the while preparing for their final act. Such is the nature of global politics, sometimes."

David looked defeated, guilt evident in his eyes, but before he could respond, Lucien added, "I need to address this immediately. We'll reconvene later." With that, Lucien departed, leaving David in contemplation of the unpredictable nature of international diplomacy.

The conference room was silent, save for the muted hum of the city outside and the low ticking of the clock on the wall.

He sat at the table, head in his hands, lost in introspection. How could he have been so naive? Every detail of his recent meetings with Lebanon's ambassador replayed in his mind. The ambassador's sincere tone, the earnestness in his eyes, the firm handshake... All of it felt genuine. David's years of training and experience in reading people told him that he had struck a genuine deal. But now, he was confronted with a stark reality. He had been duped, and the consequences were dire.

He leaned back in his chair, staring at the ceiling, battling the heavy weight of guilt and self-blame. How had he allowed himself to be misled so gravely?

He thought of the thousands of innocent lives now in jeopardy because he believed in a deceptive peace. It wasn't just about failing Lucien or The Circle; it was about failing these innocent lives.

A deep sigh escaped his lips. David was used to facing challenges head-on, but this overwhelming sense of guilt was unfamiliar territory for him. The cost of this mistake was immeasurable, and he grappled with the fear that this blunder might overshadow all the good he'd done in his career.

He reached for his phone, intending to call the ambassador, to confront him, to find some semblance of understanding or closure. But he hesitated, fingers hovering over the screen. Would it make a difference?

As the weight of the situation bore down on him, David realized that there was no easy way out. He needed to face this head-on, accept responsibility, and find a way to prevent further damage.

Chapter 34: Allies

T he operations center was an impressive display of state-of-the-art technology, with walls lined by massive screens that painted a dynamic portrait of the world's hotspots. The usually dimly lit room was illuminated by the blue hue of these screens, with analysts stationed at each one, quickly typing away and updating data points. Each station had ergonomic chairs, multiple keyboards, and communication devices, all designed for extended use. The ceiling above held retractable microphones for swift communication between the teams. The faint hum of the servers from an adjoining room and the soft clicks of keyboards filled the air.

Currently, every screen was zoomed into the Middle East, with real-time satellite imagery capturing the evolving conflict. Icons representing aircraft moved in real-time, trails of smoke indicated strikes, and different colored zones showed areas of control.

David stood, taking it all in, the weight of the situation pressing down on him. On one screen, the white trails of Israeli jets zigzagged over Lebanon, finding and targeting Hezbollah's strongholds. Beside it, another screen displayed Italian aircraft joining the operation, flying in formation, with their paths originating from the blue icon representing their aircraft carrier group in the Mediterranean.

But it was the influx of aircraft from the North and the East that caught David's attention. The sudden appearance of more jet icons, larger and more menacing, flying from Syria and Saudi Arabia, changed the dynamics of the live feed. These weren't just targeted airstrikes; this was rapidly turning into a widespread offensive.

Approaching Viktor, David asked, "What's happening here? Whose planes are those?"

Viktor, watching the screens intently, replied without breaking his gaze, "Diamond Worldwide has made certain... arrangements with Russian forces. And as for the Saudis, they're a crucial part of The Circle, keen to ensure the region's stability. They've pledged their air support."

"But this... this is massive. Look at the scale!" David pointed to the screen where the additional Russian and Saudi Arabian jets were shown to be carrying out blanket bombing runs. Cities and towns were smothered in plumes of smoke, both military installations and civilian areas hit indiscriminately.

Viktor's face was unreadable. "War isn't pretty, David. But it's effective. We're making sure the threat is annihilated."

David took a moment to absorb what was happening, the vast difference in approach between the precise Israeli strikes and the raw power of the Russian and Saudi offensives evident. He whispered to himself, "What have we set into motion?"

Lucien strode into the operations center, his presence instantly commanding attention. As Viktor began to update him, David approached, a mix of anger and despair evident on his face.

"Lucien, those airstrikes – they're not discriminating between military assets and civilian zones. It's... it's a massacre out there," David's voice was filled with urgency.

Lucien turned to David, his face impassive. "David, I appreciate your commitment to peace. You tried diplomacy with Lebanon, and what did it get us? A surprise attack on Israel."

David's frustration was palpable. "But responding like this? Indiscriminate bombings? How can we claim the moral high ground? How can we promise a new era of peace when our response is so... brutal?"

Lucien sighed deeply, his gaze locked onto the main display. "Son, look around you. For decades, centuries even, this region has been ablaze with conflict. Every Western attempt to broker peace, to mediate – what has it achieved? Temporary cessations, followed by renewed violence. It's a cycle, and it's high time it's broken."

David shot back, "So, we break it with more violence? With bloodshed?"

Lucien's voice was calm but firm. "If we need to make a drastic show of force to end decades, or potentially centuries, of further bloodshed, then so be it. The citizens of these countries elected these leaders, supported their belligerent actions, and celebrated their aggressions against neighbors. The line between innocence and complicity blurs in such cases."

David was near breaking point. "But children? Families? They didn't ask for this."

Lucien, still staring at the screens, responded, "War is tragic, David. Innocents suffer, yes, but think of the long-term peace. The end of an age-old cycle. Isn't that worth it?"

David looked torn, his belief in diplomacy at odds with the raw reality unfolding before him. "What kind of peace is it when it's steeped in the blood of the innocent?"

Lucien finally turned to David, his eyes betraying a hint of sadness. "It's a peace, David, that ensures those innocents haven't died in vain. And sometimes, for the sake of generations to come, we must take decisions that weigh heavy on our souls now."

The operations center, with all its buzz, seemed to quieten for a moment, as two men, each driven by their principles, grappled with the moral quandaries of war and peace.

Chapter 35: Prayer

The room was dimly lit, the curtains drawn tight against the midday sun. Becca sat on her plush couch, the soft sounds of Leila's rhythmic breathing providing a muted backdrop to the room's stillness. Leila's little chest rose and fell, her soft curls cascading across Becca's lap. The quiet ambiance was punctuated by the TV's low murmur.

Suddenly, the newscaster's voice took on an urgent tone, the familiar cadence of "Breaking News" capturing Becca's attention. She shifted slightly, careful not to wake Leila, and looked up. The screen was filled with images of billowing smoke and fallen debris. Rockets streaked across the sky. The headline was bold, jarring – *War Erupts in the Middle East Days Before Historic Peace Treaty*. The news anchor reported about the unprecedented military actions that had engulfed Israel and Lebanon, countries on the cusp of what many hoped would be a transformative peace.

Becca's heart sank. The weight of her mission in Lebanon pressed heavily on her. A flood of memories rushed back - the dusty streets, the anxious faces, the countless hours spent trying to piece together a roadmap for peace. She felt a pang of guilt, thinking about how she could have done more, but another part of her, the seasoned CIA agent, whispered the bitter truth - sometimes, in the chessboard of international diplomacy, pawns get sacrificed.

Closing her eyes, she tried to block out the grim visuals on the screen, but the images seeped into her thoughts, mixing with memories of her time in Lebanon. With a soft sigh, she reached for the remote and muted the television. The room returned to its hushed state, save for the gentle rhythm of Leila's breath.

Beside her lay the Bible Mark had given her, its leather cover soft from use. Slowly, almost hesitantly, Becca opened it. She pondered where to begin and then, as if guided by some unseen force, turned to 1 Peter 5. As she read, the verses spoke of sufferings, of the trials that believers face, and of the strength that God provides. It delved into why adversities were allowed and hinted at a purpose that might be beyond immediate understanding.

Tears welled up in her eyes as she read about casting all anxieties on God because He cared for her. In this moment of deep introspection, Becca found herself grappling with age-old questions about suffering, about God's will, and the presence of evil. As she delved deeper into the scriptures, a sense of calm enveloped her, reminding her that even in the darkest hours, there was always a glimmer of hope.

The evening sun painted a golden hue on the horizon. Becca, having just tucked Leila into bed, now found herself sitting on her patio, the Bible open in her lap. She'd been reading it more often, seeking solace in its teachings and trying to reconcile her tumultuous life with the divine messages it contained.

Turning the pages, she found herself reading the story of the prodigal son. The tale of a young man who strayed, wasted his inheritance, and returned home to find his father waiting for him with open arms. The unconditional love of the father resonated deeply within her. In many ways, she felt like that prodigal child—having lived a life focused on duty, danger, and service, often losing her way amid the complexities of her profession.

She continued reading, moving to the New Testament, where she found the account of Jesus' sacrifice. The concept of unconditional love, grace, and redemption leaped from the pages and echoed in her heart. She remembered Mark speaking about the power of the cross, about the incredible gift of salvation and the grace available through Jesus Christ.

As the stars began to twinkle in the night sky, Becca felt a gentle pull in her heart. She thought about the mistakes she had made, the paths she had taken, and the sense of emptiness that sometimes consumed her. The realization dawned that perhaps she had been searching for something more profound all along—a purpose, a sense of belonging, and a divine love.

In that quiet moment, tears streaming down her face, Becca whispered a prayer. "Lord, I've been lost for so long. I've tried to find my way, but I've come to realize I can't do it on my own. I need You. I need Your love, Your grace. I believe in You, Jesus, and in the sacrifice You made for me. I accept You as my Lord and Savior. Please, come into my heart and guide me."

A profound sense of peace enveloped her. It felt as if a burden had been lifted off her shoulders, replaced by a comforting embrace. She felt connected, not just to the world around her but to something much more significant.

The night deepened, but Becca remained on the patio, lost in thought, prayer, and a newfound relationship with Christ. The journey ahead would surely be filled with challenges, but with Christ by her side, Becca felt equipped to face them.

Chapter 36: Forced Peace

T he imposing Lucerne Culture and Congress Centre stood in sharp contrast to the surrounding natural beauty of Switzerland. Perched on the shores of Lake Lucerne, the building's modern architectural design echoed the reflection of the towering Swiss Alps in the serene lake waters. Inside, the grandeur was no less striking: high ceilings with ornate chandeliers, plush seating arrangements, and walls adorned with exquisite art pieces. It was a fitting venue for decisions that would change the course of history.

The expansive conference room was dominated by an elongated mahogany table, around which sat the leadership of The Circle and the political delegation from Israel. Papers, marked with annotations and official seals, were neatly stacked in front of each individual, representing long nights and countless debates.

Antoine, a tall, suave man with salt-and-pepper hair, cleared his throat, drawing attention. "Let's talk about the order of events for the signing of this landmark peace treaty," he began, but was interrupted by Lucien's assertive tone.

"There's just one more thing," Lucien declared, his cold blue eyes scanning the room. "For this treaty to be fully effective, Israel will need to join The Circle. Furthermore, the digital dollar must be adopted as your official currency."

The room turned silent, the weight of Lucien's words sinking in. Dr. Goldman, a bespectacled man known for his diplomatic finesse, replied with a palpable tension in his voice, "This was never on the table, Lucien. Israel has always been a sovereign nation. We won't compromise on that."

Prime Minister Abraham Katz, a seasoned politician with deep-set eyes that told of battles fought in corridors of power, chimed in firmly, "Lucien, we've had extensive discussions, and this was never part of our agreement. It won't be possible."

Unruffled, Lucien made a simple, commanding gesture, "Everyone, please, leave us." He fixed his gaze on Katz, "Except for you, Prime Minister."

Despite Dr. Goldman's immediate objection, Katz, sensing the gravity of the moment, acquiesced, "It's alright, Doctor."

Once the doors shut, sealing the two leaders in, Lucien paced slowly, every step deliberate. "Prime Minister, Israel's partnership in defeating Lebanon was commendable. But our strategy... it was necessary."

Katz's gaze hardened, "You went beyond our agreed-upon strategy. Civilian casualties were not part of the plan."

Lucien, pausing to gather his thoughts, then stated, "And though I know you didn't approve of our tactics in Lebanon, as a part of the peace deal, we'll be relocating all of the Palestinians to southern Lebanon. There will be a peace zone between the two countries to further provide you much-needed security."

Katz's brow furrowed in surprise. "Why is this the first I'm hearing of this?"

Lucien looked back, an air of calm confidence about him. "The details were just finalized. It's been a complex negotiation."

Stopping in front of a window, Lucien looked out at the serene lake, his voice measured, "In our quest for global peace, some sacrifices are essential. But," he turned to face Katz, "I understand your reservations. And that's why I want to offer you something in return."

Curiosity piqued, Katz responded, "Go on."

With a theatrical pause, Lucien unveiled, "Rebuild the Jewish temple on the Temple Mount."

Katz was taken aback. For countless years, this had been an unattainable dream for many Israelis. "That's... monumental. But how? The Islamic world would be in an uproar."

Lucien leaned in, his voice dripping with assurance, "I've spoken to key Islamic leaders. They've agreed. This is our chance, Prime Minister. A new world order, a lasting peace, is within our grasp."

For Katz, the proposition was tantalizing. But he wrestled with the implications, the risks, and the dream of a rebuilt temple. Lucien pressed on, "Prime Minister, this could be our legacy. Centuries of conflict put to rest. A reunified Israel with all her land. The temple rebuilt. The choice is yours."

The two leaders stood, the weight of history pressing upon them. Lucien's proposition dangled in the air, a tantalizing promise of peace, but at what cost?

Chapter 37: Invoice

D avid Mitchell sat at his expansive desk, his eyes drawn to the magnificent view that stretched beyond the large windows of his office at The Circle's headquarters. He couldn't help but get lost in the cityscape for moments at a time - a fleeting yet potent distraction from the myriad of questions that plagued his thoughts.

His office was a meticulous space, adorned with the trappings of success yet somehow void of personal touch. It was a room that told of accomplishments, but not of the man behind them. Amidst the sterile opulence, David's attention was captured by the disarray of documents before him – case files, reports, pieces of a jigsaw puzzle that seemed to defy assembly.

His concentration was jolted by the sharp ring of the telephone. A name he didn't recognize flashed across the caller ID – Accounting.

"Mitchell," he answered crisply, the businesslike tone a reflex.

"Is this David Mitchell?" A woman's voice, unyielding and curt, cut through the line.

"It is," David replied, his curiosity piqued.

"I have an invoice here, Mr. Mitchell. It's overdue by 90 days," the woman stated matter-of-factly. There was an evident lack of patience in her tone, as if the mere act of making this call was a nuisance.

David furrowed his brows. "Who is the invoice from?" he inquired, racking his brain and finding no immediate recollection of any outstanding payments.

"It's marked Security Consulting for The Wave Corporation," the woman replied, with a pronounced tone of irritation.

The mention of The Wave Corporation sent a ripple of unease through David. The Wave had been the company that had contracted Nadia to plant a sniffer, a conduit for gathering sensitive, and potentially damning information about business and political leaders. What business could The Circle possibly have with them?

"Could you send me a copy of that invoice?" David asked, his voice steady yet laced with an undercurrent of concern.

"It'll be in your email," the woman responded tersely before ending the call abruptly.

David sat motionless for a moment, the phone still in his hand, the dial tone humming softly. The Wave Corporation had been a central figure in a covert operation that could upend the power balance. Why would The Circle owe them money?

His hands moved swiftly over the keyboard as he logged into his email. The invoice from Accounting arrived, as cold and impersonal as the woman who had sent it. David's eyes scanned the document. The figures, the dates, and most unsettlingly, the client and service provider. The Wave Corporation and The Circle were linked financially, a revelation that cast a shadow of doubt and confusion over everything he thought he knew.

Was he wrong about The Wave?

Even more importantly, was he wrong about The Circle?

David picked up his cell phone and sent a message to a group chat, *Want to meet?*

Chapter 38: Realization

G eneral Porter's residence stood as a dignified testament to a life lived in the service of his country. The colonial-style house, while impressive in size, exuded a warmth and familiarity that belied its imposing facade. The exterior, painted in a muted shade of beige, was contrasted by the vivid blossoms in the well-tended garden – the touch of General Porter's late wife. The rows of roses, her favorite, added a splash of color to the otherwise austere surroundings.

Inside, the decor was a marriage of the General's austere military sensibilities and the elegance brought in by his wife. Delicate lace curtains framed the large bay windows, letting in a soft, filtered light. Ornate porcelain vases held bouquets of fresh flowers, their scent permeating the living spaces. Throughout the home, family photographs adorned the walls, chronicling years of love, pride, and shared experiences.

As David approached the entrance, he took a deep breath, steeling himself for the impending discussion. The solid oak door, beautifully polished and adorned with a brass knocker, swung open to reveal the stern yet familiar face of General Porter.

"David," he greeted, nodding slightly, "Glad you could make it. Come in."

David stepped inside, instantly enveloped by the cozy warmth of the home. A sense of nostalgia washed over him as he recalled past visits, before the world was on the brink of chaos.

"Mark and Becca are already here," General Porter mentioned, leading David into the dining room.

The room was dominated by a large mahogany table, polished to a high sheen. Sitting at one end was Mark, his face drawn and serious, and beside him, Becca, her eyes betraying a hint of worry.

David took a seat, the weight of the moment pressing on him. He paused, collecting his thoughts, before finally speaking, "I apologize for how our last meeting ended," his voice laden with genuine remorse.

Mark, ever the mediator, offered a forgiving smile. "It's understandable, David. The antichrist, if that's who Lucien is, would be a master manipulator."

David looked directly at him. "Do you still believe Lucien is the antichrist?"

Mark's response was firm. "Yes, I do."

General Porter, who had been silent until now, leaned forward, the intensity of his gaze unwavering. "I don't trust him," he began, his voice deep and measured. "While I'm bound by my duty to the President, I believe joining The Circle is a grave mistake. Lucien exhibits all the qualities of a man who could easily morph into a dictator."

The room was thick with tension. Becca broke the silence, her gaze fixated on David. "What changed for you, David? Why the sudden change of heart?"

Without a word, David slid an invoice across the table towards Becca. "Recognize this?"

As Becca scanned the document, realization dawned on her, and her face went pale. Her eyes, usually calm and analytical, widened in astonishment. "Oh, Nadia," she whispered, the weight of the revelation evident in her voice. She looked up, meeting David's gaze. "We had the right idea but targeted the wrong organization. The Circle was behind the blackmail, and we handed them the evidence of their own misdeeds."

The room was silent, the magnitude of their oversight settling in.

David's eyes were cast downward, the impact of their realization weighing heavily upon him. "I've been thinking about quitting," he confessed, his voice barely above a whisper. Every fiber of his being revolted against the betrayal, the manipulation they had unwittingly been a part of.

General Porter's stern yet thoughtful gaze fell upon David. The aged yet sturdy hands, veins mapping a lifetime of service and struggle, clasped together as he considered David's words. "Let's not be hasty, son," he cautioned. "The Circle has pulled the wool over our eyes, but recklessness is not our ally here."

Mark, his features imbued with a mix of concern and resolution, chimed in, "David, I think you might be in real danger now. We're not dealing with ordinary enemies; The Circle is a force we've not encountered before."

Becca, ever the voice of reason, expressed her agreement with General Porter. "We need to think strategically. Every move from here on needs to be calculated," she asserted, her tone conveying the gravity of their situation.

General Porter leaned back, his gaze unwavering from David. "It might be too late to disrupt the peace treaty with Israel, but the global stakes are higher than ever. Sovereign nations are capitulating, surrendering their autonomy. If we expose The Circle for what they really are, we could prevent a catastrophe."

The silence in the room was palpable; the air thick with the enormity of their task. If Lucien gained control over the global financial system, the world as they knew it would be irretrievably lost.

"We need eyes and ears on the inside," continued General Porter. "David, you're in a position to gather evidence. We need to unveil the true face of The Circle."

David's face twisted in unease. "The internal security... it's robust. Every move is watched, every conversation is likely monitored. I don't know how I'll manage to gather anything substantial."

The atmosphere in the room was heavy, charged with the understanding of the monumental challenge before them. It was Becca who broke the silence, her voice carrying a trace of hope. "What about Nadia? Could she be of help?"

David's eyes locked onto Becca's. Nadia - a resource they hadn't fully considered. Her skills, and perhaps even untapped information about The Circle, could be invaluable.

Every eye in the room was now fixed on David, awaiting his response. The silence was pregnant with anticipation, the impending decision carrying with it the weight of nations. The road ahead was perilous, the enemy formidable, but within the walls of General Porter's home, amidst the testament of a lifetime of service and sacrifice, a clandestine alliance was strengthening.

The world outside, unknowingly teetering on the brink of subjugation, was reliant upon the resolve and courage of the few within these walls. David, conflicted yet resolute, met the gaze of each individual at the table.

"We need every ally, every resource at our disposal," he admitted, the gravity of their mission etching deep lines of determination upon his face. The game of shadows and lights, deceit and truth, was unfolding, and every move henceforth would decide the fate of nations and the future of humanity itself.

The atmosphere in General Porter's house was tense, with the room's ambient lighting casting long shadows on the ornate walls. Becca, her determined features softened by a hint of worry, broke the lingering silence.

"I need to get back to my daughter," she said, her voice revealing a mother's deep-seated concern. "I'll reach out to Nadia. If anyone can help us navigate this maze, it's her."

David nodded, his respect for Becca deepening. Here was a woman, fiercely loyal, incredibly sharp, and willing to risk everything for the sake of the truth.

She rose, smoothing out her blouse. "Take care, all of you," she said, pausing at the door with one last lingering, meaningful look.

As she left, Mark, who had been unusually silent during the evening, also got up. His tall frame seemed to loom even larger in the room. "I should head out too," he said, his deep-set eyes, usually filled with playful mirth, now reflecting a deep introspection.

He turned to David, taking a moment before speaking. "David," he began, his voice gentle yet firm, "now, more than ever, I urge you to trust in Jesus. Life is fleeting, and amidst all this chaos, the eternal truth remains unchanged. Accepting Christ is the only way to eternal life."

David, although caught off guard by the sudden shift in the conversation, listened intently. The conviction in Mark's voice was hard to ignore.

"I've seen firsthand how faith has shaped you, Mark," David replied, his voice filled with genuine admiration. "I promise to think about it."

Mark, placing a reassuring hand on David's shoulder, simply nodded. "Remember, David, faith can move mountains. Put your trust in Him." With those parting words, Mark left, his departure marking a moment of profound introspection for David.

The room fell silent, save for the ticking of an old grandfather clock. General Porter, who had observed the exchanges of the evening with his characteristic stoicism, motioned for David to stay.

"Sit down, David. We need to talk, just the two of us." David could sense the gravity in Porter's voice.

In the subdued lighting of General Henry Porter's living room, framed by elegant draperies and adorned with personal mementos, David and the General sat across from each other, two men bound by duty but also by the weight of recent revelations.

General Porter cleared his throat, his stern face momentarily softening, reflecting a vulnerability seldom seen. "David," he began, "Mark's words weren't merely for effect. He's right. You know, after the 3/16 incident, when I came home to find my wife gone, I felt the depth of the mistake I had been making for years."

David leaned forward, sensing the deep personal significance of what he was about to hear. He saw in Porter's eyes a combination of grief, regret, and newfound conviction.

"All those Sundays, sitting in church," Porter continued, "listening to sermons, saying prayers, but not truly understanding or accepting the depth of a relationship with Jesus. It took the most jarring event of my life, the rapture of believers including my beloved wife, to finally make me see."

David listened, rapt. He had known the General as a figure of authority, as a soldier dedicated to his duty, but this was a side of him David had never witnessed.

Porter continued, "David, these times, they're changing. And not for the better. The signs are all around us. The prophecies are coming to life. This treaty with Israel... it isn't just a political maneuver. It's the beginning of the Tribulation, a period that will see God's wrath unleashed upon this earth."

A chill ran down David's spine. The gravity of Porter's words, the implications of what was being discussed, was staggering.

Porter leaned in closer, his eyes searching David's. "It's not too late for you, David. Don't make the mistake I made for so long. A life without Jesus is an eternity of suffering. Believe in Him, truly accept Him in your heart, and be saved from what's coming. If you don't, the consequences are... unimaginable."

David swallowed hard, feeling the weight of a decision that went beyond life as he knew it.

Chapter 39: The Dream

T he quiet ambiance of David's living room was punctuated by the soft chime of his phone receiving a notification. The room was bathed in a soft golden glow from the evening sun, filtering through the curtains. David, standing by the window, uncorked a bottle of Four Roses bourbon and poured himself a shot. The amber liquid shimmered in the glass, reflecting the dim lighting of the room.

He held the glass, feeling its cool weight, staring at the liquid but making no move to drink it. Instead, he placed it gently on the wooden coffee table, the reflections dancing within the glass. His face, usually stoic and determined, showed clear lines of tension and contemplation. The day's revelations, the weight of his newfound understanding, bore down on him.

He thought about his tenure as an undercover agent, the close calls, the adrenaline-filled moments, the many faces he wore to extract information from unsuspecting adversaries. Gathering intel on The Circle would be yet another assignment, but the stakes this time were incomparably high. It wasn't just about intelligence or national security. This was about the very soul of the world.

But once he had the information, what would he do? The institutions he once believed in – the FBI, the US government – were now intertwined with The Circle, their objectivity questionable. The UN, a supposed beacon of international cooperation, was mired in its own corrupt practices. David felt the weight of isolation; the only allies he truly had were Becca, General Porter, and perhaps Mark.

Sighing heavily, David's gaze landed on the Bible that Mark had handed him earlier. Its leather cover, slightly worn, beckoned him. He had skimmed through its pages in the past, regarding it as a text of historical significance but never really delving deep into its message.

With tentative fingers, David picked up the Bible and began to thumb through its pages, eventually landing on the Book of Matthew. The words, once mere verses, now seemed to come alive, speaking directly to his soul. Passages about faith, redemption, and sacrifice resonated deeply within him.

As he delved deeper into the teachings of Jesus, time seemed to stand still. The worries and tensions of the world outside faded into the background as David found himself engrossed in the text.

Hours, it seemed, passed in moments. The weight of his eyelids grew heavy, the words began to blur, and as the evening sun gave way to the gentle embrace of night, David, still holding onto the Bible, succumbed to a deep sleep, the book's teachings serving as a balm to his tormented soul.

Amidst the haze of sleep, David found himself standing amidst a vast crowd, a sea of faces stretching as far as the eye could see. At the heart of this gathering stood a grand temple, glinting under the sunlight, its opulent architecture radiating a sense of awe.

Lucien, dressed in pristine white, stood on a platform in front of the temple, his voice booming across the masses. "I have come to bring peace to this world," he declared. "Under my guidance, even the lion and lamb will find harmony. The serpents will dance with the sparrows, and all will be united under a single banner of tranquility."

As he continued, David's unease grew. Lucien's voice began to distort, becoming deeper and more menacing. "There are those," Lucien continued, his tone taking a dark turn, "who dare to defy me. A woman, who thought herself righteous. But she is nothing more than a whore, and she will be struck down for her insolence."

To David's horror, Lucien's form began to change. His handsome features contorted, eyes multiplying across his face, each one a blazing orb of anger. His mouth elongated, sprouting razor-sharp teeth, dripping with anticipation. Ten horns sprouted out of his head.

From the corner of his eye, David saw a figure break away from the crowd, a shining sword in hand, racing towards the monstrous Lucien. With a warrior's yell, the man thrust the sword straight into Lucien's head, piercing through with a sickening crunch. The monster that Lucien had become crumpled, falling lifeless at the base of the temple.

A collective gasp rose from the crowd, followed by angry shouts. The people, their faces twisted in rage, descended upon the man who stabbed Lucien with stones in hand, hurling them with deadly intent.

But as the scene unfolded, another creature, even more grotesque, emerged. This beast, with a roar, pulled the sword from Lucien's fallen form. To David's astonishment and horror, Lucien began to stir. Slowly, he rose, completely unharmed, his monstrous features morphing back to the charismatic leader the crowd adored.

With a look of pure hatred, Lucien lifted a massive rock and, with supernatural strength, hurled it at the man who had dared to defy him. The stone found its mark, and the man fell, lifeless.

A silence descended, broken only by Lucien's chilling laughter. One by one, the masses began to kneel, their faces filled with reverence and fear, bowing to the one they saw as invincible.

David felt a rush of cold terror. His heart pounded so loudly he could hear its echo in his ears. As the weight of the dream pressed down on him, he jolted awake. His clothing was soaked in sweat, and his breath came in ragged gasps.

Clutching his chest, tears formed in David's eyes. The chilling nightmare, the monstrous transformation of Lucien, it all felt too real, too close. The weight of the dream pressed on him, and in his vulnerability, he whispered a desperate prayer, "Jesus, save me. Save me from this darkness."

In the quiet aftermath of the nightmare, David felt a strange sense of peace wash over him, as if, even in the darkest of times, there was a beacon of hope guiding him through.

Chapter 40: Hack

In the soft glow of late afternoon, David approached the back entrance of a quaint Greek cafe nestled in a narrow alleyway. The weathered wooden door, with its chipping paint and rusty handle, bore silent testimony to its years of service. After a few moments of searching, he found the hidden key where Becca had described and cautiously entered.

The cafe, though devoid of its usual chatter and aroma of fresh food, emanated a melancholic charm. The layers of newspaper print covering the cafe's front windows let in just enough sunlight to paint a serene pattern on the wooden floor. David's eyes quickly found Becca, sitting by a corner table, her fingers swiftly moving across her phone screen.

"Favorite dish?" David initiated, taking in the stillness of the cafe.

With a faint smile, Becca replied, "Used to be the gyro and fries. Such a shame about the owners. The world lost so much that day." She glanced around the cafe, her eyes reflecting a deep sense of loss.

David took a seat opposite her. "You seem different since the last time we met," she remarked, her gaze evaluating.

Feeling a weight lifted from his shoulders, David simply said, "I feel... clearer now."

Becca nodded, sensing the change in him. "Speaking of clarity, Nadia's plan might just get us the breakthrough we need," she began. "She's been casting out phishing emails to various employees at The Circle. The moment one of them bites, and opens the attached document, it will give us a backdoor into their system."

David leaned in, intrigued. "That gives us access to their individual systems, but what about the main data goldmine?"

"That's where you come in," Becca responded, her tone serious. She produced a small device from her bag and slid it towards David. "This needs to be plugged into a network switch at The Circle. But it won't be as straightforward."

David picked up the device, inspecting it. "Security cameras watch every IT closet."

Becca nodded, "Yes, but the network switches they use have a vulnerability. If you bridge the wireless and wired networks, it sends the system into a frenzy, overloading it with data. We need you to exploit that. You need to find an unwitting fool and bridge the networks on his laptop."

David's mind raced. "So, while they're busy troubleshooting, I sneak in and install this?"

Becca hesitated for a moment, "That's the idea. But you won't be alone. The network security team will be right there, trying to identify the glitch."

David felt a rush of adrenaline. "So, I need to do this right under their noses?"

Becca met his gaze, her eyes filled with determination. "Exactly. It's a risk, but it's our best shot."

David sighed, taking in the gravity of the task ahead. The game of cat and mouse had just become a lot more complex, but with so much at stake, there was no room for hesitation.

Chapter 41: Cookies

N estled among the sea of cubicles at The Circle was Walter's modest workspace. Walter wasn't the most immaculate individual. He was portly, his clothes always seemed a size too small, and his unkempt hair looked like it hadn't seen a comb in days. His desk was no different. Amid the scattered paperwork, empty soda cans, and a forgotten sandwich from who knows when, sat Walter, usually engrossed in a movie or strategically placing cards in a game of Solitaire.

David had always viewed Walter as benign background noise. Yet now, as he observed the accountant's habits, he realized that Walter was the ideal candidate for his plan. After all, a staff member receiving a cookie delivery wasn't out of the ordinary, but it would be enough to lure Walter away for a few vital moments.

David casually positioned himself in the vicinity of the accounting department, pretending to examine some paperwork. He watched as Walter's phone rang.

Walter's eyes lit up with a mix of surprise and excitement. "Cookies for me? Really?" he said, a tinge of disbelief in his voice. Without waiting for an answer, he hurriedly got up, his chair swiveling in his haste.

David wasted no time. He swiftly, but discreetly, moved to Walter's computer. With practiced ease, he accessed the network settings, swiftly bridging the wireless and wired connections. The deed done, David made his way back to his own office without raising any suspicions.

As the minutes ticked by, the repercussions of David's actions began to manifest. The once swift and efficient network began to slow, each command taking noticeably longer to process. Whispered complaints echoed across the office. "Is your email working?" "My files won't open!" "Everything's frozen!"

The bridge had initiated a storm of network traffic, causing an avalanche of data packets with nowhere to go. These particular network switches, flawed in design, failed to activate their storm protection mechanism when faced with such an anomaly. The resulting data congestion was catastrophic.

Soon, the network on David's floor was virtually paralyzed. The digital age equivalent of a traffic jam during rush hour. Without network access, the productivity of The Circle's employees ground to a halt. Frustrated staff members flooded the IT department with service requests.

David could hear the hurried footsteps and the jangle of tools as IT technicians raced onto the floor, searching for the root cause. Their urgency was palpable, as each second of downtime could equate to substantial financial loss.

Yet, unbeknownst to them, the most significant consequence of this network failure was not the lost productivity. The IP-based security cameras, their watchful eyes always recording, had been rendered blind by the overload, granting David a rare window of opportunity in his covert operations against The Circle.

David's footfalls echoed in the sterile hallway of The Circle, a stark contrast to the chaos erupting around him. He approached the IT closet, pushing through the cluster of technicians gathered outside. The familiar, wiry form of Jim, the Director of IT Security, was unmistakable among them, busily coordinating with the team.

David called out, trying to infuse casualness into his voice. "Hey Jim, how's it going? Kinda expected you might be at the center of this."

Jim looked up, a teasing grin splitting his face. "Oh, hey David, decide to come over and see how real security professionals do their job?"

Despite the high stakes, David shot back with a chuckle, "Oh, you know, just trying to learn from the best. Especially keen on understanding how you manage to bring The Circle's productivity to a screeching halt."

Jim's chuckle matched David's, "Just give us fifteen minutes. We've got this."

David glanced to the IT closet, the door slightly ajar. Taking his chance, he inched forward, throwing a playful challenge, "Fifteen minutes? I'm willing to bet a case of beer on it."

Jim's eyebrows rose in amusement, "None of that light beer nonsense, though. If we win, I want a proper case of IPAs."

David nodded, pretending to be engrossed in their banter, even as he edged closer to the closet. His fingers itched to reach the device concealed in his pocket. But just as he was about to make his move, an exclamation rang out.

"I've got it. Port 490." Jared's voice was triumphant. David's heart sank.

Jim, caught up in the moment, motioned for David, "Come on, see some real action here."

David suppressed a groan, following the team out reluctantly. Their path led them straight to Walter's desk. Walter, crumbs of cookies dotting his shirt, looked up in bemusement, "What's going on?"

Jared didn't wait for pleasantries. He swiftly examined Walter's laptop, quickly identifying the bridged network.

"Walter," Jared's tone was a mix of disbelief and exasperation, "are you downloading movies again?"

Walter blinked, clearly caught off guard, "I, umm, I just thought..."

Jared interrupted, "You thought bridging networks would speed up your downloads? Walter, we've had this talk."

Jim and David exchanged a look, silently acknowledging Walter's penchant for such blunders. As the situation was defused and Walter's computer taken for reimaging, David realized that his golden opportunity had slipped away.

They made their way back, Jim's gait noticeably cheerier. "David, don't forget our little bet. I'll be expecting that case in my office."

David nodded, feigning disappointment, "Will do." A quick thought struck him. He patted his pockets theatrically, "You know, I think I left my phone in the IT closet. Mind if I check?"

Jim chuckled, humor evident, "Of course, of course. Always leaving something behind." With a flourish, he unlocked the door.

David entered, heart pounding, praying that Jim wouldn't linger. Quickly palming the device, he plugged it into the network switch, wiping it clean of any fingerprints. Retrieving his phone with a triumphant "found it!", he exited.

Jim locked up, shaking his head in amusement, "Always the detective, huh?"

David grinned, "Always. Thanks, Jim. And thanks for getting us back online."

As David walked away, relief washed over him. The device was in place. Now, it was time to wait.

Chapter 42: Encrypted

D avid's fingers drummed anxiously on the table, his gaze locked onto Nadia's. The weight of the mission pressed heavily on his shoulders. "Nadia, tell me the device is working. We need those files."

Nadia hesitated, her eyes darting away momentarily. She ran her fingers through her dark hair, a gesture David recognized as her way of coping with stress. "The bug you planted is working. It's streaming data consistently. But David..." She paused, her voice heavy with concern, "there's a problem."

David felt a cold knot form in his stomach. He had invested so much into this operation, and the thought of it failing was unbearable. "What is it?"

"The main servers," Nadia began, her voice barely above a whisper, betraying the gravity of the situation, "they're protected by an encryption I've never encountered before. It's sophisticated, multi-layered, almost... perfect. I can't break through it."

David closed his eyes briefly, trying to process the information. He felt a mixture of anger and helplessness. "So, all of this... all our efforts have been in vain?" His voice trembled with frustration and a hint of desperation.

Nadia reached out, placing a reassuring hand on his arm. "No, not in vain," she said, trying to infuse some hope into the bleak situation. "We're collecting a lot of peripheral information which, in itself, is invaluable. But to access the heart of their database, we'll need credentials. Someone high up in The Circle, someone with full access rights. Your account doesn't even have this level of access."

David's mind raced, trying to find a solution. The Circle was a formidable adversary, and infiltrating their inner circle seemed impossible. "But how? How can we possibly obtain credentials from one of the top officials? They're always heavily guarded, always watched."

Nadia leaned in, her eyes gleaming with a mixture of determination and mischief. David could see the gears turning in her mind, formulating a plan. "Stealing is what I do best, David. We just need a plan, a way to get close to one of them without arousing suspicion."

David looked at her, admiration and gratitude evident in his eyes. Despite the odds, Nadia's unwavering spirit gave him hope. Together, they would find a way.

Chapter 43: Humbled

T he sun cast a golden hue over Jerusalem, a city of ancient stones and stories, where every corner whispered tales of kings and prophets, battles and miracles. On this particular day, though, it was the city's present that captured the world's attention, not its storied past.

David navigated the city's labyrinthine streets, now fortified with layers of security checkpoints, sniffer dogs, snipers perched on rooftops, and an array of state-of-the-art surveillance tech. The juxtaposition of the ancient walls with the modern security apparatus gave the city an atmosphere of tension and anticipation.

In a large square, a stage was set up, with a backdrop of Jerusalem's iconic golden Dome of the Rock shimmering in the distance. The multitude of international flags flanked the stage, with Israel's blue and white Star of David prominently displayed in the center.

The ambiance was electric. Reporters from every major news network jostled for the best vantage point, their cameras pointed at the stage, awaiting the historic moment. The buzzing drone of live news choppers overhead added to the cacophony.

Lucien, ever the charismatic leader, fielded questions with ease. David watched him, admiration and doubt warring within him. Lucien had been like a father to him, guiding and mentoring him through the last few months. But recent events had sown seeds of mistrust. The Circle's intentions, Lucien's true motives, were they as noble as they seemed?

As Lucien wrapped up with the press, he spotted David overseeing the final security arrangements. The two locked eyes, and Lucien approached with a knowing smile. "Feel good about today, David?" he asked, the hint of a challenge in his eyes.

David, usually unflappable, hesitated for a moment, searching for the right words. "Yes, sir. Security is tight; I don't expect any problems," he replied professionally.

But Lucien, ever the astute observer, could sense the undercurrent of emotions in David. "That's good, David. But how do you *feel* about today?" he pressed.

David looked around, absorbing the significance of the day. "I'm... I'm humbled, sir. To be a part of something that feels like it's been in the making for millennia... It's overwhelming."

Lucien placed a firm hand on David's shoulder, drawing him in slightly. "You've been more than just a 'part,' David. You've been instrumental. You should be proud of that."

Their conversation was cut short by a security commotion near one of the checkpoints. David instinctively moved in that direction, his instincts kicking in. "I'll handle it, sir," he said, taking charge. "See you at the signing."

Lucien watched David for a moment, admiration evident in his eyes, before turning back to the awaiting dignitaries. The stage was set for a day that would change the world.

Chapter 44: Treaty

The stage was set against the stunning backdrop of Jerusalem's ancient stone walls, which had witnessed countless historical events, and today was adding another chapter. As the sun began to set, casting a warm, golden hue, Lucien Morreau, the charismatic leader of The Circle, stepped up to the microphone.

The audience, a mix of dignitaries, diplomats, and ordinary citizens from across the world, waited with bated breath. Lucien started, "Ladies and gentlemen, friends and allies, today marks a turning point in the annals of human history. The road to this moment has been long, often treacherous, filled with distrust and misunderstandings."

He paused, drawing everyone in, "But it's not the journey that's most extraordinary; it's the people who've traveled it. The brave souls from every nation, every culture, who dared to dream of a world where children wouldn't know the sound of an air raid siren, where mothers wouldn't live in fear of the next missile."

Lucien's voice carried a soft intensity, "I've been but a servant in this grand tapestry of peace, humbled to stand among giants. Giants who showed us that, in the face of adversity, hope can triumph over fear, unity can conquer division."

He paused, looking out over the assembled crowd, his voice resonating with emotion, "Bravery isn't the absence of fear but the will to overcome it. Today, I salute that bravery, the indomitable spirit of every individual who dared to hope, to dream, to work towards this moment."

The applause began softly but quickly crescendoed into a deafening roar. Lucien signaled for quiet and gestured towards the wings of the stage, "Ladies and gentlemen, it is my distinct honor to introduce a leader who epitomizes that spirit, a beacon of hope for his nation and now, for the world. Please welcome Israeli Prime Minister, Abraham Katz."

As Prime Minister Katz strode onto the stage, the applause reached a fevered pitch. The two leaders shared a handshake that radiated genuine respect.

Katz began, "Shalom. Peace. A word that has been woven into the fabric of our culture, our prayers, our dreams for thousands of years. Today, it is no longer just a dream. It's our reality."

His deep-set eyes scanned the crowd, "Israel, a tiny nation in the heart of the Middle East, has always yearned for peace.

Today, with The Circle and our new allies, that yearning is fulfilled."

Katz's voice swelled with emotion, "The path to this day wasn't easy. But through it all, our guiding star was peace. And now, under the steadfast leadership of Lucien and the dedication of countless others, peace is within our grasp."

He concluded, "Today, as the sun sets on Jerusalem, it ushers in a new dawn for Israel and the world. A dawn of hope, prosperity, and lasting peace. To Lucien, to The Circle, to all of you, on behalf of every Israeli, thank you."

As Katz finished, the audience rose in a standing ovation. The sounds of clapping and cheers echoed off the ancient walls, and for a moment, the world seemed united in its hope for a peaceful future.

The grand stage was bathed in soft, golden light from the setting sun, as the world watched what was dubbed as a historic moment. The oversized peace treaty was spread out on a magnificent table. One by one, the dignitaries approached the table, each one leaving their signature as a testament to their commitment to peace.

David, clad in his formal attire, stood to the side, taking in the spectacle. Beside him, Dr. Goldman, an older man with wisdom etched on his face and a slight stoop in his posture, observed the signing with a mix of reservation and sadness.

With the bustle of the stage as a backdrop, Dr. Goldman leaned toward David, his voice barely more than a whisper. "Woe be to Israel for seeking peace with man and not with God," he began, his tone tinged with regret. "Woe be to Israel for not placing her trust in the Almighty Jehovah in her time of need."

David, accustomed to the sounds and sights of grand political displays, turned to face the elderly professor. He listened intently, absorbing the gravity of Dr. Goldman's words.

Goldman's eyes were moist as he continued, "David, I've had the privilege of knowing you for some time. Your bravery saved my life once. I fear for our nation. True peace isn't brokered in boardrooms and on stages. It's a divine gift."

Taking a deep breath, David replied, "I understand your reservations, Professor. But what choice do we have now? This treaty... it's done."

Dr. Goldman sighed deeply, "We've traded our divine inheritance for a seat at the table with The Circle. It's a heavy price, David. Israel's spirit may never be the same."

The professor nodded thoughtfully, "We must pray for guidance and strength. Our nation is venturing into uncharted waters. We have to remember that true peace comes from Jehovah, not from any treaty."

Both men bowed their heads, lost in thought, seeking solace and guidance as the world around them erupted in applause and celebrations.

Amidst the backdrop of a rejuvenated Jerusalem, two seemingly divergent processes were setting in motion a new chapter in Israel's history.

To the north, bus after bus began their scheduled routes, transporting Palestinians to their new homes in southern Lebanon. The air was thick with a mix of emotions: some of resignation, others of hope for a new beginning, and still others of sorrow at leaving ancestral homes. Entire communities were uprooted, their old homes gradually disappearing in the rear-view mirrors of the buses. As the convoy snaked its way through the hilly terrain, children peered out of windows, their eyes wide with curiosity, while the elderly clutched onto memories of a homeland they were leaving behind.

Simultaneously, in Jerusalem, the ancient, revered ground of the Temple Mount underwent a transformation. The remnants of the mosque, which had fallen during the war, were carefully removed, each stone catalogued for potential historical significance. Bulldozers and cranes dotted the landscape, signaling the start of a monumental construction process.

The Temple Institute, together with The Temple Mount organization, had been waiting for this moment for decades.

Blueprints, drawn with painstaking accuracy, were unfurled on makeshift tables. These were not just plans; they were the culmination of years of research, based on ancient texts and archaeological finds. The organizations had even gone so far as to recreate the sacred artifacts necessary for the Third Temple. Goldsmiths had forged the menorah, the seven-branched candelabrum, with pure gold, while craftsmen had sculpted the ceremonial basins and altars.

One of the most notable preparations was the training of the Kohanim, the descendants of Aaron. Young men, identified through rigorous genealogical checks, were being tutored in the rites and ceremonies that were last performed thousands of years ago. In secluded courtyards, these future priests practiced rituals, wearing the intricate, ornate garments specially woven for them.

Around the Temple Mount, a palpable excitement pervaded the atmosphere. Tourists from around the world flocked to the city, each eager to witness the reconstruction of a temple that had been destroyed twice in history. Every day, as the sun set, casting a golden hue over Jerusalem, it illuminated the beginning of an architectural marvel, a symbol of faith that had withstood the test of time.

Israel's ambition to open the Third Temple within a mere seven months of initiating construction was as audacious as it was symbolic. This rapid timeline was set in motion through a highly coordinated approach, combining modern engineering techniques with ancient architectural knowledge.

Pre-fabricated materials, crafted over the years by The Temple Institute in anticipation of this very moment, were swiftly transported to the site, ensuring that construction could proceed without delays.

Around-the-clock shifts, employing thousands of skilled laborers, ensured that work never ceased. Advanced machinery worked alongside artisans specializing in ancient construction methods, bringing together the best of both worlds. The nation's fervor to see the temple rise was matched only by the meticulous precision with which each stone was laid and every ritual artifact positioned. Every step was choreographed to the minutest detail, driven by the collective will of a nation eager to witness the rebirth of a cherished emblem of their faith.

Yet, with every brick laid and every chant practiced, a subtle undercurrent of tension lingered. The reconstruction of the temple was not just a revival of religious fervor; it was a testament to a nation's resilience, its undying faith, and the challenges that lay ahead.

Chapter 45: Executed

The United Nations General Assembly Hall, vast and imposing, was filled to the brim with diplomats and leaders from every corner of the world. Lucien took the center stage, oozing confidence and an unnerving calm. His opening remarks about the peace deal drew applause, but as he transitioned to his criticism of the UN, the atmosphere grew tense.

"Over decades," Lucien stated coldly, "The United Nations, with all its lofty ideals, has failed to deliver on its promises. Wars continue to rage, hunger persists, poverty deepens. Instead of being a beacon of hope, this organization has become an epicenter of bureaucracy and infighting."

Murmurs of dissent spread across the floor. Delegates exchanged uneasy glances, while others openly scoffed at his words. Lucien, however, was unyielding. "The Circle," he continued, "in just a few short months, has achieved more than this institution ever did. We have brought genuine peace and progress."

The murmurs grew louder, escalating into shouts of disagreement. Lucien raised his hand, trying to calm the assembly. "I implore you to think rationally. Join The Circle. Those who join us now will reap the benefits of full membership. The others? Well, let's just say they will have a different status."

Suddenly, Dr. Aria Desai, the UN's Secretary-General, rose from her seat. With a steely glare, she addressed Lucien. "Mr. Morreau, you stand in this hall, a symbol of international cooperation, and spew such threats? The United Nations won't be dissolved by your words. Your hubris is unparalleled."

Lucien smirked, "Secretary-General, I was merely offering a choice. It's clear, however, that my words may not be enough to persuade."

Exiting the hall, Lucien's path was intercepted by Viktor. "It doesn't seem like your speech was well-received," Viktor noted dryly.

Lucien, still smirking, replied, "Perhaps, Viktor, they require a more... tangible demonstration of our resolve."

Viktor signaled discreetly to a group of men positioned nearby. Without hesitation, they pulled out automatic weapons, storming back into the General Assembly hall. As the elevator doors closed behind Lucien, the horrifying symphony of gunshots and screams rang out.

That evening, every major news outlet around the globe led with the same heart-wrenching headline. "Tragedy at the United Nations: Catastrophic Gas Leak Claims Hundreds of Diplomats." Newscasters, their faces a mix of shock and sorrow, reported the unimaginable calamity. Anchors detailed how, during a crucial session, a deadly gas leak had enveloped the General Assembly, snuffing out the lives of representatives from nations far and wide.

Chapter 46: Nexus

The rustic charm of the Greek cafe, even in its dormant state, was undeniable. The musty scent of aged wood melded with the faint traces of Mediterranean spices still lingering in the air. Faded blue and white tiles adorned the floor, and the walls showcased fading photographs of coastal villages, old family portraits, and handwritten notes of thanks from past patrons. The place was steeped in memories, making it an apt rendezvous for the old crew to reassemble.

The soft chime of the entrance bell announced David's arrival, drawing his gaze instantly to Becca and Nadia. The surprise etched on his face was clear. Nadia's deep brown eyes met his, reflecting a fusion of caution and subtle defiance, while Becca's smile, radiant as ever, seemed to lessen the room's shadows.

"We've got the band back together," Becca quipped, her voice tinged with nostalgia and humor.

Clearing her throat, Nadia leaned forward. "You know, The Circle missed a beat," she began, her voice steady. "Their hubris made them blind. They saw only what they wanted, never imagining someone like me could be lurking in the shadows."

David looked puzzled.

Nadia added, "as I looked at the data gathered from The Circle, I saw that when they hired The Wave to hack the Internet, they didn't realize the company outsourced it to me. They don't know who I am, I felt like it was safe to return."

David, moved by the weight of their past ordeals and the sheer joy of seeing Nadia safe, embraced her. "Missed you," he whispered, a sentiment deeply felt but inadequately expressed.

Soon, the cafe's door creaked open again, revealing Mark's familiar earnest face, which appeared momentarily daunted by the magnitude of their mission. A beat later, General Porter entered, his military posture intact, his aura exuding a stoic confidence.

As Becca playfully probed about Porter's secretive skills making sure he wasn't followed, the General's retort was swift, "A Ranger's training doesn't fade. It's muscle memory, just like riding a bike."

Attempting to bring some levity, Mark chipped in, his voice laced with irony, "These cloak and dagger lessons have been enlightening, to say the least. Though, I must admit, I'm a long way off from being a master spy."

Laughter bubbled up among them, albeit briefly. It was a fleeting moment of lightness in the shadow of the mammoth task ahead.

Nadia's slim fingers began tapping on her laptop, bringing up a series of blue-lit screens. "Alright," she began, pushing a strand of her raven-black hair behind her ear. "Here's what we've got."

She pulled up a series of encrypted files on the main screen. "At the core of The Circle's operations is this," pointing at a complex architecture diagram labeled 'Core Nexus.' "It's their central data repository. Everything - their plans, strategies, communications - all of it converges here."

Mark, squinting, leaned forward. "Looks heavily fortified. Multiple firewalls, intrusion detection systems, honeypots, and... are those quantum encryptions?"

Nadia nodded, a grim look on her face. "They're light years ahead. Their tech isn't just state-of-the-art; it's setting the art."

General Porter interjected, "Break it down for us, Nadia. What's our main target and what have we learned?"

Clearing her throat, Nadia powered on the projector. A digital map of the world illuminated on the wall, filled with countless dots representing The Circle's growing influence.

"Every one of these red dots," Nadia began, her voice steady, "represents a militia force loyal to The Circle. From the heart of Europe to remote regions in Africa, they've been systematically amassing forces." As she continued, the green dots popped up, showing the locations of private contractors, and blue ones, indicating nations already co-opted by The Circle.

Mark muttered, "This is far worse than I ever imagined."

Nadia nodded, diving deeper. "These forces are more than just armed personnel. They are being trained to target specific groups of people. They're not just going after what we might expect — extremists or potential threats. They're targeting religious groups, anarchists, any strong proponents for the current world order, and ironically, both far-right and far-left ideologies. Essentially, anyone who doesn't fit into their singular vision for a 'harmonious' world."

Becca's eyes widened, "They're shaping the world's narrative, deciding who gets to have a voice and who doesn't."

David ran a hand through his hair, frustration evident. "It's a sweeping cleanse of any dissidence."

General Porter's face darkened, "So, a totalitarian regime on a global scale."

Nadia clicked to the next slide, revealing an intricate web of financial systems. "And to consolidate their power, they're transitioning the world to a single digital currency – the digital dollar. This isn't just about economic dominance; it's about control. With a single digital currency, they can trace, track, and control every transaction."

Mark leaned in, "Meaning they could shut out anyone they deem unfit from the economy? Make them non-entities?"

"Exactly," Nadia affirmed. "And it doesn't stop there." She clicked again, and the web morphed into a depiction of the world's internet infrastructure. "The Circle is laying the groundwork to control the very fabric of the Internet. They're not just looking to monitor it; they want to own it."

General Porter's voice was grave, "So, in essence, they control the narrative, the finance, and the very means of global communication. They're crafting a cage around the world."

David's gaze met Nadia's, determination burning in his eyes. "Then we've got our work cut out for us. We need to expose them, show the world the prison The Circle is building."

"I know just the person," General Porter said.

Chapter 47: Mr. President

Inside the dimly lit oval office, President Marcus Kellerman sat behind his desk, hands steepled, gaze focused. The amber glow from a solitary lamp painted deep shadows across the room, giving it an air of somber importance. As General Henry Porter stepped inside, he immediately felt the weight of their coming conversation. The door closed with a quiet but definitive thud, signaling their privacy.

"General," President Kellerman began, nodding his acknowledgment. The usual formality between them was underscored by the situation's gravity. "I hope you have something concrete. Rumors about The Circle's intentions have been swirling, but no one has provided any proof."

Porter adjusted his uniform slightly before speaking, "Mr. President, I assure you, this is more than mere rumors." He unrolled a large digital tablet and displayed the map that Nadia had shown earlier, with dots indicating The Circle's growing influences.

Kellerman leaned in, eyes narrowing, "What am I looking at?"

"This," Porter began, "is the network of militia forces loyal to The Circle. Their reach is much more expansive than we anticipated. They're positioning themselves on a global scale, with both private forces and nation-backed troops."

The President frowned, "You're telling me that they've co-opted nation-states into this?"

Porter nodded gravely, "And not just for show. They're actively training these forces to target specific groups, from religious groups to political dissenters on both ends of the spectrum. Their aim is to silence opposition, to mold the narrative as they see fit."

Kellerman's voice rose with disbelief, "This is absurd! And our intelligence agencies have no hint of this?"

"They've been incredibly discreet, and, as you know, their influence runs deep," Porter replied. He then showed the financial systems slide. "To further their control, they're trying to monopolize the world's economic systems through a digital currency. With this, they can monitor, sanction, or incentivize as they see fit."

The President rubbed his temples, clearly feeling the weight of the revelation. "This... is an existential threat."

Porter continued, "There's more, Mr. President. They're not content with controlling just the physical and financial world. They're working on capturing the digital realm as well, planning to control the very backbone of the Internet."

Kellerman stood up abruptly, pacing the length of his office. "How did we let this get so far? How could we have been blind to such a comprehensive takeover?"

General Porter sighed, "Their movements were discreet, their intentions well-masked. But now that we know, we must act."

Kellerman stopped, fixing his gaze on Porter, "Tell me, General, what do you recommend?"

Porter met the President's gaze resolutely, "We need to mobilize. Inform our allies, strengthen our defenses, and get ahead of their narrative. Expose them for what they truly are. We have a window of opportunity, Mr. President, but it's closing fast."

The room was silent for a moment, the weight of decisions yet to be made pressing down. Finally, President Kellerman nodded, "Alright, General. Let's get to work."

Chapter 48: Wired

The evening was settling into its usual rhythm as General Porter returned home after his intense meeting with President Marcus Kellerman. The revelation about The Circle's sinister intentions weighed heavily on him, though sharing the burden with the President had brought a modicum of relief.

Pulling his Cadillac into the garage, Porter exited the vehicle, his steps echoing in the quiet space. Once inside his home, the familiarity of its corners and shadows greeted him. He went to the kitchen, fetched a beer from the refrigerator, and settled into his worn recliner, taking a moment to reflect on the day's events.

But just as he started to let his guard down, a cold wire looped around his neck, pulling taut. Panic and years of military training kicked in. With one hand, he wedged space between the wire and his throat, trying to relieve the pressure. His other hand found the pocket knife he always carried, and he swiftly flicked it open.

Without hesitation, he drove the knife backward, hoping to hit his attacker. He felt the blade sink into flesh and heard a muffled grunt, but the wire only tightened. The General used his weight to push himself and his assailant sideways, sending them crashing into a bookshelf. Books and keepsakes tumbled down, creating chaos and distraction.

In the ensuing struggle, the living room turned into a battleground of shattered glass, upturned furniture, and discarded memories. Porter managed to land several blows on his assailant, each one fueled by adrenaline and desperation. Finally, with one well-aimed thrust of his knife, he pierced a vital spot, causing the attacker to release his grip and stumble backward, collapsing near the fireplace.

But the altercation had taken its toll on the General. Wounded and exhausted, he tried to rise, but his strength failed him. He fell to the floor, the room spinning, each breath more labored than the last. As darkness encroached on his vision, his last thoughts were of the danger that still loomed for those he cared about. Both men lay motionless in the wreckage of a room that had witnessed their final confrontation.

Chapter 49: Discovery

The sun was setting, casting long shadows over the quiet suburban neighborhood. David's heart raced as he parked his car in front of General Porter's house. The sinking feeling in his stomach grew more profound as each second passed without a response from the General.

Sending a quick text to Becca, *He isn't answering his phone or responding to text messages. I'm pulling into his driveway. I'll let you know*, he looked around, checking for any signs of movement or disturbance. Every instinct screamed at him that something was wrong. The absence of noise, the darkened windows, the feeling of foreboding that clung to the air – it all pointed to something seriously wrong.

David didn't trust the President's administration. They seemed to eager to work with The Circle. Too far down the path of joining with the organization. Too trusting of Lucien Morreau.

His hand instinctively moved to the Glock on his hip as he approached the house. The silence was deafening. Without waiting, he knocked, hoping against hope that the General would answer. When no response came, David took a deep breath, steadying himself for what might lie inside.

With one swift, forceful kick, the front door gave way, revealing the dimly lit interior. David's eyes scanned the scene: a toppled bookshelf, shattered glass, and two lifeless bodies. The remnants of a deadly altercation.

His training kicked in. He quickly checked the General for any signs of life, but deep down, he already knew. After confirming the worst, he checked the assailant, ensuring no further threat.

Aware of the ticking clock and the potential for witnesses, David retreated quickly. Once back in his car, he drove away, merging with the flow of traffic, trying to process the gravity of what he had just witnessed.

His phone buzzed with incoming messages. Without hesitation, he texted Becca, Nadia, and Mark, his fingers moving rapidly over the screen, *Need to meet right now. Normal spot. Make sure you're not followed. Bring a go bag.* The game had changed, and they needed to be prepared for what was coming.

Chapter 50: Death

The scent of stale olive oil and herbs lingered in the air as David entered the abandoned Greek cafe. The worn-out blue and white checkered tablecloths still lay draped over a few tables, and the counter still had the residue of ground coffee.

Every instinct David honed over years in the FBI screamed at him to clear the room before his crew arrived. Methodically, he checked the restrooms, the kitchen, and the storage area. The weight of the responsibility bore heavily on him - what if he had inadvertently led everyone into a trap?

The sound of a car pulling up outside interrupted his thoughts. Mark stepped in, his usually jovial demeanor replaced by a grim expression. The brief nod they shared conveyed volumes - both men understood the stakes. Mark took his position by the entrance, scanning the street.

Not long after, Becca and Nadia arrived. Becca's hazel eyes, always sharp and alert, sought out David, her usually composed face marred by worry. Without any preamble, she asked, "What did you find at the General's, David?"

David sighed heavily, pausing a moment before answering. Years of experience at the FBI came back, helping David slow down his heart rate and calmly explain what he saw. "He's been murdered, Becca. There was a struggle. He managed to take out his assassin with him." David recounted the grisly scene he'd discovered - the signs of the fierce struggle and the eerily professional feel of the hit.

Mark's voice was taut with restrained anger. "Do you think the President ordered the hit?"

Nadia's response was swift, her eyes cold. "Whether it was him or one of his cronies, it's clear we can't trust the administration. The lines are drawn now."

David replied, "Not so fast, it could have been The Circle. Or maybe they have someone in the administration. Let's not jump to conclusions that it was the President."

Nadia's voice, thick with emotion, broke through, "They're going to pay for this." A tear trickled down her cheek, her hands clenched in fury.

Becca took a deep breath, her resolve solidifying. "Yes, they will. And we need to decide how."

The revelation of General Porter's death cast a somber shadow over the group. The air was thick with a cocktail of emotions - grief, rage, and a deep-seated anxiety about what lay ahead.

David's voice, steady yet laced with the raw edge of emotion, cut through the silence. "Your homes are off-limits until we ascertain the extent of their knowledge and reach. We can't afford to underestimate them," he declared, his eyes scanning each face - faces of colleagues who had become akin to family.

He turned to Becca, the unspoken question hanging heavily in the air - "Leila?" Every muscle in his body was taut, the protective instinct that had served him well over the years now magnified a hundredfold.

Becca's eyes, though red-rimmed, reflected the unwavering steel of her character. "She's safe. I've arranged for her to be watched. They'll protect her as long as necessary." The definitive assurance in her voice brought a fleeting, albeit significant, comfort.

The cafe, with its stillness interrupted by the occasional distant sound of a car passing by, seemed to encapsulate them in a world far removed from the chaos that awaited outside. Becca's voice, soft yet assertive, broke the silence again. "The owners lived in a small apartment upstairs. It isn't much, but it's secure. We can stay there tonight."

As the group ascended the creaky staircase, each step seemed to echo the gravity of their circumstances. The apartment, though spartan, carried the warmth of the memories of its previous occupants. It was a stark reminder of the world that once was, before the incursion of The Circle's ominous shadow.

David looked around and, sensing the exhaustion and emotional turmoil of his companions, volunteered to stand the first watch. "I'll keep an eye out. You all should try to get some rest." Yet, deep within, he knew the ghost of the evening's revelation would keep sleep at bay. The image of General Porter's lifeless body - a man of honor and integrity reduced to a casualty in a war they were only beginning to comprehend - was etched indelibly in his mind.

The stillness of the night was a stark contrast to the maelstrom of emotions surging within David. With every passing minute, memories of his tumultuous relationship with his biological father flooded his mind. Memories of harsh words exchanged, unmet expectations, and the void that stretched between them. The silence of the apartment seemed to amplify those memories, making them even more potent and painful.

General Porter had been one of the few anchors in his life since 3/16. David recalled the many nights they had sat together, with the General sharing stories of his youth, his time in the service, and the values that had guided him throughout his life. Those conversations had a profound impact on David, helping him navigate through the storm of the past several months.

David remembered a particular night, when they sat under a canopy of stars, the General had spoken of faith, of God's unwavering love, and the redemptive power of Jesus Christ. It was then that David had felt a tugging at his heart, a pull towards something greater, something divine. The General, with his wisdom and kindness, had steered David towards a path of spiritual awakening. He had introduced him to the teachings of Jesus and had been there when David had taken the monumental step of accepting Christ into his heart. It wasn't just mentorship; it was the kind of guiding light one expects from a father.

As the night deepened, anger bubbled up within David. Anger at the injustice of losing such a guiding force in his life. How could The Circle rob the world of a man like General Porter? How could they continue their nefarious activities with such impunity? And how had the world's leaders, including President Kellerman, become so entangled in Lucien Morreau's web?

Each thought stoked the flames of his anger, making them burn brighter and hotter. His fingers clenched tightly around the grip of his gun, a physical manifestation of the raging battle within him. He wanted to scream, to shout, to lash out at the cruel world that had taken so much from him. But he knew that raw emotion wouldn't help them now. He had to be strategic, smart. The Circle was formidable, and he knew that they had to be careful with their next moves.

Drawing a deep breath, David whispered a prayer. He asked God for strength, for wisdom, and for guidance in the days ahead. He prayed for his team, for their safety, and for their resolve. And he prayed for the soul of General Porter, hoping that he was at peace with the Savior they both cherished.

The night stretched before them, pregnant with the unsaid and the unknown. The silence of the cafe below and the occasional distant sounds of the city were a stark backdrop to the tumultuous storm of thoughts raging in David's mind.

Chapter 51: No Sleep

The dim morning light seeped through the gaps in the curtains, casting a grayish hue in the room. The apartment was silent, save for the soft sounds of breathing from the three figures sprawled on various pieces of furniture, exhausted from the emotional and mental strain of the night before.

David, who had been seated by the window, stood up, stretching out his stiff limbs. His gaze settled on the sleeping figures of Becca, Mark, and Nadia. The lines of worry etched on their faces even in slumber were a testament to the tumultuous events of the past few days.

Slowly and quietly, he began gathering his belongings, ensuring he made as little noise as possible. As he was slipping on his jacket, a soft voice pierced the stillness. "Where are you going?"

David turned to see Becca sitting up, searching his face for answers. There was something about the way she looked at him, a mix of concern and something deeper, something he couldn't quite place but felt drawn to. "I'm going back home, and then to work," David replied in a hushed tone, ensuring the others weren't stirred awake.

Becca's blue eyes, which always seemed to see right through him, held his for a moment longer. "But it's too dangerous. After what happened to the General..." Becca's voice trailed off, the weight of the situation evident in her eyes.

David moved closer, kneeling beside her. "I've been thinking about it all night. The best way to protect all of us and to maintain my cover is to act as if nothing has changed. If I disappear or act out of the ordinary, it may draw unwanted attention. They might start connecting the dots."

Becca frowned, clearly not convinced. "David, you saw what they did to General Porter. How can you be sure you'll be safe?"

David took a deep breath. "I can't be, not entirely. But it's the best chance we have. We need someone on the inside. And right now, that's me."

Becca looked down, wrestling with her emotions. She then reached out and took David's hand. "Just promise me you'll be careful. We can't afford to lose you too."

David squeezed her hand reassuringly. "I promise. Besides, I've got a good team watching my back." He glanced over at the still-sleeping figures of Mark and Nadia.

The two shared a long, silent moment, conveying more with their eyes than words ever could. Finally, David stood up, adjusting his jacket. "Take care, Becca. I'll see you soon."

With that, he silently slipped out of the apartment, leaving behind a heavy air of uncertainty, hope, and determination.

Chapter 52: No Faith

T he sleek exterior of The Circle's headquarters gleamed menacingly under the morning sun, its massive structure a testament to the organization's power and reach. David paused for a moment outside the entrance, taking a deep breath to steady his nerves. The events of the last 24 hours played on his mind, but he willed himself to push past the uncertainty.

As David approached the security turnstile, he noticed a few unfamiliar faces among the guards. Their eyes darted around, scanning the employees as they entered. David took extra care to appear nonchalant. He pulled out his ID badge from his pocket and tried to scan it. The scanner emitted a loud beep and flashed red. David's heart raced. Had they discovered him?

A guard, with a stern face and a shaved head, looked at him pointedly. "Problem, Mr. Mitchell?"

"Just a glitch, I guess," David replied, attempting to keep his voice steady. He scanned his badge again. This time, the scanner flashed green, and the turnstile gates opened.

The guard, maintaining his intense gaze, nodded. "Move along."

David nodded, not daring to speak, and quickly made his way to the elevators. As the doors closed behind him, he let out a silent sigh of relief. But the ordeal wasn't over. He was now in the lion's den, and he had to tread carefully.

His office, a minimalist space with a sprawling view of the city, awaited him. Before settling down, David conducted a routine sweep, checking for any bugs or surveillance devices. Finding none, he sank into his chair, his thoughts racing.

The soft rhythmic tapping on David's office door pulled him out of his focused trance. As he turned towards the entrance, the door creaked open slightly, revealing Clara, his admin assistant. She was a petite woman, always neatly dressed, with a sharp wit that was masked by her gentle demeanor.

"David," she began with a slight hesitance, "Lucien has called for an impromptu staff meeting in the assembly hall. Fifteen minutes from now."

David arched an eyebrow, attempting to mask his surprise. "Did he mention what it's about?"

She shook her head, a strand of her neatly pulled back hair coming loose. "No. But there's a buzz around the office. Word is, it's something big. Everyone's been summoned."

David nodded, processing the information. He pondered the possibilities of Lucien's sudden call for a meeting. Was it about the peace treaty? Or had his infiltration been detected?

"Alright, thanks, Clara. Anything else?"

"Oh, one more thing, IT was looking for you and your laptop. They have to update some software, they said it would only take a few minutes."

"Thanks for letting me know, Clara." David began to wonder, *What was IT adding to his laptop?*

"Ok, see you in 15 minutes, David," Clara said as she closed the door behind her.

The excitement in the assembly hall was palpable. Whispers filled the room as staff speculated about the reason for the sudden meeting. As Lucien walked onto the stage, the entire room erupted into applause, a testament to the charismatic power he wielded over The Circle's employees. A few staff members even stood up in admiration, their excitement contagious.

Lucien raised his hand to quell the applause, his characteristic confident smile on display. "Thank you," he began, voice echoing through the vast room. "Thank you for your unwavering dedication and for being an integral part of our vision."

He paused, allowing the weight of the moment to settle. "Each of you," he continued, "from the coders to the strategists, from the diplomats to the security personnel, played a pivotal role in the recent peace treaty signing. Our collective dream of a unified world, free from strife and division, is becoming a reality, and it's thanks to you."

Screens on either side of the stage lit up, showcasing images from the historic event; leaders shaking hands, joyous celebrations in the streets, and the monumental structure of the treaty itself.

He paused, letting his words sink in. The eyes of every staff member were fixed intently on him, hanging on his every word.

"It's easy for the world to look at those treaties and see only the signatures of leaders. But I see the countless nights, the endless hours of work, the sacrifices that all of you have made. It's your diligence, your commitment, your belief in our mission that made this dream a reality."

Murmurs of agreement rippled through the hall. There was a sense of collective pride in the room, a realization of the magnitude of their achievement.

Lucien's voice softened, becoming even more personal. "Many said it was impossible. That a world unified under the banner of peace was a utopian dream. But, in this hall, we dared to dream that dream. And together, we turned it into reality."

The atmosphere in the room was electric, every heart beating in rhythm with Lucien's words. He continued, "The world outside these walls is looking up to us, taking cues from our actions, our decisions. And as we grow, it is paramount that we remember our core values, our commitment to peace and prosperity for all."

Lucien took a deep breath, emotion evident in his eyes. "I want you to remember this moment. Years from now, when peace reigns and the world has changed, remember that it was in rooms like this, with people like you, where it all began."

The applause that followed was even more deafening than before. Lucien's words had inspired and solidified the belief of every individual in that room.

He took a deep breath, "But let this be clear: this treaty is not the end, but the beginning. The beginning of a new era where borders are just lines on a map, where every individual has the right to prosperity, peace, and security."

The ambient chatter of the assembly hall dimmed, as the crowd was drawn into the images unfolding before them on two giant screens on either side of the stage. The visuals of war, the KKK, angry preachers, and protestors were strikingly poignant and effectively conveyed the message Lucien sought to emphasize. Lucien's voice rang out again, filling the vast space with its deep and commanding tone.

"Throughout history, religion has been used as a tool of division and destruction, not just a means of personal salvation or enlightenment," Lucien began. "We've seen holy wars, inquisitions, persecutions, and countless acts of terrorism and hate, all rooted in differing beliefs."

There were murmurs of agreement in the audience, while some appeared to be deep in contemplation.

"From the time of the Crusaders to the modern-day conflicts in the Middle East and beyond, humanity has bled. Not because of our race or nationality, but because of our faith. The burning of witches, the discrimination against non-believers, the extremist acts we've all witnessed - all can be traced back to a singular source: religious fervor."

An image of a bombed church filled the screen, followed by that of a destroyed mosque and then a temple. The sheer destruction made many in the audience shift uncomfortably.

"However, let me be clear," Lucien continued, his eyes piercing into the depths of every individual present. "I am not condemning personal faith. Personal spirituality can be a beacon of hope, a moral compass, guiding individuals towards betterment. What I challenge today is organized religious zeal that seeks to impose its will on others and spread division."

Images of serene landscapes, people laughing, children playing, and communities coming together in harmony started playing, casting a stark contrast to the previous visuals. "But we have a vision," Lucien asserted. "A vision where humanity is united, where we prioritize understanding and collaboration over division and blind belief."

A soft instrumental played in the background, enhancing the atmosphere Lucien was crafting. "The Circle's mission is to pave a path towards a world where peace isn't just a fleeting dream, but an enduring reality. A world where one's personal beliefs don't hinder collective progress."

He stepped closer to the edge of the stage, almost leaning into the crowd. "Today, we are at the crossroads of history. With the peace treaty signed, we have begun rewriting the script of global relations. But to truly change the world, we must address the root cause of much of its strife."

Whispers rippled through the crowd, some nodding in agreement while others shifted uncomfortably in their seats. Lucien, anticipating this, raised a hand for silence. "Each of us has a role to play in this grand design. We are the architects of a new world, and together, we will build it on the foundations of understanding, unity, and most importantly, peace."

The ambient chattering and clapping had died down, and the room was bathed in darkness save for the vivid images playing out on the screen. The powerful visuals resonated with many in the hall, though there were those, like David, who felt a growing unease with each passing second. The juxtaposition of the haunting images of the past with Lucien's stirring oration had a profound impact, creating a charged atmosphere.

Lucien took a deep breath, letting the final image—a smoldering church—linger for a few extra beats. "The common thread through all these tragedies, all this pain, is religion. Centuries of bloodshed, hatred, and division in the name of faith. And today, as The Circle, we say, 'no more.'"

The auditorium echoed with sporadic claps, but a hush rapidly settled as Lucien's gaze hardened, and his words took a more decisive turn. "To realize our vision of lasting peace, prosperity, and unity, we have come to a significant decision. Starting today, organized religion, in all its forms, is banned."

Gasps filled the room. Some looked at each other in shock, while others exchanged wary glances, trying to gauge the room's reaction. A wave of murmurs spread, gaining volume, as Lucien raised his hand, signaling for silence.

David felt a knot in his stomach tighten. The implications of what Lucien was proposing were enormous. Freedom of belief and worship were foundational principles for many cultures and nations. He thought of his own journey of faith and the solace it brought him, especially in recent times.

Lucien continued, "I know this may seem radical, but our purpose is unity. We have seen how religion divides us, how it breeds conflict. As we reshape the world, we cannot carry forward elements that threaten our mission. This is a step towards the future—a world where humanity is the only religion."

Whispers filled the room, a mix of agreement and dissent. It was clear Lucien's declaration was polarizing, but the power he wielded was undeniable.

Lucien gave one last piercing look across the room, his cold eyes locking with David's momentarily, making the latter's blood run cold. "We move forward, together, as one," Lucien declared, ending his speech.

David, feeling a weight like never before, knew that the world had just changed irreversibly. The ramifications of Lucien's announcement would be far-reaching and potentially catastrophic for countless communities. As the crowd started to disperse, discussing Lucien's proclamation in fervent tones, David's mind raced. The Circle's influence had grown exponentially, and this new edict would undoubtedly face resistance. But how to navigate this new world? How to protect those who would suffer from this mandate?

Chapter 53: Terminated

The polished mahogany table glistened under the soft glow of the overhead chandeliers, reflecting the intense expressions of The Circle's executive leaders. Every face around the table showed a varying degree of contemplation, apprehension, or determination.

Lucien stood at the head of the table, his hands clasped behind his back, looking over the group with a mixture of pride and anticipation. "I cannot emphasize enough the importance of our work here. I am genuinely grateful for each one of you. Your dedication, your loyalty to our cause – it has not gone unnoticed."

David, seated third from the left, used his years of undercover experience to keep his expressions neutral. The weight of the announcement still pressed heavily on his mind. He noticed a few others, like Emily from legal and Jacob from operations, showing signs of unease.

Lucien continued, "We are on the precipice of a new world, a world of harmony. The shackles of religious division have held humanity back for too long. Our move today is just the beginning." He paused, allowing the gravity of his words to sink in.

"We've seen the destruction, the chaos brought on by dogmatic beliefs. The Circle aims to unite, to bring peace. Our militia is not just for enforcement; it is a symbol of our commitment to this new world."

Silence filled the room until Mira, head of public relations, interjected, "Lucien, while I understand the sentiment, how do we handle the inevitable backlash?"

Lucien smiled, a confident, knowing smile. "Mira, that's where our new faith system comes into play. We've seen the transformational power of psychedelics, the spiritual experiences they can induce. We'll guide people towards this enlightenment. It will be... liberating."

David fought to keep his face neutral, but internally, alarms blared. The path Lucien was setting them on was a risky one, potentially even more divisive than what they were trying to combat. The very essence of individual faith was at stake.

Lucien seemed to read the room's skepticism. "I know this is a lot to digest, but believe me, the world needs this. The Circle will show them a new way to connect, to find peace. We will replace old rituals with new, enlightened ones."

The room was thick with tension, the silence only interrupted by the soft hum of the air conditioning and the occasional shuffle of papers. Lucien stood tall and imposing at the head of the large, glossy conference table, his piercing eyes darting over each face, studying them.

"We've come so far," Lucien began, his voice cold and steely. "Our vision is unparalleled. But for us to continue, I need unwavering dedication from all of you. We stand at the precipice of a new world order, and any hesitation, any doubt, threatens our mission."

David tried to control his breathing. He had always been cautious, always made sure his doubts were concealed. He felt a bead of sweat form on his forehead.

Lucien continued, "There is a traitor among us. Someone who does not share our vision, who does not believe in our mission."

He suddenly projected an email onto the screen behind him. David skimmed through it, his heart racing. The email detailed concerns about The Circle's approach, particularly the decision to ban religions. It questioned the morality and the potential consequences of such an act.

"This," Lucien's voice trembled with rage, "was sent to several media outlets. It's a gross betrayal."

The room was in shock. Whispers spread like wildfire as the executives exchanged bewildered glances. David tried to look as surprised as everyone else.

Lucien's gaze landed on Jacob, head of operations. "Jacob," he spat out, his voice dripping with venom. "Do you recognize this?"

Jacob, a middle-aged man with greying hair and glasses, paled. He stammered, "Lucien, I... I had concerns. I thought voicing them would be... constructive."

Viktor, a towering figure and Lucien's right-hand man, moved swiftly, grabbing Jacob's arm and pulling him up from his chair. Jacob struggled, looking around desperately for support, but found none.

Someone from the far end of the table, maybe Mira from PR, spoke up hesitantly, "Lucien, what's going to happen to Jacob?"

Lucien looked around the room, a sadistic smile playing on his lips. "His role," he paused, enjoying the weight of his next words, "is being eliminated. As is he."

Gasps echoed around the room. David's heart pounded in his chest, realizing the depth of Lucien's ruthlessness. The message was clear - dissent would not be tolerated.

Chapter 54: Sip

The dimly lit bar was mostly empty, save for a few late-night patrons, the familiar clinks of glasses and murmured conversations filling the space. At the end of the bar, David sat hunched over, his whiskey glass almost empty. The amber liquid shimmered in the dim light, providing him a temporary reprieve from the overwhelming weight on his shoulders.

Madi, the vivacious bartender with a penchant for conversation, leaned in towards him, trying to catch his eye. "You know," she began, her tone teasing, "if you keep looking so glum, I might have to start charging extra for the drinks."

David glanced up, managing a half-hearted smile. "Trust me, Madi," he said, "tonight's tab will more than cover it."

She cocked her head, taking in his weary face. "You don't usually drink like this. Something happen?"

David's gaze drifted to the array of bottles behind the bar, each one promising a different flavor of oblivion. "Just a rough day at work," he replied vaguely.

Madi, not one to be easily deterred, persisted. "You can talk to me, you know. Sometimes it helps."

But David's mind was miles away. Every time he closed his eyes, he tried to picture Lisa's face — the curve of her lips, the twinkle in her eyes — but it was fading, slipping through his fingers like grains of sand. And then there was the weight of General Porter's death, a burden he hadn't anticipated.

His phone buzzed, pulling him back to the present. It was a message from Becca. "David, are you okay? Please, talk to me."

He stared at the message, letting out a sigh. He quickly typed back, "I'm alright, Becca. I'll call you tomorrow. Promise."

Setting the phone down, he motioned for Madi to refill his glass. He wanted nothing more than to drown the chaos in his mind, to escape from the guilt and pain that threatened to consume him. And tonight, in this quiet bar with a comforting bartender, David sought solace at the bottom of a whiskey glass.

Chapter 55: Concede

The abrupt pounding on the door echoed through David's dimly lit apartment. The room was a mess, with empty bottles strewn across the table and last night's clothes discarded on the floor. He'd slept in his jeans on the couch, his pounding head a testament to the alcohol he had consumed the night before.

Grumbling under his breath, David got to his feet, grabbing his Glock from the coffee table and holding it behind his back as he approached the door. The incessant knocking continued, making David's headache even more pronounced. Taking a deep breath and steeling himself, he opened the door.

There stood Mark, his expression a mix of concern and frustration. "Man, you look like hell," Mark remarked, taking in David's disheveled appearance.

"Thanks for the pep talk," David muttered sarcastically. "Come in."

As Mark stepped inside, he took a moment to survey the apartment, his nose wrinkling at the stale smell of alcohol. David shuffled awkwardly, suddenly feeling very self-conscious. "Want something to drink?" he offered, even though he already knew the answer. "All I've got is cold beer."

Mark waved away the offer, his gaze fixed firmly on David. "What's going on with you? I thought you gave up the bottle."

David sank into a chair, the weight of recent events pressing down on him. "What does it even matter anymore, Mark?"

Mark took a deep breath, choosing his words carefully. "David, you need to pull yourself together. We need you. You can't just drown your sorrows and pretend everything's okay."

David scoffed, his voice laced with bitterness. "Easy for you to say."

Mark sat down opposite David, leaning in. "Listen," he said, "you need to come and talk to everyone. They're worried sick. Plus, there's something else we need to discuss."

David looked up, his interest piqued. "What's that?"

Mark hesitated, "It's better if you hear it from everyone. But you need to be there, David. Pull yourself together. We're in this together."

The sound of water pelting against the tiles of his shower brought some temporary solace to David, helping him wash away the alcohol-induced stupor from the previous night. He dressed hastily, choosing a casual button-down shirt and jeans. As he looked in the mirror, the weight of everything he had been through made him appear older than his years.

Mark waited patiently in the living room, his posture rigid with unease. The pair exchanged a brief nod before making their way to the car.

The drive to the cafe was silent. David's mind raced, sorting through the events and deciding how best to relay them to the team. The abandoned Greek cafe came into view, its rustic charm hidden by years of neglect.

Upon entering, the familiar sight of Nadia and Becca was a relief. Becca's face was etched with concern, and Nadia's usually fierce demeanor had softened. They sat at their usual spot, the worn wooden table scarred with years of clandestine meetings.

"David," Becca greeted softly, her voice filled with relief.

David took a deep breath and began. "Lucien held a meeting today," he began, his voice measured. "He intends to ban all religions and replace them with a singular faith system."

Nadia's eyes widened, "What? How can he even suggest such a thing?"

David continued, "It's not just a suggestion. He's pushing for it. And it doesn't stop there. This new faith system? It's based on psychedelics."

Becca shook her head in disbelief, "It's brainwashing on a global scale."

The room went silent as they processed this information. David looked at the faces of his team, seeing the shock and anger reflected in their eyes. He took another deep breath, "That's not all. Our head of operations tried to leak information to the press about The Circle's plans. His name was Jacob."

"Was?" Nadia echoed, confusion evident in her voice.

David nodded, his expression grave. "Lucien found out. He had Jacob pulled out of a leadership meeting and, in front of everyone, he proudly boasted about having him killed."

The weight of David's revelation hung heavily in the air. Mark finally broke the silence, "We're in more danger than we ever realized. Lucien and The Circle are ruthlessly eliminating anyone they see as a threat. We need to tread carefully."

The team sat in somber silence, each person grappling with the reality of the situation. The world they knew was rapidly changing, and they were caught in the crosshairs of a dangerous power play.

The dim lighting of the cafe reflected off the table, painting a somber atmosphere that matched the heavy hearts of those gathered around. David's voice, normally filled with conviction and determination, wavered with doubt.

"Maybe I should just quit The Circle," he muttered, avoiding the eyes of his friends. "Maybe we should all go into hiding. Lay low. Disappear."

His words were met with silence. The atmosphere grew even more tense, the weight of the situation evident in the air.

Mark shifted uncomfortably in his seat, his gaze focused on a distant point on the floor. Becca clasped her hands tightly, her knuckles white. Nadia, always so fierce and defiant, looked lost.

"How do we even have a chance against The Circle?" David continued, his voice filled with desperation. "They have spies everywhere. Militias in every corner of the world. It feels like we're just pawns in their game. At this rate, we're all just going to end up dead."

His words resonated with the group, echoing their own fears and doubts. For a long while, no one spoke. The silence was deafening.

Becca finally took a deep breath, her voice soft but firm, "David, I get it. It's overwhelming. But we can't just give up. We've come so far."

David looked at her, his eyes brimming with tears. "I don't know if I can do this, Becca. I don't know if any of us can."

Nadia reached out, placing a comforting hand on David's. "We're all scared, David. But we have to stick together. We can't let them win."

David closed his eyes, taking a moment to gather his thoughts. When he finally spoke, his voice was filled with raw emotion. "I'm sorry. I'm just...I'm tired."

The group sat together, each lost in their own thoughts, drawing comfort from their collective presence. The weight of the situation was immense, but they had each other. And for now, that was enough.

Chapter 56: Domestic Agency

The stark white walls of the CIA headquarters seemed even colder than usual as Becca walked down the corridor to the meeting room. The apprehension in the pit of her stomach wasn't just because of the sudden summons, but because of the unfamiliarity of the venue she was being led to. Rarely did meetings occur in these secluded rooms, unless they were of utmost importance and secrecy.

Upon entering, she was met with a cold, businesslike atmosphere. The room was furnished with a large wooden table, which was currently occupied by a few familiar faces, including her case agent, Martin, and some she didn't recognize. At the head of the table was a man with graying hair and a stiff posture, who Becca knew to be Director Ames.

"Agent Lawrence," Director Ames greeted, his tone formal. "Take a seat."

After the brief exchange of nods, Martin slid a thin file across the table towards her. It was marked confidential, and the name on the cover read: *Felix Hayes.*

"This is your new assignment," Martin began, his tone steady. "We want you to monitor Representative Felix Hayes."

Becca's eyes widened in disbelief. "Hayes? Why him? Isn't he...?"

"The Majority Leader of the US House of Representatives, yes," Martin interrupted. "Also an outspoken critic of The Circle and President Kellerman."

"But the CIA doesn't operate on US soil, especially not against our own elected leaders," Becca protested.

"That's the usual protocol," Director Ames interjected, "but Hayes is currently under investigation by the FBI for espionage. This case is attached to the domestic agency, which gives us the necessary jurisdiction."

Becca looked from one face to another, her mind racing. "Why me? Why not leave it to the FBI?"

Martin leaned forward, his eyes locked onto hers. "Hayes has connections, both here and abroad. We believe you're the best person for this job, given your background and expertise."

Becca took a deep breath, processing the information. She felt trapped, caught in a web of politics and espionage that she hadn't anticipated.

"I'll need full access," she said finally. "Details on his known associates, any wiretaps, surveillance footage. Everything."

"You'll get what you need," Director Ames assured her. "This is of paramount importance to national security."

Becca nodded, the weight of the assignment pressing on her. "I'll get it done."

The dim light from Becca's desk lamp created soft shadows on the worn, yellow pages of the file before her. She had pored over every piece of information, every transcript, and every photograph several times, looking for a hint, a clue, that might justify the investigation on Felix Hayes. But, each pass left her more convinced than before – this wasn't an investigation, it was a witch hunt.

"Damn politics," she muttered under her breath, frustration evident in her voice.

The sudden ring of her office phone startled her. Glancing at the caller ID, she saw it was Martin.

"Becca," Martin's voice crackled through the line, urgency evident in his tone. "We've got intel that Hayes is meeting with a foreign agent tonight. I've got a suite set up across the street for surveillance. I need you there."

She stiffened. "A foreign agent? Do we know who?"

"No," Martin admitted, "but our sources are reliable. This could be the break we need to validate the investigation. You in?"

Becca hesitated, torn. On one hand, this could vindicate her belief in Hayes' innocence. On the other, it could lead them down an even darker path.

"I'll be there," she finally replied, determination in her voice.

Chapter 57: Stakeout

The surveillance suite was dimly lit. Soft murmurs and the occasional beep of equipment filled the air. She saw two scopes aimed at a hotel room across the street. As Becca entered, she immediately recognized Jake and Carla, two CIA agents she'd been paired with on previous assignments. Both of them looked more tense than she remembered.

However, it was the presence of two unfamiliar figures that piqued her curiosity. Both of them were dressed in crisp suits – the man, tall with a sharp jawline, and the woman, slightly shorter with piercing green eyes. Their demeanor was notably different from the usual agents Becca had encountered. There was an aloofness, an air of mystery around them.

Jake noticed Becca's gaze fixed on the two strangers. "Becca," he began, nodding in their direction, "let me introduce you to—"

But before he could finish, the male stranger interrupted. "It's best if you just know that we're from a *different* agency," he said, his voice smooth yet commanding.

The woman simply nodded in agreement, her gaze unwavering.

Carla, always the diplomat, attempted to ease the tension. "We're all here for the same reason, right? Let's focus on the task at hand."

Felix Hayes seemed uneasy, frequently checking his watch. When the door finally opened, and a hooded figure stepped inside, the room's energy shifted palpably. The agents watched with bated breath as Hayes and the mysterious visitor exchanged words, their conversation muffled by the distance and the thick walls of the suite.

"I can't get a clear visual on the foreign agent," one of the agents said, frustration evident. "And the audio is too distorted."

Jake turned to Becca. "What do you think?"

Becca frowned, deep in thought. "Not much to see here," she replied cautiously. "It's just a meeting. We're not even sure who he's meeting with."

The tense atmosphere in the surveillance suite had reached a palpable crescendo. The silence was disrupted only by the low buzz of the monitors and the sudden chirping of a phone. The taller stranger pulled out a sleek black device, answering the call swiftly. He listened intently, occasionally nodding, offering a sharp "Understood," or "Affirmative."

Once the call ended, his demeanor shifted – from professional detachment to rigid authority. "It's time for you to leave," he instructed, his voice devoid of any emotion.

His female counterpart swiftly began assembling a high-powered rifle with expert precision. Her movements were methodical, each piece clicking into place effortlessly.

Becca, her instincts on high alert, immediately confronted him, "What are you planning to do?"

He met her gaze, coldly reiterating, "Your assignment here is over. You need to leave, now."

Carla's phone vibrated, drawing her attention. Glancing at the message, she whispered to Becca, "We're being ordered to stand down."

Becca's disbelief was evident. "I haven't received any such order," she retorted. The tension in the room heightened as she swiftly unholstered her gun, aiming it at the duo. "I need you to stop what you're doing."

Almost simultaneously, the male agent drew his own pistol, leveling it at Becca with deadly precision.

Jake and Carla, sensing the imminent danger, quickly drew their own weapons, pointing them at the unknown agents, resulting in a nail-biting standoff. The room was a pressure cooker, with four guns drawn, each agent waiting for the other to make a move.

Carla, attempting to defuse the situation, broke the silence, "We're all on the same side here. Let's not do something we'll regret."

The female agent, while continuing her assembly, remarked coldly, "We have our orders. And so do you."

The tension in the room grew as Becca met the mysterious agent's gaze. "I'm not leaving until that rifle is disassembled. And I won't let you endanger Hayes or anyone else," she asserted, her voice steely.

"You're in over your head, Agent Lawrence," the agent said in a calm manner.

Without missing a beat, Becca responded, "Been there before." In a swift move, she fired at the window of the suite, shattering the glass. Another bullet went straight into the window across the street, causing chaos and forcing Hayes and his guest to escape.

With the situation across the street momentarily diffused, Becca turned her attention back to the two agents. "Your move."

The first agent, realizing they were at an impasse, lowered his weapon. The second agent swiftly started to disassemble the rifle, her eyes never leaving Becca's. As they exited, the first agent paused, "Pleasure meeting you, Agent Lawrence. Give my regards to Leila."

Becca's heart skipped a beat. How did he know about her daughter? She watched them leave.

"We need to get out of here." With that, the three CIA agents quickly exited the suite and the hotel.

Chapter 58: Released

B ack at CIA headquarters, Becca felt the weight of the day's events bearing down on her. She had expected retribution, a harsh reprimand, or at the very least an urgent summons to the director's office. But the halls were silent, and her phone remained eerily quiet.

She finally broke the silence, dialing Martin's extension. "Martin, it's Becca."

There was a pause on the other end. "You're off the Hayes case," he said tersely.

She took a deep breath. "And what's happening with Hayes?"

"That's not your concern anymore. The order's from the top." Martin's voice was cold, detached.

Becca's mind raced. She knew the implications. The fact that she was being kept in the dark wasn't a good sign. She thought of all the late nights, the undercover operations, the sacrifices she'd made for the agency, and felt a pang of bitterness.

She looked around her office, filled with plaques, commendations, and memories of past missions.

Becca hung up, her thoughts heavy. She had joined the agency with a clear sense of purpose, a burning desire to protect her country. But now, she felt lost amidst the shifting sands of political agendas and global conspiracies. The realization dawned on her: perhaps her time at the CIA was coming to an end. But if not here, then where did she belong?

Chapter 59: Fellowship

D avid and Becca walked up to the nondescript building in Arlington, Virginia. Mark was leaning against the building. David joked, "Is there some sort of suburban criminal racket that you need a washed-out former FBI agent and the CIA's best undercover agent to help you break apart?"

"No," Mark said, "Something much better than that."

The dim lighting from the entrance barely reached the bottom of the stairs. As David, Becca, and Mark descended, the atmosphere grew colder and more mysterious. At the bottom, the gruff guard looked them up and down, his face barely illuminated.

"You sure about them?" the guard grunted, his eyes narrowing on Becca.

"They're with me," Mark replied with a reassuring nod.

The guard hesitated for a moment before unlatching the heavy door and swinging it open. As it did, the stark contrast between the black-walled room and the next was striking.

David and Becca exchanged a surprised look as they walked through a thick curtain and into a room filled with a vibrant congregation. The once-old dance club, with its mirrored walls and disco ball still hanging from the ceiling, was alive with the sounds of worship. Rows of folding chairs had been set up, and people of all ages were clapping, singing, and dancing to the praise music.

"It's... a church?" Becca asked, her eyes wide in amazement.

Mark smiled, "A safe haven for believers."

As they made their way through the crowd, a tall man with a shaved head and tattoos down both arms approached them. He wore a warm smile and a cross pendant around his neck.

"Mark!" he exclaimed, embracing him. "Glad you could make it. Who are your friends?"

"Becca, David, meet Chaz," Mark said, gesturing to the man. "He's the heart and soul of this place."

Chaz shook their hands warmly. "It's an honor to meet you both. This church is a testament to the resilient faith of its members. In these times, having a place free from prying eyes where we can worship is more valuable than ever."

David looked around, moved by the community's strength and commitment. "It's incredible what you've created here, Chaz."

Chaz nodded. "It's not just me. It's everyone here, coming together, supporting each other, and keeping the faith alive."

Becca added, "In times of darkness, it's places like this that bring hope."

Chaz smiled, "That's the idea. Welcome to our family. We call ourselves The Fellowship."

After a couple of worship songs and prayer time, the room settled into an anticipatory hush as Chaz made his way to the front. The dim, ambient lights from the old club danced around the room, casting a soft glow on the faces of the gathered congregation.

Chaz paused, taking a moment to scan the room, making a silent connection with many of the eyes that met his. He then began, "The prophet Jeremiah wrote a letter to the people of Israel when they were living in exile in Babylon. It wasn't the message they were expecting."

He projected a scripture onto a screen behind him. "Jeremiah 29:4-7 says, 'This is what the Lord Almighty, the God of Israel, says to all those I carried into exile from Jerusalem to Babylon: Build houses and settle down; plant gardens and eat what they produce. Marry and have sons and daughters; find wives for your sons and give your daughters in marriage, so that they too may have sons and daughters. Increase in number there; do not decrease. Also, seek the peace and prosperity of the city to which I have carried you into exile. Pray to the Lord for it, because if it prospers, you too will prosper.'"

He paused, letting the words sink in. "We live in a time of spiritual exile," Chaz continued. "We feel the weight of a society shifting away from the foundational truths we hold dear. But just like the Israelites in Babylon, we are not called to retreat or abandon our mission. We are called to engage, to build, to plant, to marry, to seek the welfare of the place God has put us."

The room was silent, punctuated only by the occasional murmur of agreement or a softly uttered 'Amen'.

"We might feel out of place," Chaz continued, his voice rising with passion, "but we are right where God wants us to be. Our exile is not a punishment, but an opportunity. An opportunity to be a light in the darkness, to show love where there is hate, and to bring hope where there is despair."

He paused again, letting the weight of his words hang in the air. "Let us not grow weary in doing good, for in due season, we will reap if we do not give up."

Chaz's words struck a chord with many in the room. As he closed in prayer, there was a palpable sense of renewed determination and purpose among the congregation. They may have been living in a time of exile, but they were not alone, and they were not defeated.

The service ended and the last attendees milled around until Chaz encouraged them to head home. The faint hum of the old club's air conditioning was the only sound as the remaining five people settled into a semi-circle of old, mismatched chairs. The air was thick with the weight of the evening's worship and the message that had been delivered.

Chaz leaned forward, hands clasped, elbows resting on his knees. "I know it might sound crazy to some, but with everything that's been happening, especially with the peace treaty... I believe we're in the Tribulation. The signs are all there."

Anthony, an older man with silver hair and deep, thoughtful eyes, nodded in agreement. "I've been studying eschatology for years," he began. "The patterns, the prophecies, they're all lining up. Israel, always a focal point in end times prophecies, has signed this peace treaty. And with the rise of The Circle and their anti-religious sentiment... it's like we're seeing the pages of Revelation come to life."

Mark interjected, "And with that treaty, it's like the world's been given a false sense of security. But we know it's just the calm before the storm."

David, ever the analyst, responded, "But there's always been conflict, rumors of wars, natural disasters. What makes now any different?"

Becca, her face pensive, replied, "The scale, David. The global unity against religion, the push for a single economy, the technological advances that make things like the Mark of the Beast feasible... it's all converging."

Chaz took a deep breath, "We need to be prepared. Not just physically, but spiritually. This is going to be a time of testing like the church has never seen before."

Anthony placed a comforting hand on Chaz's shoulder, "But we also know how the story ends. It's our job to keep the faith, to support one another, and to spread the message of hope."

Chaz's eyes clouded with distant memories as he began to share his story. "You know," he began softly, "I was one of those kids who grew up in the church. Sunday School, youth group, the whole shebang. But when I hit my teenage years, I rebelled, hard. I wanted to experience the world, to feel freedom without the constraints of religion."

Mark, David, and Becca exchanged glances, each recalling their own stories, the unique paths that had led them to this underground sanctuary.

"I remember that day so vividly," Chaz continued, his voice cracking with emotion. "3/16. People I'd known my whole life, good people, just... died. My parents, my little sister, friends from my childhood. Gone. The world plunged into chaos. The realization hit me like a brick wall; the rapture had happened, and I was left behind."

He paused, swallowing hard. "The guilt, the regret, it was overwhelming. I thought of ending it all. But," he lifted his head, determination gleaming in his eyes, "God had other plans for me. In my darkest moment, He reached out. It wasn't a grand vision or a booming voice from the heavens. It was a gentle whisper, a nudge, a feeling deep down that there was still hope."

Becca, her eyes moist, whispered, "The transformative power of His love."

Chaz nodded, "Exactly. He saved me, not just spiritually, but physically too. And now, every day, I wake up with this burning passion to share His message. The world may be in turmoil, but it's also ripe for harvest. There are so many lost souls out there, searching for meaning, for hope. And we have the answer."

Anthony added, "And this place, this underground church, it's our base. A beacon of light in a world that's growing darker by the day."

David, ever pragmatic, mused, "But we have to be careful. The Circle is growing stronger, and we're prime targets."

Chaz met David's gaze. "I know the risks. But this mission, it's worth it. Because every soul we bring to Christ is one more victory against the darkness."

David took a deep breath. "There's something I need to share, something Becca and Mark are already aware of, but it's important you both know as well. I work for The Circle."

Chaz and Anthony exchanged glances, their expressions unreadable. The weight of the revelation hung heavy in the air. The Circle was the very antithesis of everything they stood for.

David continued, "I joined them in the beginning when their intentions seemed noble. Peace was the goal, and with my past experience in the FBI, I thought I could contribute to a better world. But over time, I've come to see their true colors."

Becca interjected, "David's been our inside man. He's been risking his life every day to provide intel on The Circle's plans."

Mark added, "And he's been instrumental in helping us avoid their surveillance and traps."

Chaz leaned forward, eyes sharp, "How deep are you in? Do they suspect anything?"

David shook his head, "I've been careful, covering my tracks. I've had to make some... difficult decisions to maintain my cover. Every day, I walk a tightrope."

Anthony looked contemplative. "We knew they were powerful, and their reach was vast. But to have someone on the inside, that's a game-changer. David, know that we are with you, praying for your safety and guidance."

Chaz nodded in agreement, "God has placed you in a unique position, David. You have a purpose, and while the path is perilous, you're not walking it alone."

Chapter 60: Lies

"Let's begin, Mr. Mitchell," she said, her voice devoid of emotion. "Are you David Mitchell?"

"Yes," David responded calmly, trying to keep his breathing even.

David was strapped to a chair, electrodes attached to his fingers and chest. Across the table sat a stern-faced woman, a polygraph machine by her side, its needle dancing over the paper with every heartbeat. Her cold, piercing gaze fixed on David, creating an atmosphere of intimidation.

"Are you currently the International Director of Security for The Circle?" she continued.

"Yes," David answered, doing his best to maintain his composure.

The polygraph needle danced a little, but then steadied.

"Are you a woman?" she asked.

David looked at her side-eyed, but knew this was just to try to catch him off guard. He replied "No."

The needle reacted in the same manner as before.

The interrogator leaned forward, her gaze becoming more intense. "Now, Mr. Mitchell, let's get to the crux of the matter. Were you aware of a recent hack where a video of Lucien Morreau was leaked on the Internet?"

David's heartbeat raced a little faster, but he tried to remain calm. "Yes, I am aware of it."

The polygraph needle made a slight jump but steadied itself quickly.

The woman's eyes seemed to pierce deeper into David's. "Did you have any involvement in the leak of this video?"

"No," David replied firmly.

The needle barely jumped.

"Have you ever shared confidential or compromising information about The Circle or Lucien Morreau to any external sources?" she pressed on.

"No," David reiterated.

Again, the needle barely jumped.

The interrogator leaned back and asked a final question. "Are you a Christian?"

The needle jumped slightly. David wasn't expecting the question but maintained a peaceful and serene landscape in his imagination. Throughout the interrogation, David had pictured himself at an old cabin he frequented as a teenager in the Catskill Mountains. It was the most peaceful part of his teenage years.

He replied firmly, "No."

The interrogator leaned back, studying the polygraph readings. "Mr. Mitchell, on behalf of The Circle and Mr. Morreau, I'd like to thank you for taking the time to answer our questions today. As you know, finding and eliminating the source of these leaks is vital to the mission of The Circle. As our head of International Security, it'd have been quite embarrassing for us to find out you're the mole, wouldn't it?"

She let out a little laugh, the first time her gruff personality had broken into something a little more personable.

"I can imagine. If you're done, I'd like to get back to work tracking this leak down."

"Of course," she replied.

The door to David's office was slightly ajar.

As he pushed the door open, he saw Lucien and Viktor helping themselves to a glass of his 30-year-old whiskey while they shared a laugh about something.

"David," Lucien began with a smile that didn't quite reach his eyes, "I'm so glad you're here." He stood up, opening his arms and embracing David. David felt a chill run down his spine but forced himself to remain calm.

"You know, I've always had a great deal of trust in you," Lucien exclaimed while grabbing both of his hands. "You know, when I was in the Belgium Special Forces Group as a young man, they called me the 'human lie detector.' In Desert Storm, I successfully interrogated three Revolutionary Guard officers by just feeling their heart rate and observing their breathing."

He looked at David intently, still holding his hands, and asked, "David, are you a spy?" He held his gaze there until he and Viktor cracked up laughing.

Lucien motioned to the chair opposite him. "Please, sit."

Viktor, who had remained silent up until now, finally spoke, "The video leak has caused considerable damage. It's tarnished our reputation and made our mission harder."

David nodded, "I'm aware. And I'm ready to do whatever it takes to identify the person or persons responsible."

Lucien leaned forward, placing both hands on the desk. "David, this is of the utmost importance. We cannot have further breaches. Our unity, our vision for a new world is at stake."

David straightened up, "What's the plan, Lucien?"

Lucien took a deep breath, "We need to go through every employee's records, cross-reference them with possible affiliations that could hint at a motive to leak the video. We need surveillance on key personnel, and we need a team that can discreetly monitor online activity."

David felt the gravity of the situation. "I'll assemble a team immediately. We'll start with the IT and Communications departments. If there's a trail, we'll find it."

Viktor added, "And when we do, they will be dealt with. Severely."

David met Viktor's gaze, recognizing the cold determination in his eyes. "Understood."

Lucien stood up, signaling the end of the meeting. "David, we've placed immense trust in you. Do not let us down."

David nodded, "I won't, Lucien."

As Lucien and Viktor left the office, David took a deep breath, relaxing his muscles. *Why did I agree to do this?*

Chapter 61: The Recording

A week ago

B ecca, still processing the information, leaned forward, her voice laced with disbelief. "So you're telling me, Lucien sat in a room full of executives and openly ridiculed the Israelis?"

David nodded, "He didn't hold back. He went on and on about how 'pathetic' and 'feeble' they were. Said they owe everything to The Circle. That without us, they'd still be struggling, forever caught in their petty skirmishes. He probably spent five minutes talking about how Katz is always calling to ask for permission to do anything. He remarked that Katz doesn't even take a crap without checking in with The Circle first. But the worst parts were the terrible things he said about the Jewish people."

Mark's face contorted with anger. "The audacity! After everything they've been through? I wish we had video evidence of this. It would be the perfect ammunition against Lucien and The Circle."

David glanced around, then gave a sly smile. "Funny you should mention that..."

Nadia, quick to pick up on David's hint, gasped, "You recorded the meeting, didn't you?"

David shook his head, smirking, "Not me. But Janice did. She always records when she's on a video conference for notes later. And since she was attending virtually..."

Becca let out a triumphant laugh, "So we have Lucien on tape, disparaging an entire nation and its people. This is gold!"

David raised a finger, cautioning them, "It won't be easy getting that footage. Janice's files are encrypted and stored in a secure server."

Mark, always the problem solver, said, "We have Nadia. And if anyone can crack into a system, it's her."

Nadia added, "It's a lot easier than that. Those files get recorded locally. They're on Janice's laptop. We just need to break into that, download the video, and put it on the Internet."

Nadia sat hunched over her keyboard, her fingers moving rapidly.

David and Becca sat on a nearby couch, anxiously watching her progress, their eyes darting between Nadia and the screen.

"Okay, I'm in her Wi-Fi network," Nadia murmured, her tone neutral but focused.

Becca leaned forward, "That was fast."

Nadia smirked without looking up, "It's a basic home network. Nothing fancy."

"Elementary question, but this can't be traced back to you?" David asked.

"You think I'm a noob? First off, I'm using a VPN that hops to a different server every ten minutes. Second, I hacked into some unpatched servers and infiltrated from them. When I'm done, I'll wipe the servers clean and there won't be a record of this ever happening."

"Got it. What's next?"

Nadia replied, "Now, I get into her laptop. That's where she would've stored the video."

Every so often, an encrypted line would turn green, signaling Nadia's successful bypassing.

Minutes felt like hours. Then, suddenly, a folder icon appeared on the screen, labeled 'Meeting Videos.'

"We're in," Nadia whispered, a hint of triumph in her voice.

David let out a sigh of relief. "Find the one from the meeting with Lucien."

Nadia quickly skimmed through the list of video files, selecting one with the date of the meeting. "Ok, I'm going to upload this directly to several file-sharing sites from her laptop so there's no tracing it back to anyone else. If they track it down, it will look like Janice uploaded it."

The city of Jerusalem was a hive of activity, the streets echoing with outrage and disbelief. TV screens in shop windows broadcast Lucien's incendiary comments on a loop. Every word, every sneer seemed to amplify the indignation. From young students to elderly residents, every Israeli felt the sting of betrayal.

There were signs of unrest and protest everywhere.

The few remaining newspapers not controlled by The Circle displayed blaring headlines condemning Lucien and Prime Minister Katz. Crowds gathered at Rabin Square in Tel Aviv, holding banners that criticized the alliance with The Circle and demanded Katz's resignation.

The uproar wasn't just confined to the streets. Social media was abuzz with debates, commentaries, and calls to action. Influential leaders from various sectors, including business, academia, and the arts, publicly condemned Katz's association with The Circle. University students organized rallies, and artists painted murals capturing the national sentiment.

Within forty-eight hours, the relentless pressure bore fruit. A beleaguered Katz appeared on national television announcing his resignation. The video of Lucien had not just toppled a Prime Minister; it had exposed the vulnerability of The Circle's vast empire.

From their vantage point, David, Becca, and Nadia could sense the shifting sands. The release of the video had sparked a national, and potentially global, reevaluation of The Circle's intentions. The streets of Jerusalem, usually resonant with history and faith, were now also channels of political upheaval and resistance.

Lucien's palatial office, adorned with contemporary art and the emblem of The Circle, was buzzing with an unprecedented sense of urgency. His massive desk, usually the place where he made deals that altered the destinies of nations, was now a battleground. Papers were strewn around, and multiple screens streamed news broadcasts from across the globe.

His closest advisors, all dressed sharply, were huddled together, discussing strategies and damage control. Viktor, his most trusted aide, stood to the side, making a series of urgent calls.

"I don't get it!" Lucien thundered, his blue eyes darting with fury. "They were mere jests! How can the world blow it out of proportion?"

His advisor, Helena, hesitated before speaking, "Sir, in the age of information, nothing remains confined. The comments, however unintentional, have hit a raw nerve. The sentiment on the ground was already simmering; this video was just the catalyst."

Viktor disconnected his call and chimed in, "We are also getting intelligence that certain factions are using this opportunity to rally against us. It's not just Israel; the resentment is snowballing globally."

Lucien paced the room, his tall stature casting a shadow over the elegant décor. "Find the leaker. I want them found and brought to justice. No one undermines The Circle."

His head of IT security, Jim, stepped forward, nodding. "We have already begun tracing the origin of the leak. Every person who had access to the video conference will be scrutinized."

"And what about the Israeli Prime Minister?" Lucien inquired, narrowing his gaze.

"He's resigned, under immense pressure," Helena updated, "Israel is in political chaos."

Lucien paused, the weight of the moment evident. "I underestimated the sentiments of the people. This needs to be handled. Quickly and discreetly."

Viktor moved closer, his voice low, "Lucien, this might be bigger than we imagined. We should be prepared for all eventualities."

Lucien sighed, "Just find me that mole."

Viktor replied, "We're having everyone take a polygraph. Starting with our leadership team, today."

David perked up when he heard that comment.

The room buzzed into action, everyone understanding the urgency. The Circle, which always seemed unshakeable, was now at the precipice of a crisis, and Lucien felt the weight of the world he tried to control pressing down on him.

Chapter 62: Shots Fired

The majestic backdrop of the Colosseum was stark in contrast to the scene unfolding before it. Thousands had gathered in Rome, holding signs and chanting slogans that called for the removal of The Circle and the restoration of Italy's sovereignty. The cobblestoned streets were awash with a sea of humanity: young students, elderly couples, workers, mothers holding their children's hands, priests, nuns, and even some tourists who felt moved by the energy of the crowd.

The atmosphere, while charged, had remained peaceful. Speakers took turns addressing the crowd from a makeshift platform, each echoing the sentiments of freedom and self-determination.

However, as the day wore on, armored vehicles rolled in, surrounding the protesters. The local militia, armed and faceless behind their riot helmets, began to encircle the crowd. A loudspeaker blared, asking the protestors to disperse, but their response was to sing their national anthem louder.

Suddenly, without provocation, a militia officer struck a protester with a baton. The man, an elderly gentleman holding a simple placard, crumpled to the ground, blood oozing from a gash on his forehead. The crowd erupted in anger. More militia moved in, batons swinging. Screams pierced the air as more and more protesters were beaten.

A young woman, Martina, quickly began filming the brutality. Around her, chaos ensued as unarmed protestors tried to defend themselves using whatever they had - signs, water bottles, even their own fists.

Without warning, the unmistakable sound of gunfire echoed through the streets. Bodies fell, cries of horror and grief rose, and the once peaceful protest transformed into a battleground.

Martina, shaky hands still holding her phone, captured it all. The raw, unfiltered brutality of a regime against its own people. She managed to send her video to several contacts before being chased down an alleyway.

Within minutes, the video began appearing on social media platforms. Despite immediate removals citing "disinformation," it was too late. The video had been downloaded, shared, mirrored, and re-uploaded thousands of times. Alternative platforms, direct messaging, encrypted chats – every means was used to circulate the footage.

The repercussions were immediate and global. Major cities - Paris, Berlin, New York, Tokyo, Sydney - saw spontaneous protests erupting. The video from Rome served as a rallying cry, a stark reminder of the price of freedom and the lengths to which The Circle would go to suppress it.

The world watched, and for the first time since The Circle's dominance, it united not under its banner, but against it.

At The Circle's headquarters, an imposing skyscraper that overlooked Washington, D.C., Lucien was surrounded by his core team, watching the scenes play out on multiple screens. With each passing second, his frustration grew.

"This is spiraling out of control!" He snapped.

His aide, Helena, approached cautiously, "Sir, political leaders from various minority parties have been joining the protests. We've even seen some religious groups participating. They're uniting people, giving them hope."

Lucien's icy gaze met hers. "Then we must strip them of that hope."

Clearing his throat, his closest advisor, Viktor Stahl, presented a solution. "We must act swiftly, sir. A show of force, a clear message that we won't tolerate insubordination."

Lucien pondered for a moment before taking a deep breath, "Declare martial law. 30 days. No one goes in or out of major cities. Strict curfew. The militias have complete authority."

Helena intervened, "Sir, this will only escalate matters. The people—"

"They need to be reminded of who's in charge!" Lucien cut her off. "And those religious fanatics, they're the root of this. Round them up. Detain anyone spreading dissent."

Viktor responded with a firm voice, "It will be done, sir."

As the decree of martial law was broadcasted globally, an eerie silence fell upon cities worldwide. The night was illuminated not by the moon or stars but by the patrol lights of militia vehicles, the stark beams of searchlights, and the occasional flare from a distant conflict. The world, once buzzing with resistance, was forced into a tense and fearful silence, as the heavy hand of The Circle sought to crush any glimmer of rebellion.

The St. Andrew's Church, one of Toronto's last bastions of faith, had become a refuge for many in recent times. It was a place where community members could gather, pray, and find solace in the midst of the oppressive regime of The Circle. However, the serenity and faith that the church embodied became its very undoing.

On a cold winter night, hushed whispers and soft hymns echoed inside the church. People from various walks of life had congregated there, seeking peace in these troubled times.

Outside, the snow was falling gently, covering the city in a blanket of white.

Suddenly, the silence was broken by the roar of engines. Bright lights illuminated the stained-glass windows as several military vehicles belonging to the local militia pulled up outside the church. A loudspeaker announced a curfew, demanding the immediate dispersion of those inside.

But the congregation didn't budge. They believed in the safety of their sanctuary and the power of peaceful resistance. With hands held and voices joined, they started singing, hoping that their songs of unity and faith would deter the militia.

However, their hopes were in vain. A rock, allegedly thrown from the crowd, became the militia's pretext. But footage captured by one brave soul from a window above showed the grim reality: a peaceful gathering was violently disrupted by the militia, unprovoked.

Tear gas filled the church, causing panic and chaos. People scrambled, choking and crying, desperately trying to escape the noxious fumes. Amidst the turmoil, a Molotov cocktail was thrown, setting the historic wooden structure ablaze.

The inferno that consumed St. Andrew's was symbolic of the greater battle between the oppressed and The Circle. The burning spire, which once reached out to the heavens, became a beacon of resistance for the city.

As news of the incident spread, the already strained relationship between The Circle and the public worsened. The Circle became more aggressive in shutting down "disinformation" on the Internet, banning user accounts and even IP addresses of people sharing opposing content. Militias started receiving lists of dissenters, and squads started forming to eliminate those who opposed The Circle.

Toronto's loss became the world's rallying cry. The blatant act of violence was not just an attack on a church but an attack on humanity's fundamental rights and freedoms.

Chapter 63: Militia

The atmosphere in the underground church in Arlington, Virginia was one of unity and peace. Soft candlelight flickered, casting a gentle glow on the congregation. David, Mark, and Becca sat side by side, their voices rising in harmony with the others, singing hymns that spoke of hope, faith, and deliverance.

Suddenly, the serene ambiance was shattered by the chilling sound of a gunshot. The hymns came to an abrupt halt, replaced by a hushed silence. Eyes darted in fear, looking for an exit, as the reality of their dire situation sunk in. Chaz, who had always been their pillar of strength, took charge immediately, his voice firm but calming. "To the back door, now!" he shouted.

But before they could move, the back door burst open. Masked militia members, armed with batons, stormed in, their intent clear from their menacing demeanor. A wave of panic surged through the congregation as they scrambled to find a way out. Some were trampled, others screamed, and chaos reigned.

David instinctively reached for the pistol he had concealed, but a glance from Becca stopped him. Her eyes, always so full of determination and resilience, now conveyed a single message: "*This is not the time.*"

As the trio made their way towards the front door, they saw Anthony, the elder, being cornered by a militia member. The brute was swinging his baton with ruthless force, each blow landing with a sickening thud. David felt a surge of anger and instinctively moved towards Anthony, but Becca's firm grip on his arm pulled him back. "We have to go, David," she whispered desperately.

Outside, the cold night air filled their lungs as they ran through the narrow streets, trying to put as much distance as possible between them and the church. Behind them, they could hear shouts, screams, and more gunshots. The world they knew was collapsing around them, but for now, all they could focus on was survival.

The door of the Greek cafe creaked as Becca, David, and Mark walked in. The warm scent of freshly baked bread and brewed coffee greeted them, but the trio was too preoccupied to notice. They found Nadia sitting at a corner table, her laptop open in front of her, typing away furiously.

As they approached, she glanced up with a bright smile, her eyes shining with excitement. "Guys, you won't believe what I've managed to do! I've built a new secure network, completely bypassing The Circle's surveillance. We can communicate, share, and organize without them ever knowing!" she exclaimed.

She was about to dive into the technical details when she noticed the expressions on their faces. Becca's eyes were rimmed red, David's jaw was set in a hard line, and Mark's face was ashen. The weight of their collective exhaustion and trauma hung heavily between them.

Nadia's smile faded as quickly as it had appeared. "What happened?" she asked, her voice now filled with concern.

David cleared his throat, struggling to find the right words. "The church... it was attacked," he began, his voice barely above a whisper.

Mark took over, detailing the horrific events of the evening. The armed militia, the chaos that ensued, the people they saw being beaten, and their narrow escape. Becca described the feeling of helplessness as they watched Anthony being brutally attacked.

As they recounted the events, Nadia's face drained of color. She closed her laptop and leaned back in her chair, taking a moment to absorb the gravity of what she had just heard.

"We need to act fast," she finally said, determination burning in her eyes. "They're escalating their tactics, and we can't afford to be caught off guard again."

In the dim light of the Greek cafe, Nadia's laptop screen glowed as they surfed through official news websites. Each headline mirrored the next: "Terrorist Cells Exposed," "Successful Crackdown on Extremist Groups," and "World Peace Closer Than Ever." But as David dove deeper into the underbelly of online forums and encrypted chat rooms, a different story emerged.

"These aren't 'terrorist groups,'" David said with a heavy sigh. "It's every religious gathering, every place where faith is being practiced."

Nadia nodded, scrolling through personal accounts from people across the world. There were tales of home churches in Beijing being raided, prayer groups in Nairobi being disbanded, and religious gatherings in Buenos Aires being shut down.

"The narrative is all wrong," Becca murmured, her fingers clenched around a now cold mug of tea. "They're painting us as the villains, as if practicing faith is a crime."

Mark, exhausted by the day's events, had drifted off on the cafe's old couch. His steady breathing provided a stark contrast to the tense atmosphere in the room.

Nadia redirected the conversation to a more hopeful topic. "Let me show you CALEB," she said, her fingers dancing across the keyboard. The screen displayed a simple, user-friendly interface, but behind its simplicity was a sophisticated encryption protocol.

"CALEB stands for 'Covert Advanced Link Encrypted Broadcast,'" Nadia explained. "I named it after one of the spies Moses sent into Canaan, someone who saw the challenges ahead but remained faithful and hopeful."

Becca raised an eyebrow, impressed. "So, it's an encrypted communication tool?"

Nadia nodded. "Exactly. We can send messages, videos, and documents without being tracked or intercepted. It's decentralized, so even if one node is compromised, the entire network won't be."

Nadia's excitement was palpable as she explained further, "So, when we send a message using CALEB, we aren't just sending a straightforward piece of data. Let's say you want to send a video message. That video is fragmented into thousands of tiny chunks, almost like creating a jigsaw puzzle from a painting."

Becca leaned in closer, intrigued. "And then?"

"Those chunks, or pieces of the puzzle, are then replicated thousands of times," Nadia continued, her fingers moving rapidly over her laptop keyboard to pull up a visual representation. "Each of these replicated chunks is then distributed to nodes across our network."

David interjected, "By nodes, you mean?"

"Hacked routers, servers, even personal devices," Nadia replied. "So, instead of having one path for our message, we create hundreds of thousands. This not only ensures our message gets to its intended destination but also makes it virtually impossible to stop."

Becca frowned, trying to process the information. "But how does the recipient put all these chunks back together? It sounds like a massive jigsaw puzzle."

Nadia grinned, "That's the beauty of it. You need a private key to reassemble the message, much like you need a reference picture to complete a jigsaw puzzle. Without this key, all those chunks are just random, meaningless data. It's a level of encryption that makes our communications secure."

David looked impressed, "So even if one node, or a hundred nodes for that matter, are taken down or compromised..."

Nadia finished his thought, "The message can still be reconstructed from the remaining chunks. And if we lose a node, the system automatically sends out another copy from the active nodes to maintain that level of redundancy."

Becca's eyes widened in realization, "This means that if someone were to leak a video or some information, it could potentially reach thousands, even millions of people in mere seconds, without being stopped."

Nadia nodded, "Exactly. The potential is vast, and it gives us a fighting chance against the censorship and control The Circle is trying to impose."

David leaned in, examining the system. "This could change everything. We can coordinate better, share real news, and perhaps even organize larger-scale resistance."

The three of them spent hours delving into the intricacies of CALEB, brainstorming ways to safely distribute it, and ensuring that its encryption couldn't be cracked. The night wore on, and the weight of their mission pressed down on them, but there was also a spark of hope — a belief that with tools like CALEB, they could make a difference.

The low hum of the laptop fan filled the quiet as Becca leaned forward, her blue eyes locking onto David's. "Look, while I'm incredibly impressed with CALEB and the potential it has, we need to stay focused on The Fellowship. We have a community in crisis."

David nodded, rubbing the back of his neck in thought. He loved the fierceness that Becca had for defending those she loved the most. "You're right. Our first priority is ensuring everyone is safe. We need to regroup and find our people."

Mark, half-asleep and listening in, yawned and then chimed in, "First, we need to find Chaz. He's not just our pastor but a beacon of hope for many in The Fellowship."

David looked over to Mark. "Do you have any idea where he might be? A place he'd consider safe?"

Mark slowly sat up, stretching. "Yeah. I remember him talking about a place. He once mentioned the home where he grew up. It's in a small town, about an hour's drive from here. If he got out, he might've headed there. It's secluded, and very few people know about it."

David stood up, determination in his eyes. "Then that's where we start. We'll go check it out. Hopefully, he's there, and we can strategize on the next steps."

Becca shot them both a stern look. "Be careful. It might not just be The Circle we're up against. There could be informants, snitches, anywhere."

David nodded, acknowledging the weight of her words. "Don't worry. We'll be discreet."

Feeling a sudden surge of emotion, Becca stepped forward and wrapped David in a brief but tight hug. "Just... come back safely," she whispered. David, taken aback by the unexpected gesture, felt a warmth spread through him. "I promise," he murmured back.

As David and Mark made their way out, Becca turned back to Nadia. "While they're gone, let's get CALEB up and running. We need it now more than ever."

Nadia nodded in agreement, her fingers already flying over the keyboard. The two women, each fueled by a mix of fear and determination, set to work, knowing that the fate of many rested in their hands.

Chapter 64: Chaz

C haz's childhood home was an old brick house, two-stories, with a slightly worn-out appearance. The windows were covered with faded drapes, and the yard, though large, was wild with overgrown shrubs and grasses. As David and Mark approached the door, they noted the silence that enveloped the town.

Knocking gently, they waited, scanning the area to ensure they weren't followed. The door opened slightly, and Chaz peered out, his face wearing an expression of surprise and guarded skepticism. He looked even older, with dark circles under his eyes revealing the weight of recent events.

David immediately saw the doubt in Chaz's eyes and realized he had to be transparent. "Chaz, I know what you're thinking, but I swear on everything I hold dear, I had no part in what happened."

Chaz's gaze shifted between David and Mark, the weight of his suspicion evident. "David, you're part of The Circle. Why should I trust you?"

David took a deep breath, trying to find the right words. "Because if I were here on their behalf, I wouldn't come with just Mark. I'd have a team. We're here to help you and everyone else."

Mark stepped closer, placing a reassuring hand on Chaz's shoulder. "Chaz, David is with us. He's trying to do right. We all lost something last night. We want to figure out what we can do to help."

Chaz took a moment, clearly battling with his emotions before sighing deeply. "I know, Mark. It's just... I saw them, our people... getting hurt. I feel so powerless."

David nodded understandingly. "We all feel the weight, Chaz. But right now, we need to regroup, strategize. And for that, we need you. What can we do to help?"

Chaz looked at both of them, the determination returning to his eyes. "We find a safe place, regroup, and we fight back. But first, we need to get as many of our people to safety."

David put his hand on Chaz's shoulder. "We have a place in the city where we meet, come with us, let's find out what happened to our people."

The dim lighting of the abandoned Greek café barely illuminated the dusty corners, but the central table had been cleared and was now covered in laptops, routers, and screens displaying rapidly scrolling code. The faded murals of Greek islands on the walls contrasted starkly with the high-tech scene in front of them.

Nadia and Becca looked up as the door creaked open. David, Mark, and a shaken-looking Chaz stepped in.

"Chaz," Becca whispered, rushing over and hugging him tightly. The others greeted him with nods and comforting pats, fully aware of the trauma he had recently endured.

"Welcome back to the war room," Nadia quipped with a half-smile, trying to lighten the mood.

Chaz, regaining some composure, glanced around and remarked, "Seems you all have been busy."

Nadia beckoned everyone over to the main screen. "We've developed something revolutionary. Meet CALEB."

The screen showcased a beautifully designed interface, vibrant against the gritty backdrop of the café. It was sleek and seemed to radiate a sense of hope.

"CALEB is our countermeasure to The Circle's stranglehold on communication," Nadia began. "Every message, video, or file sent through CALEB is broken down into thousands of parts, replicated, and then sent through hacked routers and servers globally. Only the receiver, with a unique key, can piece them back together."

Chaz, trying to keep up, frowned, "So it's a secure messaging system?"

David nodded, "But not just that. It's a beacon. We can reach out to believers, underground churches, and groups worldwide without the fear of being intercepted or shut down by The Circle."

Mark added, "It's our underground railroad of information. A way to keep our communities informed, safe, and more importantly, connected."

Chaz, lost in thought, mumbled, "You can give hope to so many in hiding…"

Becca squeezed his hand. "That's the plan. We are the light, Chaz, even in the darkest of times."

Chaz took a deep breath, "Then let's shine brighter than ever."

Becca's encrypted phone vibrated, startling her. The caller ID showed "Ephraim Goldman."

She answered, "Dr. Goldman?"

"Becca, I'm in town," his voice conveyed urgency, "I have something critical to share. We need to meet."

She immediately turned cautious, "With your profile, The Circle will surely be tailing you. I have a plan. Go to 'Brewed Thoughts' on King Street. Order a coffee and then make your way to the restroom. There's a backdoor leading to the alley. I'll meet you there."

Professor Goldman's voice was low, "Alright, I trust you. I'll be there in 20."

As Becca hung up, David glanced over, "Everything okay?"

She relayed the conversation to the group, "Dr. Goldman reached out. He has some information. I need to meet him."

David straightened up, "Dr. Goldman's here? I should come with you. It's been ages since I've seen him, and two pairs of eyes are better than one."

Chaz, looking concerned, remarked, "Sounds serious. Stay safe."

Mark nodded in agreement, "Be cautious. The Circle is everywhere."

Grabbing her jacket, Becca replied, "Don't worry, we've done this a million times. We'll be back before you know it."

With that, Becca and David left the café, ready to unravel another piece of the puzzle.

Chapter 65: Yeshua

The dim lighting of the old Greek café gave a warm glow to the worn wooden tables and chairs. As David and Becca escorted Professor Goldman inside, the atmosphere was thick with anticipation. Mark, Nadia, and Chaz waited, their expressions a mixture of concern and hope.

"Professor," Chaz began, offering a seat. "We were worried when we heard you were in town."

Goldman sighed, looking around, taking in the makeshift command center, "I had to see you all. Recent events, my studies... they've led me to a revelation."

Nadia, curiosity evident in her eyes, inquired, "What kind of revelation?"

Goldman hesitated, his voice wavering slightly, "You all know I've spent my life as a devout Jew, studying our scriptures, teaching our traditions."

David nodded, "Yes, your insights have been invaluable for us. One of the leading scholars in Israel."

Goldman looked at David, then to Becca, "But there's something I've realized. A truth I can't ignore any longer."

Chaz leaned forward, "What is it?"

Taking a deep breath, Goldman confessed, "I believe Jesus... Yeshua... is the Messiah. Our Messiah. The Jewish people's Messiah."

The room went silent for a moment, the weight of Goldman's declaration hanging in the air. Becca was the first to respond, her voice soft, "Professor, that's a profound realization."

David smiled, placing a reassuring hand on Goldman's shoulder, "It's heartening to know you're seeing the truth about the Messiah. It only strengthens our resolve."

Goldman's eyes watered slightly, "It's been a journey, David. A difficult one. But the scriptures, the prophecies, the undeniable signs all around us... How could I ignore the truth?"

Mark chimed in, "It's a difficult pill to swallow, especially given your background. But we're here with you, every step of the way."

Nadia, her voice gentle, added, "It's not an easy path, Professor. But the truth has a way of shining through the darkest clouds."

Goldman nodded, wiping a tear, "Thank you. It's a new beginning for me, and I'm ready to stand alongside all of you in this fight."

"I've delved deep into eschatology for years, exploring the mysteries and prophecies surrounding the end times," Professor Goldman began, adjusting his glasses and opening one of the scriptures. "The patterns, the signs, they've always fascinated me. But now, they terrify me."

David responded, his voice gentle, "We've always believed Lucien to be the antichrist, Professor."

Goldman nodded, "I've come to the same conclusion. The rise of The Circle, the peace treaty, the way he's been idolized by the masses. It all points to him."

Chaz, leaning back in his chair, added, "It took us time to see it too, Professor. It's a hard truth."

Goldman sighed, "It's not just the prophecies, it's the way he operates. The deception, the charisma, the way he's twisting peace into something malevolent."

Becca placed a comforting hand on Goldman's, "Your realization is a significant step, Professor. We're just glad you're here, realizing the truth with us."

Goldman looked at each of them, his eyes glistening, "It's more than just realizing the truth about Lucien. It's about accepting the truth about Yeshua, Jesus. It's been a spiritual awakening."

Mark smiled warmly, "That's the most important realization of all, Professor."

Nadia added, "It's never too late to find the path. We're just grateful you're finding it now."

Goldman closed his scriptures, taking a moment to collect himself, "I always prided myself on understanding the scriptures. But now, it feels like I'm reading them for the first time. Truly understanding them."

David nodded, "With everything happening in the world, we'll need that understanding more than ever."

"But that's not the reason I came here today," Dr. Goldman said, his tone becoming even more serious. Everyone looked at him with heightened anticipation.

He reached into his coat pocket and pulled out two sleek thumb drives, laying them on the table.

"This first thumb drive," he pointed to the black one, "contains all of the data that Mossad has amassed on The Circle. As much as we appreciated the peace, Israel has had its reservations about The Circle's motives from the beginning. This data will give you insight into their operations, their influence, and the international connections that they've been cultivating in secret."

Mark raised an eyebrow, "Sounds like Mossad has been busy."

Goldman continued, "And the second one," he pointed to the silver thumb drive, "contains files from the heart of The Circle. All the data that Prime Minister Katz had access to. It's everything: their agendas, plans, insider communications. Everything."

David's eyes widened. "This is a gold mine, Dr. Goldman. How did you get your hands on this?"

Goldman looked somber, "There are many in Israel who were uneasy with The Circle's growing influence. Some channels were opened, risks were taken."

Becca leaned in, intrigued, "And the encryption?"

Goldman smiled wryly, "Ah yes, the infamous Circle encryption. Nearly unbreakable, unless you have the passcode. And thanks to a brave soul deep within The Circle's hierarchy, Mossad has it."

Nadia's eyes shone with excitement, "This could change everything. With this information and the encryption key, we can expose The Circle's true intentions." She gave a glance at David and a quick smile.

David smiled at Nadia and chimed in, "This is monumental. It's exactly the break we've been praying for." He thought about all of the encrypted files Nadia has gathered since he installed the network sniffer on The Circle's internal network. The passcode will unlock petabytes of data that will help them take down The Circle.

Goldman nodded, "I've done my part. Now it's up to you to use this information wisely. The world needs to know the truth."

David clasped Goldman's hand, "We won't let you down, Professor. And we won't let the world down either."

As the weight of Professor Goldman's revelations settled in, Becca looked at him, concern evident in her eyes. "Dr. Goldman, you've given us something invaluable, but at what cost? Will they trace this back to you?"

Goldman met her gaze, his old eyes filled with a mix of determination and weariness. "Miss Lawrence, I've lived a long life. I've seen wars, experienced betrayals, and witnessed miracles. At this point, my concerns are not for myself, but for the generations to come."

"But surely, there will be repercussions. The Circle won't just let this slide." Becca pressed on.

He nodded, "True. But remember, I've been in the game for a long time. I have allies and friends in places one wouldn't expect. There are still those who will aid an old friend."

Mark interjected, "Still, we should consider a plan to get you somewhere safe. We've got networks and connections."

Goldman chuckled, "I've already made arrangements. There's a growing underground movement in Israel, resistance fighters who've been opposing The Circle discreetly. They've offered me refuge and support. Besides, the underground tunnels and old routes through Jerusalem are not unfamiliar to me."

Chapter 66: Dissolved

Inside the abandoned Greek café, Nadia sat hunched over her laptop, surrounded by a maze of tangled wires and routers. The dim light from her screen illuminated her face, her eyes reflecting determination and hope. With a few keystrokes, she activated CALEB, her masterpiece, into the world.

Within hours, the digital landscape had changed. Millions around the world were drawn to the promise of CALEB: secure, untraceable communication, free from the prying eyes of The Circle.

The few news outlets still independent from The Circle's control started reporting the emergence of a new digital sanctuary where free speech thrived. Whispered conversations in hidden corners led more and more to CALEB's domain.

A week later, the team gathered around the long wooden table in the café, the mood was tense but hopeful.

David cleared his throat, "The momentum is on our side. We have the platform, and now it's time to release the truth."

Becca nodded, "Starting with the identities of the abusive militia. The world deserves to know who they are."

Chaz added, "People should know who's enforcing this tyranny. Unmask them, let them be accountable for their actions."

Nadia took a deep breath, "Releasing this information is going to create a massive stir. Once it's out there, there's no going back."

David placed a hand on Nadia's shoulder. "We know the risks. But it's the only way to weaken their grip and expose the truth."

With a nod from David, Nadia began the upload. Profiles, names, addresses, and documented instances of abuse by the militia members started flooding CALEB.

It was an avalanche of truth, and the world was watching. Within hours, outraged citizens started protests, demanding justice against the identified militia. Families, torn apart by the actions of the enforcers, now had names to their pain.

As the news spread, many militia members went into hiding, while others were confronted by the very communities they once terrorized.

The Circle's iron grasp was slowly weakening, and the tide of rebellion was rising.

The team, watching the ripple effect of their actions, knew this was just the beginning. The real battle was still to come.

The atmosphere across global cities was charged with a palpable tension. With CALEB's revelations and the incapacitation of the militias, the citadels of power that once stood invincible were now being challenged by a renewed spirit of resistance.

In various capitals, protestors began gathering, their chants and slogans echoing through the air. The faces of the dictators were painted on placards, often distorted in mockery, serving as a focal point for the people's ire. It was the power of a populace unshackled, pushing back against their oppressors.

Broadcasts from state-controlled media attempted to downplay the unrest. Anchors spoke of minor disturbances, emphasizing the need for order and unity. But the visuals, captured on smartphones and disseminated on CALEB, told a different story.

At the heart of the storm was Lucien. The once-magnetic leader, now seen as a puppet master, had lost his sheen. Washington D.C., which had once welcomed him with a red carpet, now had crowds chanting outside his quarters, demanding his departure.

As dusk set over D.C., a convoy of armored vehicles left the heart of the city. Inside the lead car was Lucien, his face void of the usual confidence and charisma. His destination was Belgium, a return to his roots, but under starkly different circumstances.

Once airborne, Lucien summoned his closest aides aboard the private jet. "These religious zealots and troublemakers have ruined everything!" he exclaimed, frustration evident in his voice.

An aide tried to comfort him, "Sir, the world is just not ready for The Circle."

Lucien's eyes flashed angrily, "They were on the cusp of a new age! We offered them unity, peace! But these fanatics..."

He trailed off, staring out of the jet's window, watching the lights of the East Coast recede.

The next day, an announcement shook the world. The Circle was officially disbanding. Lucien blamed "bad actors" and "religious fanatics" for the organization's demise. His statement was filled with lament, speaking of a lost opportunity for global unity and peace.

The world watched with a mix of emotions. Many cheered, relieved to see the end of The Circle's influence. Others, though opposed to Lucien's methods, mourned the loss of a vision, however flawed.

But for the majority, it was a moment of victory. The resilience of the human spirit had triumphed over a singular vision of unity.

The sun hung low in the sky, casting long shadows over the Greek cafe. The group sat in a circle, the weight of their past victories and future challenges evident in their eyes.

David cleared his throat. "The Circle might have disbanded, but the spirit that drove it still lingers. Lucien might be in hiding, but we all know he'll be back."

Nadia nodded, tapping her fingers on the table, her eyes lost in thought. "He's just biding his time, strategizing. But this time, he'll be even more dangerous."

Chaz leaned forward, "The scriptures warn us about this. The antichrist will return with more power, deceiving even the elect if that were possible."

Mark, taking a sip of his coffee, said, "So, what's our plan? We've had a victory, but it's a small battle in a larger war."

Becca, looking at each face around the table, responded, "Our focus remains the same. We save as many souls as we can. We show them the love and truth of Christ."

David nodded in agreement, "We also prepare ourselves for the spiritual battle ahead. We need to be rooted in the Word and covered in prayer."

Nadia chimed in, "And we must ensure CALEB remains operational. It's our best tool to counteract any propaganda Lucien throws our way."

Chaz, looking somber, added, "I've heard whispers among the faithful. Dreams and visions suggesting that a time of great persecution is coming. We need to fortify our communities and establish safe houses."

Becca took a deep breath, "All of this, while ensuring we maintain our own spiritual health. We can't help others if we ourselves are not strong."

Mark placed his hand on the table, palm open. One by one, each member placed their hand on top. "Together," he said, "with Christ at the center, we'll face whatever comes our way."

The group nodded in unison, a renewed determination in their eyes. The sun had set, and the room was bathed in the soft glow of the overhead lights. They knew the battle was far from over, but their unity and faith would see them through the challenges ahead.